how it's done

For Diane M.

how it's done

Christine Kole MacLean

Woodbury, Minnesota

First Edition
Second Printing, 2007

Book design by Steffani Chambers
Cover design by Gavin Dayton Duffy
Cover image © Picture Quest
Editing by Rhiannon Ross

Flux, an imprint of Llewellyn Publications

Library of Congress Cataloging-in-Publication Data (pending)
ISBN-13: 978-0-7387-1029-7
ISBN-10: 0-7387-1029-6

Flux
2143 Wooddale Drive, Dept. 978-0-7387-1029-7
Woodbury, MN 55125-2989, U.S.A.
www.fluxnow.com

Printed in the United States of America

If we are faithless, He remains faithful,
for He cannot deny Himself.

2 Timothy 2:13

Sometimes, when I'm weeding a row of peas or beans, my leg will start to ache again. I'll crawl down the row to the lawn and roll onto my back. Lying there beside my crutches, listening to the *tick-tick-tick* of the corn leaves in the humid breeze, I think about Michael. If my concentration is good, I can almost feel him dragging his finger lightly—so lightly—along my jaw and down my neck to the dip in my collarbone, and I can bring on that flash of longing.

I don't know why I do it to myself. Maybe to make it all real again.

Then I'll hear a voice calling to me from the porch, "Ace! Ace!," reminding me of the way things are. And I'll wave idly without opening my eyes, wondering if I could have figured everything out differently, in a way that was more true to myself. Maybe the way I did it *was* true to myself. It's hard to say, when you're eighteen.

It's not like there's a "find yourself" kit or road signs that say "This way to being your own person." If you're lucky, maybe there's someone who can help you, like a fat lady on the beach might yell, "Keep going! You can do it!" if you're a lousy swimmer and in way over your head. The funny thing is, that person is never who you think it's going to be.

It's never who you want it to be.

One

Rebecca felt herself swoon as Conrad wrapped his muscular arms around her and held her fast. Every part of her wanted to give in to him, to claim him, finally, as her own, but summoning all her strength and her will, she clawed at his chest.

"Let me go!" she cried. "You know I am betrothed to another!"

His face clouded with anger. "Why is he tending to another now and not to thee?"

Rebecca averted her eyes, not wanting him to see her uncertainty. "She's ill and in need of him."

"In need of him, perhaps," said Conrad, brooding, *"but not ill."*

Rebecca slapped him sharply across the cheek. "How dare you! He's a better man than you'll ever be."

Conrad released her, roughly pushing her away from him. "Why do you fight me so?"

"And why do you tempt me so?" she cried in anguish.

When he looked down at her, his eyes were full of longing but his voice was bitter. "It's not me that does the tempting, lass. It's thee."

"I've done nothing to encourage you!"

His expression softened. "Nay," he said tenderly. "All that you do—all that you are—encourages me." He reached down and fingered the tendrils of hair that had come loose from her braid, then dropped his hand to caress her—

Oh, Conrad, tempt me, I thought, holding my breath and turning the page. I was so lost in the thought of where his hand was going that I didn't hear my father until he was right behind me.

"Still reading *Moby Dick?*" he asked, walking past my chair and sitting down in his own at the head of the table.

I jumped, sloshing some orange juice out of my glass. "Yes, uh-huh, *Moby Dick.*" Steady, I told myself. Remember, to him it's just *Moby Dick.* After learning a while ago that my father hadn't ever read it, I had cut the cover off a paperback copy I bought and used it as a fake cover whenever I read a romance novel.

I shoved *Rebecca's Folly* into my backpack, before he could get a closer look. He thinks that romance novels are written by the devil himself and has told me not to read them. "They'll put a wall between you and God," he'd told me once, plucking *Keeping Courtney* out of my hands with his thumb and index finger like it was dirty Kleenex and dropping it into the trash in the kitchen. "Is that what you want?"

Knowing what he wanted to hear, I'd said no. But I'd been thinking, *What I* want *is to find out if the Earl will discover that Courtney is really his long-lost daughter before he kisses her.*

My father picked up his newspaper. "Seems like you've been reading that book for a long time."

"It's a long book," I said.

"You're so good about staying on top of your studies, Grace," said my mom, bringing my dad his coffee. "Never causing us a single worry. Isn't that right, Dan?"

Now? I wondered, tucking my hair behind my ears. *Should I ask my dad about the concert now?* It seemed like the right time, since Mom had just said what a good student I was. If I waited too long to bring it up, it would mess up his routine, and he was all about routine. 7:17: Brush teeth, trim nose hairs (as needed). 7:22: Put on coat and rubbers. (Liv can't walk past them without snickering, "Doesn't your dad know you shouldn't re-use *rubbers?*" But that's Liv for you.) 7:26: Fake-kiss Mom and say goodbye to me.

My dad grunted, already lost in some article in the business section. "People complain about Michigan winter potholes, but then they complain about taxes!"

Mom slid a plate of eggs under the edge of the newspaper. Seeing them, my father sighed and set the paper down beside his fork. There was lots of room for it there, since our table is big enough for eight people. I don't know why they bought such a big table when there has only ever been the three of us. All it does is make the house feel empty.

Dad bowed his head. Mom and I automatically did the same, but I'd stopped closing my eyes a long time ago. The first time I kept them open, when I was five or six, I squinted my eyes and looked at the ceiling, wondering if God would smite me with a bolt of lightning. When he didn't, I was a little disappointed. Where was the God who knew my every thought and watched my every move? Maybe he was distracted, or away watching someone else being naughty.

After that I sometimes tested God, lying about having said my nightly prayers, or, much later, about where I had been with Ryan. It was like having a conversation with God. I was saying, "What will happen if I do this? Nothing? Okay, what about *this?* What will you do to me now?" And he was saying . . . well, nothing.

"Lord God Almighty," my father prayed. "Give us the strength to stay on the straight and narrow path that you have set before us, wavering neither left or right, but always keeping our eyes fixed upon you, the great giver of peace and life. May thy will be done on this and every day. Amen."

"Amen," said my mother.

I let out a sort of sigh, "Ahm," then leaned back in my chair and watched my father eat. *Cut, cut, chew. Cut, cut, chew.* "Geez," Liv said once, after going out to dinner with me and my parents and watching him eat. "He's the only person I've ever seen who can make *eating* look like work."

I waited until he had finished his eggs. Then, trying not to sound too eager, I said, "Did you think any more about the concert? Today is the last day to get tickets, so I kind of need to know."

His coffee cup made a little clink as he set it on the saucer. He wiped his mouth with a napkin. "I don't want you to go."

I tried again, thinking that he just wasn't remembering how tame the concert was going to be. "But there's nothing wrong with the music," I said. "There's no bad language or anything. And it's totally chaperoned. Remember? I gave you the list of parents who are going to chaperone? It's the senior class party."

"Grace," he said, like we'd been over this before, a million times. "You came home late last night when—"

"Five minutes! Just five minutes! Liv asked me to listen to the argument she has to give for debate team." My feet were freezing because of the cold linoleum—our house never felt warm in the winter—but my cheeks burned.

"Still. You know how I feel about keeping your word. It's our responsibility to teach you responsibility. I just want what's best for you," he said, shaking his head, like he was sorry to have to say no. "People pushing and shoving to get close to the stage, to get a closer look at half-naked rock stars—"

"Half-*naked*? They're not—"

He held up his index finger, reminding me that I was interrupting. "*Half-naked* rock stars," he said, "with everyone either wedged up against each other or trampling over each other. I've heard about them. That concert is no place for a girl like you."

Stunned, I concentrated on the line of pulp scum that ringed the inside of my juice glass. *No?* He was really saying *no*? I had stayed home almost every weekend for two months to make it more likely that he would say yes to this concert and he was saying no because I had been *five measly minutes* late? And only because I was helping Liv!

"I'm 18," I said, not looking at him. "And it's the biggest event of the year. Everyone is going. Everyone."

"All the more reason for you to stay away."

I still believed I could make him understand. "What about when you were in high school? Wasn't there like a big class picnic or field trip or something special you did at the end of the year—your whole class? That's what this is, Dad. This is our big thing!"

"That's true, Dan. We did," my mother said. My father and I both turned to look at my mother at the same time. She's quiet, my mother, and good at staying out of things. She was standing behind the stove, the island between her and us, wiping around and around the burners.

He turned back to me and said, "There are really two things going on here. One, you didn't respect your curfew. Two, you could get hurt."

"So what?" I said under my breath.

In my family, no one talks back to my father. "What did you say?" he asked.

"I just don't get what the point is if you can't have fun sometimes."

Stabbing his index finger onto the tabletop, he said, "The *point* is to glorify God in all that we say and do. That would be the *point*, Grace. But since you and I can't agree on this, let's see what the Good Book would say. Exodus 20:12."

My father loved playing this game, rifling through all the Bible verses in his head and pulling out just the right one, the one that would show me he was right. I'd figured out a long time ago that the game was rigged, but I plunged ahead anyway. "It's just a concert—with adults!"

"Exodus 20:12. What does it say?"

I knew I should just give in. But I had been so sure my plan would work that I couldn't. The disappointment churning in my stomach turned to anger as it rocketed toward my mouth. The only way I could throttle it back was by clenching the muscles at the back of my throat.

"I'm waiting," he said.

So am I, I thought. *Waiting to get out. Waiting to get away from you. Waiting for my life to begin.* I sensed my mother hovering behind me, silently urging me to do what my father wanted.

I closed my eyes and gritted my teeth. "'Honor thy father and mother, that your days may be long in the land which the Lord thy God giveth you.'"

When I opened my eyes, my father was sizing me up from across the table. "Good," he said. "Now we understand each other."

Not hardly, I thought, as he pushed back from the table and walked to the bathroom.

My mother handed me a plate piled with eggs and toast and smiled like she wished she could make things better.

"Thanks," I said, spooning a thick layer of Cheez Whiz, my favorite condiment, onto my eggs.

I leaned forward and started wolfing down large chunks of the eggs. The waistband of my skirt cut into my stomach, reminding me that I had recently gained a few pounds. I didn't really care. Liv thought the weight looked good on me. "It all landed on your butt and boobs. You look like G.D. Marilyn Monroe. The guys are going to be all *over* that!"

Still, I looked at the last slice of bacon and considered not eating it.

My father walked by again on his way to the door. He stopped behind my chair and dropped his hands onto my shoulders. "We just want what's best for you," he said again.

I stared out the window, down the row of ranch houses that were exactly like ours. When I was a kid, I thought it was neat that no matter which house I was playing at, the bathroom would always be inside the back door, to the left. But now, in the washed out winter morning light, the houses looked like cells on a prison block. They looked like a suburban Alcatraz out in the middle of nowhere.

My father squeezed my shoulder lightly. "You know that, don't you? Parents who let their kids do whatever they want—those are the parents who don't care," he said. I dropped my head, hoping that he would mistake it for a nod. "That's my girl," he said.

Walking to the door, he said under his breath to my mother, "And have her change her sweater."

After the door closed behind him, I looked down at my sweater. It was snug but not really tight. "What's wrong with it?" I asked.

She glanced at my chest. "I think he's objecting to it because . . ."

"Because what?"

"Well, you've really . . . filled out, honey, and your father . . . it's going to take him a while to adjust to thinking of you as a woman."

She was trying to be tactful, but I didn't have the energy right then to figure out what she was saying. "So I have to change my sweater . . . why?"

She sighed. "It's obvious that you're cold." Then, even though it was just the two of us, she whispered, "You can see . . . *everything*. Maybe you should wear a camisole or a thicker bra."

Normally I would have been mortified that my father had noticed, but I was too angry to care. When my mom tried to clear my plate, I snatched the last piece of bacon and shoved it into my mouth.

Licking the grease off my fingers, I watched the letters of my father's "Warning! In case of Rapture this vehicle will be unmanned" bumper sticker grow smaller as he drove away. If the Rapture had happened right then, if my father had been sucked up into heaven with the righteous, it wouldn't have been soon enough for me.

And I would've been thrilled to have been left behind.

Two

"Come on," Liv called, walking backwards in front of me. She cocked her head playfully, trying to make it impossible for me to say no. "You know you want to—oh, shit!" she said, slipping on a patch of ice and almost going down. She caught her balance just in time and laughed at the near miss. "You know you want to go."

It was so cold that the air hurt my chest if I breathed too deeply. All I wanted right then was to get to school, where it would be warm. I buried my face in my wool scarf. It smelled like my mother's cedar hope chest, which was stuffed with our hats and scarves and gloves, even the ones without mates. My mother could never give up on the missing glove.

"No, I don't want to go. I don't want to hang around Corbin College listening to lectures all day, unless I have to—and I don't." The scarf muffled my voice, but not so much that Liz missed the edge in it.

Liv flipped me off, kidding, but not. "What's your problem? It's not like I'm asking you to do something immoral or illegal or something. And it's not all day. It's only for a few hours. I need the extra credit."

"I don't have a problem. It just sounds boring and I don't feel like going." As I said the words, I pictured their molecules crystallizing as soon as they hit the air, breaking apart, and scattering. I wondered if that made it hard for Liv to hear me.

She stopped and waited for me, slinging her arm around me when I caught up. "But it will be more fun if you're along," she said, squishing me into her. "Just come. You know I'd do it for you. I'll loan you Fave Jeans."

That was an old joke, since Liv's favorite jeans (aka Fave Jeans) never had and never would fit me. We'd borrowed each other's clothes a lot when we were in grade school—even underwear, which Liv forgot to bring almost every time she came for a sleepover—but suddenly one summer, her pants didn't fit me any more. Now when she offered to loan me Fave Jeans, it was her way of saying that she really, really wanted me to do something.

Going with her to the conference at the college wouldn't be a huge deal, except that I wouldn't be able to go to Lila's

Greenhouse after school. It wasn't just a greenhouse. It was an escape from winter, which I hated. The cold days and frigid nights. The bare black branches that looked like overgrown fingernails clutching at the grey sky. The way it got dark at 5:30, and there was nothing to do, if you didn't like to ski or skate. I spent the entire winter every year bracing myself against it.

Except when I was at Lila's. The peaty smell of moist dirt and all its secrets and promises filled me up in a way I couldn't explain. It was almost like eating. At the greenhouse, where something was always ready to bloom, I could relax and take a deep breath. I always knew that winter wouldn't last forever, but at Lila's, I *felt* it.

I had been trying to get to Lila's ever since she reopened after New Year's. I was hoping she could tell me how to cheer up my African violet. I'd rescued it from the hallway outside the art room, where it was sitting between an empty bottle of red tempera paint and a wire sculpture on the last day of school before Christmas vacation.

The janitor was getting ready to haul everything away, so I'd brought it home and put it with my Boston fern, under my spider plant. My mom knew nothing about plants, so I had to figure out how to take care of them on my own with a little help from Lila. I liked doing it, and Lila said I had a green thumb—just a little underdeveloped. But lately the violet had been looking dejected. I was worried it was slipping away.

But what Liv said was true. She would go for me, just like she stayed home with me the night of the homecoming dance because I couldn't face seeing my old boyfriend Ryan with Megan, the girl who broke us up. I sighed. "All right. I'll go."

"I knew you would," she said. She turned on her high-beam smile and linked her arm through mine. I felt the way a cat must when someone pets it from tail to head—loved, but loved all wrong.

* * *

The Corbin auditorium was packed with kids from Honors English classes at other high schools in our part of the state, but Liv and I finally found two seats together. Right in the middle of "Pour Some Sugar on Me: The Manifestations of Love in Contemporary Literature," I had to go to the bathroom—as in *now*. To get to the aisle, I tripped over a backpack, stepped on a teacher's foot, and slipped on someone's down jacket. "Just call me Grace," I said to the person at the end of the row, who I recognized from school. I guess she didn't know me, though, because she didn't get the joke.

After I finished using the bathroom, I didn't feel like doing the obstacle course all over again to get back to my seat. The lecture was half over, anyway. I read a bulletin board for finding rooms and roommates for a while. When I got bored with that, I walked around in the building until I found a door out to a courtyard. There was a wire chair someone had dragged out and put in a spot that was protected from the wind. It was warmer there than I thought it would be, and I sat in the chair, sliding down until the back of my head rested against the top edge of the chair back. My skirt hiked up, but I was alone and didn't care. I closed my eyes and, feeling like a crocus trying to push its bud through the crusty snow, tilted my face to the thin sunshine.

I was drained from the fight with my father and it was so quiet there in the sun that I started to doze. Just then the door squeaked and I opened my eyes a sliver. A man wearing black wool pants and a black turtleneck strepped out. He was tall and, I guessed from the fit of the turtleneck, sinewy.

Because of where I was sitting, he didn't see me right away. I watched as he ran his fingers through his wavy hair, then fumbled in his pocket for a cigarette. Although there wasn't any wind, he huddled over his cigarette as he lit it.

It wasn't until he straightened up and inhaled deeply that he finally looked around and noticed me. His gaze swept over my face, down my body, and actually *lingered* on my thighs. When he looked me in the eye, I felt an electrical current between us, like I had tapped into a new source of energy. I could tell from the look in his eyes that he knew the effect he'd had. He smiled. "Mind if I smoke?"

I shrugged, thinking it was a little late for him to ask, since he already was smoking.

"I know what you're thinking," he said.

"You do?"

He looked away from me, then nodded, exhaling a strong, thin stream of smoke. "You're thinking I don't look like a smoker."

I hadn't been thinking anything at all—only wishing I were older, prettier, and more sophisticated—but it was true he didn't look like a smoker.

He scratched the base of his neck with his free hand and sighed. "I'm not, usually. A smoker. It's just that I like one before I speak at things like this. It relaxes me. So I'm a pack-a-semester kind of smoker." He smiled sheepishly. "Don't tell my students. They all think I'm perfect."

"All right, but it's going to cost you," I said. It was Liv's line, but it popped right out of my mouth, like I flirted with men every day.

"Fair enough," he said. He put out his hand. "I'm Michael Irving."

His grip was firm. I felt the current again, surging from him to me. "My name is Grace," I said. Then, remembering he had said his last name, too, I added, "Passedge!"

I started to pull my hand away but he gripped it tighter for a moment before letting go. "Grace Passedge," he repeated. "It's mellifluous. And religious. Are your parents poets or preachers?"

I tried to use context to figure out the meaning of *mellifluous*. Easy to say? Lyrical? "Neither," I said. "But you're right that they're religious."

He was almost finished with his cigarette. I suddenly realized that when he was, he would leave and this thing happening between us—whatever it was—would be over.

I said, "My mother wanted to name me Joan. She thought it was a stronger name. But then I almost died during delivery. My dad said it was by God's grace alone that I hadn't so my name should be Grace. What could my mother say to that?"

He grinned and tipped his head to one side. "She could have said it was your strength that got you through."

"You don't know my mother."

His laugh was genuine. "You have me there," he said.

No, I don't have you there or here or anywhere, I thought. *But, oh, what I wouldn't give to have you.*

"You don't have to wear uniforms at your school?"

I laughed. "At Corbin High School? Not hardly."

He bumped the heel of his hand against his forehead. "I'm sorry. I made the assumption that you go to a private school because you said your parents were religious."

"In the world, not of the world," I said, without thinking.

He furrowed his eyebrows. "I don't follow."

I laughed, embarrassed. "Oh, sorry. It's no big deal—it's just how my parents think about life. 'In the world, not of the world' means that it's okay for Christians to be around non-believers, but not to act like them. I guess that's why my parents didn't make me go to a private school."

He flicked his thumb against his cigarette and watched the ashes scatter across the snow. "It's an interesting philosophy."

I wrinkled up my nose. "You think?"

Grinning mischievously, he nodded. "So let's say I'm a non-believer and I saw a homeless person without any shoes and gave him mine. You couldn't do the same?"

He was teasing me, maybe even flirting. "Why would I?" I said. "He already has your shoes."

The skin at the edge of his eyes crinkled when he laughed that time. It was like he was pleased with me but also pleased with himself. Right from the start, I liked making him laugh like that.

"Judges, award another point to the young lady in the skirt," he said.

I dropped my chin and closed my eyes for a second, graciously accepting the point. "Thank you very much."

"Grace Passedge, it was nice meeting you, but I've done my damage here," he said, holding up his cigarette butt, "and now I have to do my damage in there. Are you coming or are you skipping my session, too?"

If it had been any other day, I would have given him a straight answer, but I was still seething over the fight with my father. I had been a good girl—more or less—my whole life, and what had it gotten me? A seat on the perimeter of life. I crossed my legs so my skirt edged up. "That depends on your topic," I said.

He smiled in that pleased way again and my heart lurched. "It's about transformation. The Romantics—Byron, Shelley, Wordsworth—who eschewed reason and believed that we could change the world if we could tap into our feelings and creativity. They believed in man's potential—in what he could become."

Wordsworth, Wordsworth, Wordsworth, I thought, scrambling to remember something about him. *He was a writer—a poet. He wrote about . . . nature!* "Wordsworth. He was into nature, right?"

"The references to nature in their work was nothing more than foreplay," he said. "It was a means to an end, a way to explore the most human of all our activities—thinking."

With every bold thing I said, it got easier. "And why should I come?"

"Because it will open your eyes, and you never know where that might lead," he said, opening the door for me. He nodded toward the doorway. "After you."

Without hesitating, I stepped through it.

Three

"He was like a dog in heat," Liv said to me that night as we sat on her bed. "The way he hunted you down after he gave his talk."

"Stop exaggerating," I said, but secretly I was pleased. When I had walked back into the auditorium with Michael, even after he suggested I sit in the front row, I'd thought that would be the end of it. But when he looked at me during his lecture, that *thing* I had felt when he shook my hand was still there, arcing from him to me.

"I'm not. All those adoring, suck-up teachers were lying in wait for him, but he came out of the auditorium and practically sniffed his way to you."

"Oh, please! All he did was thank us for coming."

"No, he thanked *you* for coming. No one else in that room existed for him," she grumbled. "Not even me."

I leaned over to adjust my tights so Liv wouldn't see me smiling.

She bent over, too, so close I could smell the Altoids on her breath. The mints were too overpowering for me, but she was addicted to them. "Maybe he really *likes* you!" she said, pinching my leg, hard.

"Ouch! Liv! I hate it when you do that."

She ignored me. "What if he did?"

"I don't know. It's stupid to even think about." He was probably at least twenty-six. He was tall and cute and funny, which meant he could go out with anyone he wanted. *And we've talked for a total of ten minutes,* I thought, feeling miserable.

Still, I wanted her to be right so much that my chest ached. And I couldn't stop hoping maybe he'd been attracted to me, too.

* * *

I spent the next few days replaying every minute of that afternoon. Why had I blurted out all that stuff about how my parents named me? I wished I'd been quieter and more mysterious. I remembered every word he said and the way he said it, and then tried to read between the lines. Had he really wanted me at his session? He was probably just being nice. Then again, he had pointed me to the front row. But did he do that just because it was the easiest seat to get to?

I went to the library and Googled him, but the only thing I found online was a bunch of academic papers he had written and talks he had given. When I was on any of the streets that led to campus, I watched for him. I tried to tell my English teacher how much I liked his talk, hoping she'd know more about him. But instead of "talk" I said "walk," and all she did was smile and ask me if that was a Freudian slip.

I tried everything, but none of it gave me what I was looking for—the rush I had gotten from being with him, from the feeling that he was pulling me in without even touching me.

* * *

Waiting for Liv inside the door to Chez Café, I told myself for the millionth time to just stop it.

The chimes on the door clanged and I turned toward it, ready to give Liv a hard time about being so late.

Only it wasn't Liv. It was Ryan. "Hey," he said softly, looking at me through his bangs. He was wearing his hair longer now, and it made him look shy. Megan was right behind him, brushing the snow off her coat and ignoring me.

"Hey!" I said, forcing a brightness into my voice. "Here I am, waiting for Liv—as usual."

He shoved his hands into his pockets. "Yeah? I don't think she's coming. I just saw her in the parking lot. She and Ben had something going down in his car."

"Oh." I felt awkward and stupid, like I was the only person who didn't have something to do after school. Now Ryan and Megan—the two people I'd most like to convince I was too busy to even remember who Ryan was—knew I was there alone.

Ryan didn't seem to be in any hurry to move along. In fact, it looked like he was enjoying the moment. "How're you doing?" he asked.

"Good!" I said. "Really good. You?"

"Good," he said. "We finished second in the league for the season, which isn't too bad, I guess. I scored a couple of goals. So . . ."

I wasn't listening. I was thinking how there should be a law against talking to anyone you've broken up with in the last six months. All it does is to humiliate even more whoever has already been humiliated the most. Me, in other words.

"Congratulations," I said, desperately working on an escape plan.

"It's too crowded here," Megan said, hitching her backpack higher on her shoulder. "Let's go someplace else."

Ryan shrugged. "Okay. Whatever. See you, Grace." He gave me that stupid victory sign on his way out, just like he used to after we'd kissed goodnight in his car, kissed in a way that made me understand why my father had given me a "true love waits" bracelet for my twelfth birthday and why he always checked to see if I was wearing it before I left.

Then Ryan would walk me to the front door and say, "I'll call you." He'd saunter back to his car, holding up the victory sign. It was his final goodnight, to just me. Back then, I thought it was cocky but sweet. Now it was stupid. Still, it made me miss him a little, which is why he did it.

I couldn't stand leaving at the same time as Ryan and Megan, so I got in line. Then, of course, they saw someone else they knew and changed their minds. *Great.*

The line was long so it took a while to get my hot chocolate. I was holding it, looking around the room for an empty seat and hoping for one far away from Ryan, when I saw one of two people at a corner table getting up to leave. I wandered over, wanting to get the table but not hawk over it if the second person wasn't going to leave with his friend. And once I saw the other person was Michael, I didn't want him to leave at all.

He glanced up at me and then around the crowded room. "It seems our paths are destined to cross. I'm still grading papers," he said, standing up and pulling out a chair for me, "but you're welcome to sit down . . . Grace, right?"

"Right," I said, surprised he remembered and relieved I wouldn't have to sit by myself, reading a book and pretending to be enjoying it.

"Here, let me take that for you." He held out his hand for my cup and set it on the table. I suddenly wished I'd ordered Chai tea or at least a latte—anything would seem more mature than hot chocolate.

"Thanks," I said.

As he helped me struggled out of my coat, I saw Megan staring at me from several tables over. Her jaw had dropped to the top of her charcoal cashmere turtleneck. She said something to Ryan and he twisted around in his seat and then pushed his bangs out of his eyes. I couldn't resist. I flashed the victory sign his way before turning my back on him. The tables had just turned.

Quickly smoothing my hair, I sat down across from Michael. The radiator heat made the air moist, and condensation formed on the inside of the window beside our table. Droplets of water started and stopped, started and stopped, like it was up to them whether they would slide into the puddle forming on the windowsill. Like they actually had a choice.

"All set?" Michael asked, nudging my drink closer to me. I wrapped my hands around the cup to warm them and to stop them from shaking. It felt like we were on a date.

I nodded. "Thanks. I can't believe how crowded this place is today."

"Really? I've never been here before so I don't have anything to compare it to."

"No, it's really crowded. Normally we wouldn't have had to do shares-ies."

"Shares-ies?" he said, wincing.

"When you have to share with somebody you don't know—like on the bus or like now."

"Why are students compelled to mutilate the language? 'Share' would work just as well."

I took a sip of hot chocolate and wiped my mouth to make sure there wasn't any whipped cream there. "Maybe." But the more I thought about it, the more I disagreed. "No, I don't think so. When you share something, it's like you don't mind. Shares-ies is different. Shares-ies infers that you'd rather not share, but you do it anyway."

"Implies. Not infers." Then he smiled apologetically, like he couldn't help correcting me. "It's what I do for a living."

"Oh. I always get those mixed up." I stared down at my cup, wishing I'd just stuck with my first answer—"maybe." "You can go ahead and do your work," I said. "I'll just sit here and finish and then I really do have to go."

But I think then he felt bad about correcting me and wanted to make up for it. "It's nice to have a diversion. They are kind of hard to come by in a small town. For example, what do we have here?" He picked a flyer up off the windowsill and read it. "'How about you stop by My house before dinner?–God,' Would you like to go?" he deadpanned, holding it out to me to see.

"No!"

Michael leaned back in surprise.

"I mean, it's not that I wouldn't want to go with you, but not *there*." To make sure he understood, I added miserably, "It's my parents' church."

"Oh, God! I'm sorry," he said. Then he said quickly, "Strike that first part. The God part. Talk about making an ass of yourself."

"No, it's all right."

"In the world, not of the world, right?"

"Yeah," I said, thinking, *He remembered something besides my name!*

A stroller slammed against the leg of the chair I was sitting on, jarring me. *"Excuse* me," the mother said. "Could you *move* your *chair?"* I scootched my chair closer to the window. The baby stared at me and Michael with wide eyes, as the mother pushed by us and bumped into the next table. *"Excuse* me," I heard her say just as bitchily to the man sitting there.

Wanting to laugh, I first looked at Michael to see his reaction. We locked eyes for a minute and then the woman said it again, from across the café, *"Excuse* me!" Both of us burst out laughing at the same time.

Michael leaned in close to me and said in a low voice, "How much you want to bet her fender has a dozen dents?" I beamed at him like an idiot, I'm sure. We watched her bump her way out the café door then Michael wiped his hand across his forehead, pretending to be relieved.

"So what else do your parents believe?" he asked.

Laughing relaxed me a little. I remembered that talking to him could be fun. "The usual," I said.

"There are hundreds of religions. There is no *usual.*"

"Well," I said, wondering where to start. "'Nobody comes to me but through the Son.'" I took a sip of my hot chocolate and then, because Michael wasn't saying anything, I added, "God said that."

"I figured," he said, looking amused.

I covered my face with my hands and groaned. "I can't believe I said that." Then I felt his hand touch mine. I hadn't seen it coming and I startled, jerking my hand away. "Oh!" I said.

He laughed. "Caffeine is the *last* thing you need."

"I know," I said. "Does hot chocolate have much? Maybe I should just have water."

"Not much. Look, is there something about being here with me that's making you nervous?"

I almost choked. *Everything about being here with you makes me nervous,* I thought. *What if someone who knows my father sees us? What if I blow it and you decide you don't like me? What if you decide you* do *like me?* If I thought about it all too much, I was sure I would start hyperventilating.

To get a grip, I thought about Liv and then about Rebecca, the heroine in the book I was reading. "No," I said. "Sometimes I just say the dumbest things, and then I get embarrassed. I'm sorry."

His shirtsleeves were rolled up and he rubbed his bare forearms. His bare, *muscular* forearms. "No need to be sorry. I think it's charming."

I decided then that it was probably better for him to know "the way things are." That's how Liv and I referred to our situations at home—"the way things are." I took a deep breath and said, "About my parents . . . They believe that the Bible is the word of God. They also believe in the Rapture, my dad, especially."

"When Jesus will transport true believers into heaven."

I nodded, holding my breath, wondering how he would react.

"In a post-9/11 world, with all the fear and global political unrest, I can see the appeal," he said. "It's comforting. People can then see order and purpose in the chaos, instead of just chaos."

"Right," I said, like I had conversations like this all the time with guys. Ryan had talked only about sports, TV shows, and gaming.

"Fascinating," he said. "Do you believe in it?"

"No. But I've grown up with it. I know a lot of people think the Rapture is strange, with believers being taken up to heaven but their clothes and everything being left behind."

He leaned forward again, frowning a little. "But otherwise do you share their beliefs?"

Corbin is a small town where almost everyone knows most everything about each other, including what church they go to. No one had ever actually asked me what I believed. I had been raised in my parents' church and everyone just assumed that I believed the same things as my parents. When it came right down to it, lots of times I kind of assumed it, too.

"I'm not sure, but they think I do. It's just easier that way," I said. "My dad's pretty strict—he won't even let me go to the senior class party because it's a concert. It's just a fake one. But he's made up his mind, laid down the law, whatever you want to call it."

Michael's eyes narrowed and he pressed his lips together. "Hmm," he said.

"Anyway, I'd rather not get shredded by him every day, so I work around him and let him think we all believe the same stuff."

A dark look crossed Michael's face. I wondered if I was coming off as spineless. "How do you feel about God?"

"Love and gratitude—that's the right answer according to my father."

"I'm sure that's a fine answer for your father. What about you, though?"

"I believe in him, if that's what you want to know," I said, wondering if this was some kind of test.

"Too easy," he said, waving his hand dismissively. "If you don't feel love and gratitude, which is what you've been taught, then what do you feel?"

I couldn't look into his eyes and think clearly at the same time, so I looked out the window into the late afternoon gray. It always amazes me how many different colors of gray there can be in the winter, depending on the light and the snow and the temperature—slate gray, iron gray, mule gray. And every one of them is still gray. Since I wasn't looking right at him, I forgot to think about acting mature or sophisticated. I just told him what I thought, straight out.

"I don't know. Some of it feels like false advertising, I guess. All that about how God knows and cares about even the sparrows and even more about me. But I don't feel it. I don't feel like he knows anything about me. I guess I feel let down."

"Disappointed?"

I nodded. "He just doesn't seem to . . . come through that often. You probably think I'm saying that because I don't get what I want, like for Christmas. But it's not that. Well, sometimes it's like that. But . . . I don't have any brothers or sisters. My mom wanted another baby. She knitted all these little baby things—always yellow, because she didn't know if it would be a boy or a girl. The thing is, she always had hope or faith or whatever. And because everyone said that God answered prayers, I prayed. Every night it was the same. 'Please, God, bring us another baby for our family.'"

My voice cracked and pressure was building behind my eyes. Not wanting to cry, I took a deep breath. "Because, you know . . . I loved my mother. I thought she was the best mother anyone could have."

I had been staring out the window the whole time I had been talking. I finally turned back to Michael, who was watching me intently, and held up my hands. "But here I am, and it's still just . . . me. I know we can't always get what we want, but why wouldn't he give my mother another baby?"

Michael didn't say anything, but his expression softened and I knew he understood.

Suddenly I remembered who I was talking to, and I blushed. I was surprised and embarrassed I'd said so much, all of it serious. I smiled. "Sorry. I don't know where all *that* came from."

"It sounded very much like it came from your heart."

"I just think my mom deserves better." I reached over and straightened the stack of papers he'd brought along. "Do you have any brothers or sisters?"

He grimaced. "I don't think so. Not anymore."

"Not anymore?"

"It's a long story. Let's save it for another time."

"Sorry, I didn't mean to . . ."

"No, I know. It's all right," he said, but then he was quiet, like he was thinking about something else.

It was probably my fault his mind was drifting. Why did I always say too much when I was with him? If he'd say something about himself maybe it wouldn't feel so weird and out of balance. Shifting awkwardly in my chair, I cleared my throat. "What about you? Do you believe in God?"

He took a drink of his coffee, squinting over the rim of his mug at me like he was trying to decide something. "Are you sure you want to get into this?"

"Ummmm, I think we kind of are into it. At least I am."

There was that smile again, the one that meant maybe I wasn't crazy to think he could like me, date me, love me. "I wouldn't normally be this direct until I know a person better—it's the kind of conversation that's sure to offend—but you strike me as someone who can have a thoughtful conversation about religious beliefs."

There was nothing more I wanted right then than to be exactly what he wanted me to be—or, at the very least, to keep looking like I was. I nodded.

Michael spread his fingers and laid his hand across the center of his chest. *"This* is what I believe in," he said, tapping his index finger on his breastbone. "I believe in *me.* I believe in Man—that we can transform ourselves from within if we just tap into our imagination and use it as a tool. It seems like so many people who believe in God are passive. They are waiting for things—waiting for answers, waiting for guidance, waiting for the second coming. Think about it!"

Wait on the Lord, I thought. *Be of good courage, and he shall strengthen thy heart.* Psalms 27: something. My parents did do a lot of waiting. Advent, the weeks leading up to Christmas, was a whole season that was all about waiting.

Michael was talking fast, pelting his ideas at me. "Christians believe God works through people. I believe we work through *ourselves.* We have the power to create and *act.* We have it within us to make ourselves better, to make the world better. I think it's all about *us,* Grace, and what we do, not about God and what he does."

Without seeming to realize what he was doing, he put his hand over mine. "I know this probably doesn't make any sense to you yet, at your age."

This time I didn't pull back. "Yes, it does," I said. "It makes perfect sense."

We sat there, our eyes locked, and even though I was nervous, I left my hand where it was, just to see what would happen. He trailed his thumb along the underside of my wrist. Once. Lightly. I gasped, then tried to cover it up by sighing. Afraid he'd feel in my pulse that I would have done anything for him right then, I pulled my hand out from under his.

The café was starting to clear out and after the blood stopped pounding in my ears, I could actually hear the *We're Skewed* CD that was playing on the stereo. I hummed along, quietly.

"You like this band?"

I nodded, kept humming.

"I know them," he said. "The lead singer used to be in Mensalot, right? They have that really great song . . . How does it go again?" He used his index fingers as drumsticks and beat out the rhythm on the table as he sang quietly, "Striking out on my own, looking back but never going ho-oooome. No, never going hooo-oooo-oome." He raised his eyebrows. "How'd I do?"

I said the first thing that popped into my head. "Stellar."

He smiled. "Good word. Stellar, from the Latin *stella,* meaning star. Of or relating to a star performer." I nodded, like I'd known. "We should go see them," he said. "If you think you can get away—you know, arrange things on your end. I'll try to find out when they'll be in Chicago."

I tucked my hair behind my ear and tried to sound casual. "That would be great."

Michael drummed the table again. And he seemed so genuinely happy that it was like a glimpse of what he must have looked like as a kid right after he'd caught his first fish.

"All right," he said, smiling and nodding. "All right."

Four

I lost track of time after that. Mostly all I thought about was when I would see Michael again. We met up as often as we could—a couple of times a week and always after school, so it was easy to hide him from my parents. I was home by curfew, and I learned to always keep a half-truth in mind.

My favorite half-truth was that I had to go to the library to do research online. Before, I had complained bitterly about not having Internet access at home, but now it was a perfect alibi. Getting good grades made my parents happy, even though I'd already been accepted into the teaching program at St. Clair Baptist College.

At home, I was the perfect student, Christian, and daughter—the person my parents wanted me to be. I wanted them to think it was just life as usual around our house—no worries, no cares, everything running on autopilot. It was easy to pretend. We didn't even have small arguments anymore, because I never asked to go on a date or to a dance. I didn't care about missing the senior class party or about hanging out with my friends. I did what I needed to do—went to school, finished homework, cleaned my room—knowing it would buy me time for the only thing I couldn't live without. Michael.

Things just kind of unfolded between us, a little more every time we met up. It reminded me of the way tulips, for weeks before they actually open, *look* like they are going to burst open and everyone worries that a late winter frost will kill them before they bloom. But they always open exactly when they are supposed to.

It took him forever to kiss me for the first time. I was starting to wonder if he ever would. It seemed like he wanted to, but kept holding back, like he was afraid of what would happen. Finally he did one day when we were walking through a wooded park together. One of my socks had worked its way down my ankle, bunching itself up over my foot. I stopped and took off my boot so that I could pull up the sock. Trying to balance on one foot, I put my free arm on Michael's shoulder to steady myself.

"There!" I said, after I'd pulled the boot back on. I looked up at him, my arm still on his shoulder. "Thanks. Let's—" But, looking at him, I couldn't remember what

I'd been going to say. It was the weirdest thing—like my mind had been wiped clean. The late afternoon sun sliced through the trees, making his hair glow. The effect mesmerized me. I couldn't look away. I couldn't even blink.

I tried again. "Let's—"

Michael seemed to sense the change in my mood. "Yes," he said. "Let's."

He leaned in and kissed me on the lips, then softly behind my ear, then down around the base of it, sending the current through me again.

Ryan, who was the only guy I'd ever dated seriously, had never done that. But in my romance novels, Conrad and Drake and Ethan had done just that to Rebecca and Elizabeth and Lorelei, which is why I knew to arch my back and turn my head so Michael could kiss my neck. I wondered if he could smell my perfume, which was lavender and supposedly had pheromones, and if it screamed *high school senior* to him.

"Mm," Michael said, his lips still close to mine. "Fresh." He slipped his hand between my unbuttoned jacket and sweater, pausing when his hand was right below my breast. I leaned into him, letting my body answer his question. He cupped my breast and slowly skimmed over the curve of it with his thumb. He did it so lightly that I sensed it more than felt it. The current intensified, humming, arcing, crackling down my spine, down further than I'd ever imagined it could go, down and around, racing through me and into me until it jolted the very center of me. Suddenly, instead of just feeling the current, I *was* the current. The hum was me and I was the hum and Michael was the one who set it all off.

I'd made out with Ryan, but it had always been rushed and awkward, squeezed in while his parents were out but coming home soon, or while parking in his beater car, lying on spiral-bound notebooks, after we'd cleared the seat of empty Coke bottles and his soccer cleats.

With Michael, though, making out was *this*—an event, and during it all my senses and emotions were keen and electrified. With Michael everything was and is and would be different, now and forever more, Amen. With Michael . . . but then he kissed me slow and deep, and Ryan and school and my parents and Liv and even I receded, until all I knew was the rush of him wanting me.

* * *

I spent that evening trying to concentrate on my homework at Liv's, but it was impossible. Michael was in my head and my heart and suddenly there wasn't room for anything else.

Around 9:00, I gave up and walked home. Before going inside, I closed my eyes and took a few deep breaths to remind myself that I was switching worlds, going to the one where Michael didn't exist.

When I opened my eyes, I saw that the mail was still in the box, and I grabbed it for my mom, who probably hadn't thought to get it.

Only the light over the kitchen sink was on. Thinking my parents had already gone to bed, I stood there sorting through the mail—a phone bill, a postcard from church reminding my dad of a meeting, a flyer of coupons from Pizza Pete's, which I tucked under my arm so I wouldn't lose it. When I got to a yellow envelope from "Everywhere the Word," I stopped and flicked at it with my finger, thinking. How long had it been since the last time Dad and I had gone? Three years? Four?

"Everywhere the Word" was an activity my church had been doing since I was a kid. A bunch of families would go to another town and go door-to-door, passing out tracts and telling people about God. In the evening, after dinner, we'd form a big circle, hold hands, and sing and pray for all the people we'd met. We'd spend the night at a motel, and the next morning, we'd get up and do it all over again.

The three times we'd gone before, my mom had said it would make her too tired and had stayed home.

So it was just my dad and me and a bunch of other families. For me, it was one big adventure. The first trip, I remember holding my dad's hand, swinging his arm in a wide arc as we walked to the next house, just happy to be with him.

But then Pastor Mark had caught up with us. "This is the most important job you'll ever do, Gracie," he said, patting his Bible. "Pray that the Holy Spirit will soften these people's hearts, so they come to know the Lord Jesus Christ. Otherwise, they'll spend eternity in hell."

Later, I worried that I hadn't prayed long enough to save anyone because my best church friend, Bethany, had skipped up behind me and, giggling, pinched my arm, then darted away.

"Can I chase her, Daddy? Please?"

He looked around to make sure Pastor Mark wasn't watching, then winked at me and said, "Okay. Just keep it between you, me, and the Trinity."

Once we were inside the house, I listened to what my dad said, even though the kids who lived there were watching cartoons. "It's not complicated. It's simple. There's only one thing you need to know." He turned to me and asked, "Isn't there, Grace?"

I nodded. "Believe in the Lord Jesus Christ and thou shalt be saved, and thy house. Acts 16:31." He flashed a proud smile at me before he turned back to the unsaved and said, "That's right. All you need to do is believe."

That night, after the prayer meeting, after I'd put on my Cinderella pajamas in the bathroom and brushed my teeth, and we'd called my mom, my dad tucked me into one of the big double beds, and we talked for a long time about things that were important to me. We talked about why Lake Michigan is so many colors of blue, and how I really wanted a frog sleeping bag before going to Bethany's sleepover, and the locket I thought we should buy Mom for her birthday.

And it was like that the other times we'd gone, too—special, even fun.

Until the last time we went, a few years ago. By then, Bethany had moved, and I was embarrassed by going door-to-door. By then I knew people didn't really want us in their homes. They were just being polite. I got through the day by thinking how much fun my dad and I would have hanging out in the hotel room later.

Walking down the hall with our luggage that night, he handed me a key. He stopped in front of a door and said, "Here we are."

I unlocked the door and hauled in my suitcase and pillow. "I guess you want the bed closest to the bathroom, as usual," I said, throwing my stuff onto the far bed, then turning to help him with the cooler full of snacks we had brought.

He was still standing in the hall. "I'll be in room 153. It's just a few doors down."

"But . . . why?"

He shifted his weight from one foot to the other, looking uncomfortable. "That's the way it'll be now. You're getting older. It's time."

"Time for what?"

"Just . . . right there is where I'll be," he mumbled, cocking his head toward the end of the hall. "If you need anything."

"Wait. Aren't we going to, you know, hang out? Like we always do?" I questioned, feeling puzzled and a little hurt.

"It's been a long day. I think I'll just go to bed." He shoved the cooler inside my room. "But here. You keep this. Have whatever you want out of there."

* * *

Now, standing there at our kitchen counter, softly tapping the corner of the "Everywhere the Word" envelope against my palm, I thought how what I'd wanted wasn't in that cooler. It was weird to remember, given how I felt about him now, but what I had wanted back then was to spend time with him.

"Grace?" my mom said from the living room.

I made my way to the living room, flipping on lights as I went. "I thought you and Dad had gone to bed already."

"He forgot something," she said, nodding at the window, which looked out on our street. "At church. He went back."

"You shouldn't sit in the dark. It'll ruin your eyes."

Smiling just made her look more tired. "But I'm not reading."

I gave her the stack of mail, leaving the "Everywhere the Word" envelope on top. "I don't have to go on that trip, do I? Please say I don't."

"Why, yes," she said, sounding surprised. "Your father is planning on it. He'd be so disappointed if he knew you didn't want to go with him."

I groaned again. "It's embarrassing."

"Don't let your father hear you talk like that. It'll be good for you and him to go together. Maybe it'll make things better between you. You used to love going."

"That was before."

"Before what?"

Before he stopped cutting me some slack once in a while, I thought. "Before I outgrew it."

"Don't be sullen about going, okay?" The lights from the car swept the room as my dad pulled into the driveway. "Here he is. Just act a little excited about it. It would mean so much to him."

I sat down on the couch, feeling like I might as well get it over with. My father came in holding up a file folder. "Found it," he said. "Right where I left it on top of the coat rack. Grace, I picked up those forms that you still have to fill out for St. Clair today, and I deposited money in your bank account. I also talked to Brent Laslow about a summer job."

"Mr. Laslow—at your office?"

"That's right. I told him you could do clerical."

"But I was going to talk to Lila about a job at the green house!"

"I know that, but you'll never be able to use those skills in the real world. If you work at our office, you'll learn how to organize, keep track of things, work with people—the kinds of things you'll be able to use when you're a teacher. Don't worry about interviewing. I've set it up for you already," he said, picking up the pile of mail from my mom's lap. "All you'll have to do is show up the week after graduation."

I watched miserably while my father sorted the mail into two neat stacks. Between having to work with my dad all summer and having to go on the "Everywhere the Word" trip with him, I wasn't sure how much worse things could get.

He paused when he picked up the yellow envelope, like he was trying to decide which stack to put it in. My mother raised her eyebrows at me and nodded. I knew she was waiting for me to say something positive.

Finally, he pursed his lips and threw it on top of what I guessed was the "throw out" stack.

"Grace and I were just talking about that and how much she's looking forward to going," my mom said. I glared at her, but she refused to look at me.

"Sorry to disappoint you, Grace. We're not going this time."

Inside, I was thrilled. "That's all right," I said, getting up. Then, wanting to make my mother happy and figuring I had nothing to lose, I added, "Maybe we can go next time."

Still concentrating on my father, my mother didn't even notice my extra effort. She folded one hand over the other and said, "Just last week you said—"

"I have a work conflict," my father said, picking at the front of his shirt. "That I just found out about."

My mom's face was calm. "Oh—over a weekend?"

"Yes," my father said in a curt voice, pulling at his shirt again.

"Is that shirt bothering you?"

"What?" my father said. "Oh, no. Nothing. Just an itch, I guess." He dropped the bills onto the kitchen table and threw the rest of the mail into the trash can, letting the lid close with a clank.

I said goodnight. Feeling like a person on death row who had just been given a stay of execution, I had to work hard to keep the bounce out of my step as I escaped to my room.

Five

The next time we saw each other, I went to Michael's house for the first time. The inch or two of lake-effect snow that had been predicted had turned into a late-winter snow-storm, taking plow crews by surprise, and the back roads were still buried under six inches.

All the snow muffled the road noise, and the ride out was quiet and dreamlike. Even if the car slid off the road and into a ditch, I was sure the landing would be soft, like driving into a big down pillow. No one would get hurt.

I looked out the window at the pristine snow as Mi-chael's car cut a path through it. Illuminated by the bright headlights, oversized snowflakes rushed at the windshield and when I looked at them head on, I felt like I was traveling through space, hurtling past stars and planets toward another galaxy. After a few miles I got dizzy and had to look away.

Michael fiddled with the heater control. "Comfortable?" he asked.

"Mm-hmm," I said, unbuttoning my coat. "Is it far?"

He lifted his briefcase and moved it to the backseat, so only my backpack was between us. I tried to move it so I could sit next to him, but it was heavy and at an awkward angle.

Just a few days before, Michael had made fun of a contemporary novel. He'd said it was "the literary equivalent of white trash, just like horror books and romances." After that, I stopped hiding the romances in my backpack. Instead, I left them at home, hidden from my father in an empty Tampax box. Still, all the books I was using to research my paper on the *Odyssey* for English made my backpack heavier than usual and unwieldy. I finally just shoved it onto the floor and slid over next to him.

He smelled like stale smoke, leather, and fading aftershave, and, when I tipped my head back so he could kiss me, his stubble scrubbed against the skin on my cheek. He moved the bottom of my coat aside and laid his hand high on my thigh.

"Is it far?" I asked again.

"Yes, but it won't seem like it." He accelerated and the car surged ahead.

"I'm hungry," I said. Deep snow always made me hungry. It was like something in my brain that was left over from prehistoric times. As soon as my body saw deep snow, it started to worry about starving.

"That's good," he said. "It's a sign of a healthy appetite. I'll make you something special when we get there."

We drove past a pond that we had visited on field trips every year in elementary school. "I've always liked water striders," I said, suddenly. "Those bugs that skate across the water?"

Michael squeezed my leg playfully. "Now there's something you don't hear every day—someone saying they like water striders."

"I think it's something about how their looks are deceiving. They are all spindly and look harmless, but you know how they eat their prey? They use a sharp thing—a rostrum, I think it's called—to suck the juices out."

"Voilà!" Michael said. "A tasty first course!"

"Exactly," I said. "But they don't look like they have it in them to be that strong. I mean, there is nothing to them. And they are always moving. If they don't keep moving, then something further up the food chain will eat them." I wondered if Michael thought all my talk about bugs was dumb, if it bored him.

But then he leaned over and kissed me. "You're so good for me," he said.

"I am?"

"You take me out of my ivory tower," he said. "I'm always thinking about nature because of Wordsworth and the other Romantics, but it's not anything you can really touch. It's conceptual. But nature speaks to you in a very elemental, real way, not theoretical. Maybe that's why I feel like you keep me grounded."

Something inside of me broke loose when he said that. Until then, I had tried not to think too much about where our relationship could or couldn't go. I'd just been inhaling it, living my own secret fairy tale. But when he said I was good for him, what he meant was that he liked me. I *did* something for him. I suddenly realized what had broken loose. It was hope.

I knew we were north of the library, where he had picked me up, but I had stopped recognizing landmarks a few miles back. I liked the idea that there were still parts of town I hadn't seen before and I was seeing them with Michael.

His tree-lined driveway was flat by the road but quickly became steep as it wound through the woods. The house was perched on a clearing at the top. When we reached it, Michael cut the lights and the engine but didn't move to get out.

I pulled up some strands of hair that had come loose from my hair clip, coaxing them back into place, then went through my pockets and backpack for a mint, which I couldn't find, even though I was sure I had some that morning. I finally gave up, figuring that Liv had probably taken them. Shifting in my seat, I sighed.

Michael laughed. "You're like a little rabbit, darting this way and that. Just sit and *be.*"

"I guess I'm not used to sitting out in the middle of the woods in the dark. Aren't we going to go in or something?"

"In a minute. I'm just looking at you."

"It's dark. You can't even *see* me."

His coat squeaked against the seat as he angled his body towards me. "Do you want to sit over here with me for a minute?"

I slid up onto him and sat with my back against his window. I draped my arm across his shoulders. He ran his hand over the top of my thighs around my hips and then up my back.

"I can't see you," he said, "but I can feel you. You're curvaceous—"

Suddenly self-conscious, I sucked in my stomach. "No, don't," he said. "God, your curves are refreshing! And you're so soft. It's the softness that I love."

That he loves! But before I had time to turn it over in my mind, he said, "We've sat in the car so often that it's habit. For a while, I felt like I was back in high school myself—although I can't remember what it was like to be a virgin."

"Michael!" I said, glad that he couldn't see that I was blushing.

"Come on," he said, opening his car door. "I'll make you my signature dish."

When we got inside, I saw that snowlight was streaming in through the floor-to-ceiling windows. The windows and the openness of the rooms made me feel like I was on a widow's walk, high above everything and out in nature, rather than in a house. "It's like we're still outside," I said, pivoting slowly to take it all in. "Like there aren't any walls at all."

"I'm used to it, I guess," Michael said, helping me take my coat off. "It's not mine." He turned on the recessed lights in the kitchen. "I'm just renting it for this term, until I go back to Amberton in June. I was lucky to find someplace fully furnished. The people who live here are spending a year abroad."

"It's nice," I said, following him into the kitchen and watching as he put some cheese and crackers on a plate. I ate them all, one after the other.

"Don't they feed you at home?" Michael asked, cutting more cheese and handing it directly to me.

"Mom cooks, even though food isn't really her thing. It's just that lately I've been so hungry. Maybe it's just some kind of late growth spurt or something." I groaned. *Had I really said growth spurt?*

He ran his hand over my butt and gave me an appreciative smile. "A siren's appetite for a siren's body."

I wrinkled my nose. I had always wanted a body like Liv's—naturally thin with little breasts and no hips—but that wasn't the way I was turning out, and I didn't feel like fighting nature.

"Let me get you a glass of wine. I have a nice chard that's cold. How about that?"

"Sure," I said, thinking *Chard? What's chard?* I knew a little about beer and rum because of high school parties, but my parents didn't drink and I knew nothing about wine. So I did what I always did when Michael talked about something I didn't know—I waited and hoped for a clue.

"Some chardonnays have a bite," he said. *Oh, chardonnay*, I thought with relief. *White wine*. "But this one is older so it has mellowed. In fact, it's dangerously smooth. By the time you feel its effect, you're already drunk."

"Thanks for the warning." The wine glass glittered in the light when he handed it to me. Afraid that I'd break the stem if I gripped it too tightly, I held the glass gingerly.

"Wait," he said. He lifted his glass and touched it to mine. "To what can be, instead of what is."

I took a small sip and, knowing he was watching me, tried not to make a face. "It's . . . interesting."

"It's okay if you don't like it. Wine is an acquired taste."

I took another sip. I wanted to acquire the taste.

Michael pulled a barstool away from the island. "Have a seat," he said.

I looked around the kitchen. "I could help you."

"Do you cook?"

"I make a mean macaroni and Cheez Whiz."

"Cheez Whiz?" He shuddered, making me laugh. "I hope you know that's not real food. Anything that's misspelled is never real food."

"I don't care. I like it. It goes with everything—eggs, broccoli, crackers, chips . . ."

"I can see I have my work cut out for me," he joked, putting a pan of water on to boil. He disappeared into the pantry and called, "And stay away from the stove! I'll be doing the cooking for the foreseeable future."

When he came back he had an avocado. "Do you like these?" he asked.

"I don't know." I watched him slice through the skin of the avocado and slide his thumb between the skin and the flesh. The top layer of the avocado gave way under pressure of his thumb, but the flesh itself was firm.

"Do you mean you've had them but were undecided about them? Or that you've never had them?"

"I've never had them."

Michael skimmed the surface of the peeled avocado with his finger and held it up. "It's good," he said. "Try it."

I knew I wouldn't like it. Using my finger, I took a bit from his finger and tasted it. "It's all right."

He laughed. "You barely tasted it!" Bringing the naked avocado with him, he came up beside my barstool. "You need to savor an avocado in order to fully appreciate it. Like this," he said. He picked up my hand and guided my index finger over the avocado's buttery surface. I felt the urge to giggle, but swallowed it. By the time he took my finger into his mouth, closed his eyes, and slowly circled my finger with his tongue, lightly sucking on it at the same time, I felt a different kind of urge.

I closed my eyes and relaxed into it for a moment, until I realized that I didn't know what to do next. *When should I pull my finger out? Thirty seconds? Ten? And how many seconds have gone by?*

I sometimes read Liv's *Cosmopolitan* but I had never seen anything about how long to leave your finger in your boyfriend's mouth. Liv, who had made out a lot with guys, had never said anything about it, either. And even though Rebecca's bosom heaved a lot and Conrad "swelled" against her, I couldn't remember any mentions of fingers, except for when they were on the trigger of a pistol.

So I guessed. When my fingertip was almost out of his mouth, Michael bit down lightly on it and ran his tongue over the top of it. The tingling sensation I felt there scattered to my wrists, the back of my neck, and the inside of my thighs and higher, where it set a part of me vibrating.

So this is how it's done, I thought. *This is the way it's supposed to be.* Other guys headed for the obvious places. Michael knew about secret places hidden in plain view. And he knew how to navigate them.

"Now do you like avocados?" he asked.

"I do," I said, sure he would kiss me then, desperately wanting him to.

He went back to dicing the avocado, as though nothing had happened. "Aztecs called them *ahuactl*—testicle—because the pit looks like a testicle and because they thought it aroused passion."

"Maybe I should put some in my macaroni and cheese."

"What kind of food do you eat at your house? Other than that?"

"The bland kind."

"Like what? Give me specifics."

I took a sip of wine. I didn't like the taste any better, but the effect was nice. It made everything easy. "Chicken, chicken, and chicken. And then there are the nights where, just for a change of pace, we have chicken."

"Is it any good?"

I laughed loudly. "It's awful. My mom tries really hard, but the chicken is always dry." I suddenly realized that I had to go to the bathroom. "Where is the . . . ?"

"The restroom is through the living room to your left," he said.

I felt a little unsteady when I stood up, like I was walking on a puffy moon walk instead of the kitchen's firm slate floor. I kept my balance by concentrating, and suddenly it seemed hilarious to me that it was so much work to do something as simple as walking. I giggled all the way to the bathroom.

By the time I got back, Michael had lit candles, dished out the pasta, and poured himself another glass of wine. I was disappointed to see that there was only a large glass of water next to my plate.

The words escaped as soon as I thought them. "Aren't you going to get me drunk and take advantage of me?"

Smiling, he shook his head and pulled the chair out for me. "You've had enough wine, I think. Drink the water or you'll get dehydrated."

Even though my mind was a little fuzzy, it hit me then that Michael cared about me. Other guys had been nice to me on dates, but there was something different, almost tender about the way Michael treated me. Sometimes, when

I couldn't push aside my guilty feelings about lying to my parents, I would kind of disappear into a quiet zone. Michael would ask me, "Do you want to talk about it?" And if I shook my head, then he'd just hold my hand or put his arm around me and we'd be together that way. He was so laid back then, so perfect for me.

I leaned over the steaming dish of pasta, closed my eyes, and inhaled. "Mmmm," I said. "It smells great."

"I hope you like it," he said, putting the linen napkin over his lap.

I tasted my pasta and then stared at Michael. "This is really amazing," I said. "I'm serious. I've never had anything like it."

Michael beamed. "I do all right, for a bachelor. I actually learned to cook when I was pretty young." He poured himself a glass of water and ate a few bites. "And where are you tonight?"

I knew he meant where had I told my parents I'd be. "At Liv's. Studying for a history test."

"Learning much?"

"Only about the history of avocados."

He broke off a piece of French bread and handed it to me. "Will they check on you?"

"I don't think so, but if they do, Liv will cover for me. They're at church tonight," I said, through a mouthful of bread. I brushed away the crumbs that fell onto my cardigan, hoping that Michael hadn't noticed.

"Again?"

"Always." I ticked off my dad's priorities on my fingers. "God, country, family."

"Just like the Boy Scouts."

"Wait—you were a Boy Scout?"

"For a while, when I was young, before . . . things disintegrated." He picked up his glass of wine and moved it in small circle, so the wine swirled in the glass. I propped my elbows on the table and rested my hand on my chin.

"Actually, things had been disintegrating for a long time."

"What happened?"

"My mother died when I was six—breast cancer."

"But that's so young!" I said.

He smiled sadly. "I was young. She was, too—just forty-eight. To say that I wasn't a planned baby is an understatement. My sister, Elise, was already sixteen."

"So that's when everything fell apart?"

"I told you it was a long story. I'm getting to that."

"Sorry," I said.

"It's all right. In truth, that's probably when it did start falling apart. My dad held it all together for a while after Mom died. Our family was different, obviously, but at least it still felt like a family. Elise tried to be a surrogate mom for me. It was working moderately well.

"But Dad, instead of unraveling, got more tightly wound. He had always been driven, but it had been okay because my mom buffered us. After she died, his ambition was like a laser and he directed it at us. He was determined that we'd go on to 'make something of ourselves'—that her dying wouldn't be a setback that way. He pushed us—nothing was ever good enough. My sister got the worst of it. 'The Princeton admissions committee is not going to care that your mother died.' That's what he'd say." Michael pressed his lips together until they were a hard, thin line.

"That's pretty harsh."

Michael took a drink of his wine and shook his head. "My father was always right, as far as he was concerned. Eventually Elise gave up trying. She rebelled—stopped studying, drank, hung around with a crowd of misfits. My father and Elise started arguing—frequently. Everything escalated. And then, one night, she threw some things in a bag and left."

"Where is she now?"

"I don't know. I thought she might turn up at my high school graduation or at Dad's funeral a few years ago, but she didn't. Even if she was mad at him, I think she would have gotten in touch after he died. I think something must have happened to her. She didn't have any money, and she was probably too proud to call Dad for help."

I sat quietly, not knowing what to say, but feeling flattered that he'd confided in me. I had never felt as close to anyone as I did to him right then. The hum I always felt when I was with him suddenly seemed like something I could hold instead of just feel. I put my hand on his arm. "It must be awful for you."

"Not so much anymore. It all happened a long time ago." He ran his fingers through his hair and sighed. "How did we even start talking about all that?"

"I was telling you what was most important to my father, which led to Boy Scouts, which led to your sister." I was pleased with myself that I could trace it all back for him. I took a big bite of pasta.

"Right, and it all leads back to you—back to us," he said, smiling.

I savored all the new flavors in the pasta and then washed it down with a big gulp of water. "This is so incredible!"

"Thank you," he said. He seemed grateful to be talking about the food again.

"Is there anything you're not good at?"

He leaned back in his chair and stroked his chin. "Hockey. I tried it once and ended up almost impaling myself." He thumbed the center of his chest once with his fist. "Right here."

I didn't believe him, so he showed me his jagged three-inch scar on his chest. It made him seem even more perfect to me. I had the sudden urge to taste it, but instead I ate another bite of my pasta while he tucked his shirt back in. In fact, I ate every bit of my pasta. And if I'd been by myself, I probably would have licked the bowl.

* * *

Michael said he'd do the dishes later, but I wanted to do them for him. The dishwasher wasn't working, so I squirted some lemon dish soap into the fancy kitchen sink and filled it with warm water until it was up to my elbows. I carefully slid each piece in and then washed them all, taking my time, enjoying the feel of the water against my skin.

I felt loose and alert at the same time, hyper-aware of Michael's every move in the other room. I heard the bathroom door open and close and open again, then the hiss of the gas fireplace. He came back into the kitchen, heading for the bottle of wine and our wine glasses, but stopped right behind me and fit himself against my back. Resting his head against my hair right above my ear, he wrapped his arms around me and then put his hands into the sink, too. He ran his hands down my slippery arms and twined his fingers through mine when he found them at the bottom of the sink, washing spoons.

I had thought about being alone with Michael in his house for a long time. Liv and I had talked about it. "You think he's going to be content with a little kissing?" she had asked. "Once a guy has done it, anything less makes him frustrated and restless."

Michael already knew I wanted to stay a virgin. He said he respected my decision ("as long as you're thinking for yourself," which I thought I was), even though he didn't really understand it. "People get so stuck on sex when it's just two people connecting and getting close," he'd said. "Making love is a simple, natural thing, but they give it so much power and so much baggage. But it's your decision."

That's what worried me. We had never been alone together in a house, with a fireplace, and wine, and a bed. Every night for the past week I had been practicing saying no, mostly on my African violet and spider plant.

"No," I'd whisper to the violet. "You know I can't," I'd say to the spider plant. And then I'd lie awake and worry about being strong enough to say no, not to Michael, but to myself.

When I had balanced the last pan atop all the dishes on the drainer, we went into the living room and sat down on the couch that faced the fireplace. Michael put his arm around me.

"What are you supposed to be doing tonight?" I asked, snuggling into him.

"Grading English Comp papers. And writing a report for the department chair."

"A college professor who's single and good looking," I said, teasing him a little. "Girls must come on to you all the time."

He stared at the fire and nodded, like it was no big deal. "Sometimes they do," he said. "But I don't want them anymore."

My heart lurched—*did he not want them anymore because he only wanted me?*—but I kept my voice steady. "Liv worries you're just using me."

Michael threw his head back and laughed. "For what? We haven't done anything except kiss." Still holding his wine glass, he brushed the back of his hand across my breast playfully. "And I have managed to get to first base—is that what it's still called?"

I looked out the window behind the couch, making sure I could still see him out of the corner of my eye. "She wonders why you don't go out with women who are your own age."

Michael unclipped my hair and it fell to my shoulders. "I have," he said, tucking my hair behind my ear and then letting it slip through his fingers until he reached the top button of my sweater. "But they are too hard. There's no 'give' to them. They already think they know everything." He put his hand on my chin and turned my face toward him, so I had to look at him. "With you, there's this incredible sense of discovery and openness to things. To me."

His gaze was so intense, like he wanted to lock me in and keep me from looking away.

"Listen," he said. "I don't make a habit of cradle-robbing, if that's what you want to know. This—*you*—took me by surprise. I'm glad it happened, but I didn't plan for it to be this way."

"But you . . . with me. It's—" I stopped and sighed, not wanting to say *It's incredible, impossible, unbelievable that someone like you wants me.*

"It is what it is," he said. "We don't know yet what it could be."

He leaned in and kissed me then for a long time. After a while, without even looking, he unbuttoned my cardigan in five smooth moves then pushed it aside so he could look at me. His gaze felt more personal than Ryan's touch ever had. Suddenly self-conscious, I folded my arms over my chest.

He shook his head and gently pulled my arms away. "You don't know," he said earnestly. "You're beautiful and you don't even know it." He stroked my collarbone, then using just his pinkie, slipped my bra strap over my shoulder.

"Grace," he said, lightly stroking my skin. "I want to lie together."

I closed my eyes and it was only because I had so faithfully practiced on my plants that I could say, "Michael, I can't—"

"I know you don't want to make love. I'm not asking you to. I just want to see you. I feel so close to you, Grace. I just want to lie together, with nothing between us." He rested his forehead against mine. "Please," he said. "I won't try anything."

Yes, my body said. *Yes, yes, yes*. I said, "Michael—"

He traced my lips with his finger to stop me, setting in motion a wave deep inside of me. "Please," he whispered, his lips still close to mine.

I thought about Liv, who was practically dying of envy. "He could have anyone," she'd said. "And he wants you." But how many things could I say no to him about before he got tired of being with me? That night Michael had opened up so much with me. I felt so connected to him, like what we had was something real. I wanted to be close to him and to feel him close to me. I liked the feeling of the wave building inside of me. All he wanted was to lie together. My father would have said it was the devil's voice I was hearing, but I was sure it was finally my own. Plus, I'd already proven that I could say no. That I would say no.

I looked around the living room. "Here?" I asked.

He shook his head and stood up. "'Arise, my love, my fair one, and come away; for lo, the winter is past, the rain is over and gone,'" he said. It sounded familiar, but I couldn't place it.

"Keats?" I guessed.

He smiled and shook his head. "Song of Solomon."

"Wait. The Bible? You . . . ?"

"I thought you'd like it," he said, taking my hand and pulling me up. I did. Even more, I liked the way his voice had come out, smooth and low, like he was caressing me with the words.

He slung his arm low around my hips and guided me into the bedroom. While he dimmed the recessed lights, I stood there wondering what to do. I knew from books and movies that this should feel incredibly romantic, but instead it felt awkward.

I wished there was a way to skip over this part. As he slowly undressed me, pausing after each item of clothing to look at me and kiss me, all I could think of was how I must look to him. Pale, uncomfortable, and not exactly thin.

"You're shivering," he said. He turned back the covers and I lay down, trying not to look as stiff as I felt. He pulled the down comforter up around me. While Michael took off his own clothes, I looked out the window at the falling snow. There were some things I just wasn't ready to see yet.

When I felt him lie down beside me, I knew it was safe to roll onto my side and look at his face.

He propped his head up on one arm and kissed my eyelids and forehead and lips while he moved his hand up my thigh. Over my hips, along my waist. Up and over my back, to the nape of my neck, then back down again, gently. He did that again and again until I had finally relaxed against him.

"Am I really okay?" I whispered, wishing I didn't have to ask the question.

"Oh, Rabbit," he said into my hair. "You're better than okay. You're perfect. You're just what I've been looking for. Believe me."

I believed. I believed like I had never believed anything before. He said other things then, and I listened to and believed all of them.

And when he stopped using words and let his lips talk to me in a different way, another Bible verse came to me. "Set me as a seal on your heart, for love is as strong as death; ardent love is as unrelenting as the grave. Love's flames are fiery flames, the fiercest of all." For the first time, I understood it.

Six

"*Well?*" Liv said, after Michael dropped me off at her house and we were safely in her room. "Tell me *ev*erything."

She flopped backward onto her bed, sucked in her breath, and unzipped her jeans. The waistband and snap had left angry red imprints on her flat stomach.

"How do you breathe in those things?" I asked, perching on the edge of the bed.

"It's not easy. But if I don't wear them this tight it looks like I don't have any ass at all. And don't change the subject. Spill." Liv's foot began to wiggle. Even when she was relaxing, Liv was in motion, like a pacing tiger watching for her chance to make a break for it.

I smoothed out the red bedspread. "It was nice. He made me dinner and we had some wine, and we just . . . talked."

"You didn't make out?"

"Sort of."

"Which means?"

"I guess you could say that we ended up in bed together. And our clothes . . ." I paused for dramatic effect. ". . . didn't."

Liv laid her hand on her hip, then jerked it away quickly as though it had been burned. "Sssss!" she said. "That is so hot. *He* is so hot. He wants it, right?"

"Probably not as much as I do," I said.

"Was it different than with Ryan?"

"Different?" I thought back, back to the bed, back to the current, back to the swelling wave. "Yeah, it was completely different."

"And?"

I realized then that I didn't really want to talk about it. If I said too much, Liv would probably make fun of me or find a way to spoil the whole thing. "And nothing."

"Right," she said, sarcastically. "You didn't get it on."

"It wasn't about getting it on or not getting it on."

"I'll bet. He may not be ringing your bell yet, but he is definitely on your doorstep knocking."

"It wasn't like that. He didn't push me to make love. He just wanted to get close to me." I lay down next to Liv and rolled over onto my stomach. "You know, when I first started dating, my mom told me that all I had to do was ask boys about themselves and they'd like me," I said, stuffing a pillow under my chin. "I always wondered how can they like me when they don't know anything about me? But Michael wants to talk about me."

"You mean he's interested in *who you are?*" Liv said the last words in a dramatic whisper, teasing. Liv was always accusing me of being too serious.

I chewed my bottom lip. "Kind of. He . . . *pushes* me, in a way. He's big into self-help or something. He talks a lot about man's potential."

"What? Like the Army commercial? BE! All that you can BE?"

"In a way," I said. "It's hard to explain. I guess it's good for me. He forces me to think. Last week he asked me why I wanted to be a teacher."

"Uh-huh," Liv said, chipping the green polish off her nails.

"So I said because I like to help people. He asked if I've done a lot of babysitting, and then I realized that I haven't for a while. The Livingstons and Carsons used to call and ask me all the time, but I guess they stopped because I started saying no all the time. And he asked me why I always said no, and I said, 'Because I didn't like it.'"

"So?"

"So maybe I don't even really *like* kids."

"Maybe you just don't like those kids," Liv said. She fanned out her fingers, looking for any nail polish she'd missed. "They're all brats."

"That's not the point. The point is that now it seems like I decided in—I don't know—second grade or something that I wanted to be a teacher and my parents liked that idea and I never looked back. And now I wonder if that's what I really want to be."

"All because of Michael?"

I nodded.

Liv stretched her arms up over her head and hooked them over her pillow. "He's too good to be true. Even the way you met is like out of a book. 'Their eyes met across a crowded room and in that instant they both knew.'" She lowered her voice to a whisper. "*Destiny* had brought them together and nothing—not war or pestilence or an age gap or even overprotective, praise-*Jesus!* parents—would ever come between them.'"

I frowned. "It didn't seem like it was that way for him."

"It was exactly like that for him! I was with you at Corbin, remember?"

A large crash followed by the sound of shattering glass startled us and we both rolled off the bed and onto our feet.

From another room in the house we heard Liv's father shout, "Get over here, you lazy bitch!"

I could only make out a few words of Liv's mother's shrill reply. None of them were polite.

Liv looked at her watch. "Thursday, 9:50. Right on schedule. It's nice to be able to depend on your parents, isn't it?"

"I'd better go." I stood up and hiked my backpack over one shoulder. But before I could open the door, we heard what sounded like a chair skitter across the linoleum and crash into a wall, then more slurred shouting.

I knew that Liv's parents yelled a lot, but she had never said anything about them getting vicious. I looked over at Liv, who was gnawing on her cuticles. "When did they start throwing things?"

"Thirty seconds ago? Dad lost his job today."

"Why didn't you tell me?"

"It's more fun to talk about you and Michael."

"But it's your life!"

She shrugged and stood up. "I know. But it's such a downer. And anyway, I thought maybe now they'd stop fighting. Before, they were always fighting about where to spend the money. Now there's no money to spend, so I thought there'd be nothing left to fight over. Maybe they'd actually, like, pull together in a crisis. Stupid, huh?" Liv pretended to be straightening my hood for me so she wouldn't have to look me in the eye.

"I've got to get out of here," she said.

"Want to sleep at my house?"

"I was talking about forever. I've got to get that scholarship so I can get out of here. Otherwise, I'll end up just like them."

"No you wouldn't. Never."

"What do you know?" she said, bitterly. "Nobody dreams of being a drunk when they grow up. It's what happens when you're weak, when you don't have the will to get out."

"You'll get out."

Liv's eyes narrowed. "Yeah," she said. "I will."

Then we did what we always did. We listened at the door until everything got quiet so I could slip out the side door without anyone noticing.

When I was almost to the sidewalk, I turned back to ask Liv again to come home with me, but she had already closed the door.

Seven

From the far stall, I heard the girls' bathroom door squeak closed and then someone said, in a low voice, "Julianne told me he left a single white tulip and a note on her windshield."

"I heard he left it in her locker," said a second voice. I knew from the way she said *lock-ah* that it was Carrie, which meant that the other voice was Melissa's. They were in the popular group, so I didn't know them well, but our school was small enough that we all knew each other's names.

Something—probably their books—landed on the counter with a thud. "I don't get it," Melissa said. "Why is he going out with her? She's not super attractive or anything, and what is she? Like a size twelve or something?"

I wanted to say, "No, but I do fill out my clothes—not like you with your bony ass—and real men think curves are hot," but I just stood there staring at *4getU or 4giveU?* scrawled on the inside of my stall door, holding my breath.

"It's obvious. There's only one thing he can possibly want." I heard a rhythmic, dull slapping and then, "Uhh! Uhh! Uhh!" as Carrie groaned with each slap.

I winced. It seemed like everyone thought Michael only wanted me for one reason.

"Don't do that, Care. It's so vulgar. Besides, he could probably get that with anyone."

Yeah, I thought.

"Maybe he is getting it with someone else. If she's not putting out—" Carrie snapped her fingers. "That's what he sees in her!"

"What?"

"Think about it. A single *white* tulip? A good virgin is hard to find and he's—"

"Found one," I said, stepping out of the stall. My cheeks were hot and my stomach was churning wildly, like a blender filled with anger, hurt, and embarrassment—but also worry that my father would find out about us.

If kids at school knew about Michael and me, it was only a matter of time before my father would. What then? I thought we'd been so careful.

The tulip had probably been a bad idea. Michael, knowing that I would be riding home with Liv that day, had left it for me on Liv's windshield. But—well, who at high school had ever even noticed me? Liv and I had a few other friends, but basically we were invisible to the popular crowd. Why were they watching now?

But as soon as I asked myself the question, I knew the answer. Michael. It was stupid to think that I could keep him to myself, that others wouldn't notice him everywhere he went.

Melissa dropped her blush brush mid-stroke and it clattered onto the tile floor. I squirted the foam soap into my hand and turned on the water, letting them squirm.

Carrie giggled nervously and said, "God, Grace, I didn't mean that like it sounded. No offense or anything. It's just . . . well, look at yourself."

"Shut up," Melissa hissed at her from the floor, where she was groping for her makeup brush.

I didn't have to look at myself in the mirror to know what she meant. I knew there was nothing remarkable about me. My mom said once that I was a classic beauty, pretty in a way that kids my age don't recognize. She was probably stretching the truth on that one, although I do have interesting eyes that can look either blue or green, depending on what color I'm wearing.

I wanted to tell Melissa and Carrie to get a life instead of invading mine, but I was afraid that I wouldn't be able to stop with just that, and then it would turn into a big, ugly scene, which would set off more gossip. So I didn't say anything. I just punched the button on the hand drier and rubbed my hands together vigorously.

Melissa and Carrie clutched their books to their chests and scurried out the door. *Like the rats they are*, I thought. I couldn't wait to be done with high school and its stupid "who's in and who's out" games.

I hated how Carrie's comment ate away at my confidence the way aphids had chewed holes in my mother's hostas the only time that she had tried to do a little gardening. *Carrie doesn't know anything about the way it is with me and Michael*, I thought angrily. In a way, he'd already said he loved me, when he had talked about loving my curves. The tulip and the dinner he'd made just for me—they all added up to him loving me, didn't they? But if Carrie was right and Michael was getting it on the side, that would explain why he wasn't pushing me to go all the way.

I got a splitting headache in fifth hour. Then in sixth hour I got back my history exam—the one I didn't study for because of Michael—with a large C on it. And if that wasn't bad enough, Mr. Tyce humiliated me by reading one of my "less-than-*stellar*" answers out loud in front of the class.

"You can do better, Miss Passedge. Apply yourself—to your lessons," he added, tapping his pen on my desk with each syllable. It was a day straight from high school hell.

By the end of it, I had to see Michael. I was sure that if I could just talk to him, even if it was about the weather, I'd stop obsessing over Carrie's comment. I felt funny about going to find him, though. He'd never told me not to come to the college but I knew that if I did, I'd be mixing our two worlds—something we hadn't ever done before, or even wanted to do.

Twice I started down the street in the direction of Corbin College, and twice I walked back to the front steps of the high school. Finally I promised myself I would just walk through the campus, just walk by the big white building with pillars where he had his office, and that would be enough for me.

When I got there, I sat down on a cement bench and watched as one girl after another came out of the building and walked by me. Flipping open their cell phones and checking their messages, they all looked so sure of themselves. Some of them were in pairs, others were with boys, some walked by themselves. And one, one was with Michael, her head tipped toward his, listening to something he was saying. I heard Carrie's throaty voice again in my head, "Or maybe he's getting it from someone else," and I could feel my eyes starting to fill up. *Of course he's getting it!* I thought. *How stupid and naïve could I be?*

Just then, Michael looked up and saw me. He smiled and held up his finger as if to say, "Wait a minute." I thought about bolting—I'd been humiliated enough for one day—but I couldn't make myself go. It was like even though I knew how it would end, I was too stubborn to quit it. I had to hear him say it.

I watched as he eased himself out of the conversation and edged away from the girl. "Grace!" he said. His voice was warm but he stopped a foot or so in front of me. "This is a surprise. I was just leaving. Walk me to my car?"

I was afraid that if I tried to talk I'd just start blubbering, which wasn't the way I wanted him to remember me, so I just fell into step beside him, slogging through the slush piles rather than going around them. He caught my mood and we walked without speaking to a crosswalk at the outer edge of campus. From there, I could see Michael's car, flecked with springtime mud, parked in the lot across the street.

I stopped in front of a grove of pine trees and dropped my backpack. I took a deep breath, thinking that the smell of pine was poetic in a way. A fresh smell to go with the fresh start I'd be making after he dumped me.

"Just do it," I said, wanting it to be over quickly. He looked puzzled for a second, then scanned the sidewalk and the street. "What? This?" Grinning boyishly, he pulled me into the trees and into his arms and kissed me. It wasn't a pitying, breaking up kiss, either, like the kind Ryan had given me after he had said, "I'll always have feelings for you," on the night he broke up with me. Michael's kiss was passionate and forceful. I couldn't have resisted him, even if I'd wanted to.

"I'll be needing a cold shower now," he said, pretending to stumble backwards when I finally let go.

Even though I was starting to feel silly about doubting him and I knew the answer to the question, I still had to ask it. "Michael, are you . . . seeing anyone?"

"You mean seeing as in dating?"

"Or as in sleeping with?"

Michael's eyebrows shot up in surprise. "Grace, no. No one. I haven't even thought of it. What makes you ask that?"

"Oh, it's just there were these girls in the bathroom at school and then the girl you walked out with back there was coming on to you . . ." I let my voice trail off, realizing how insecure I sounded.

He shook his head. "Students are my job. I can't help it if they like me. There's a big difference between walking out with them and making love to them." With his fingertips, he pushed the hair away from my face. "Do you want me to explain it to you in physiological terms?" he asked, pretending to be serious.

I smiled, relieved that I had been wrong and grateful he knew how to get past the awkwardness. "I've had biology, thanks."

Michael cleared his throat like he wanted to say something. When he finally spoke, his voice really was serious. "There is something I should tell you, though. I've been wanting to tell you, but I was afraid you wouldn't believe me or that it would frighten you and you'd end it."

Suddenly I felt like I was on a haunted-house roller-coaster ride where witches and skeletons jump out when you least expect them to. Just when I thought everything was okay, now there was some kind of secret that he thought was terrible enough to make me not want him. I stared down at my muddy boots and ran through the possibilities in my head. He's married. He's gay. He's dying. He's an alien. It's like Liv said. He's too good to be true.

I thought about what Elizabeth, the heroine in the romance novel I finished the night before, had said to Sean when he had ended it—"I can't stop you from ripping out my heart, but I don't have to watch you do it"—and I closed my eyes. *Say it, Michael,* I thought. *Whatever it is, say it so this awful day can end.*

"To be honest with you, I was hoping the feeling would pass. You're only eighteen, you know? But I've got it, Rabbit. And I've got it bad."

Oh, no. AIDS! It's AIDS. The awfulness of it and my certainty that I was right made me light-headed.

He cupped my jaw with his hand and ran his thumb over my lips. "I'm in love with you."

Everything except Michael faded out then—the people slogging by, the sound of wheels in slush, the smell of damp pine—as I searched his face, questioning without asking. He understood and nodded. "It's true," he said.

I let out a single sob and fell against his chest as the words sank in. Even though it was what I had dreamed of and longed for, Michael being in love with me was more shocking than any of the other things I'd imagined he might say.

* * *

By the time I got home, my cheeks hurt from smiling but I couldn't stop—even after I reminded myself that I was switching worlds again. The elation of hearing Michael say he loved me had not faded, and I had never been so completely happy.

To keep my parents from being suspicious, I forced myself to frown. For good measure, I stomped through the door, startling my mother and making her drop the knitting she was carrying through the kitchen.

"What's wrong?" she asked.

Both my parents were watchful, but they watched for different things. My father was determined to keep me on the straight and narrow path and he was on the lookout for major things like sex, drinking, stealing. But my mother watched me for something else—changing colors, maybe, like you would a mood ring. She was quieter and more understanding than my father, but she was also harder to fool.

"Nothing's wrong. Why?"

"You look flushed and your face is twisted. You don't look like yourself. Are you angry?"

"No. I had a rollercoaster kind of day. That's all." I bent down to pick up her knitting. "Is this what you're working on?" I asked.

She nodded. "It's nothing, really." She had been knitting with the same skein of tan yarn all winter, knitting up a hat or a scarf or even just a square until the skein was gone, then pulling out the yarn, unraveling the whole thing so she could use it again. I'd asked her once why she didn't finish it. "You know how your father hates it when I'm frivolous," she'd said.

"We can afford yarn, Mom," I said. "Dad wouldn't mind."

"I know we can afford it. I know that. But it just doesn't matter to me. I like to do the knitting itself. I don't need to have anything to show for it."

I was used to the way my mother picked at her food and moved around the house without a sound—Liv sometimes referred to her as "the Vapor"—but this new oddity worried me.

I rubbed my fingers lightly over the weave. "What are you making this time?"

"A scarf again, but you see it's a little different pattern from the last—"

"Yvette!" The front door slammed, and the walls of our ranch house shuddered as my father burst into the room. "Have you seen Gra—" He stopped short when he saw me. "Who is he?" he said.

No, I thought. *This isn't happening. Not now. Not when things are perfect.* "Who is who?" I asked.

"Do *not,*" he sputtered, jabbing his middle finger at me, "Do not play dumb with me. Do not *lie* to me. I saw the two of you. I saw him put his hands on you."

I scrambled to rewind the day. *Where had he seen us?* We had been so careful. Both of us had wanted to be—me because of my parents and Michael because the college would disapprove. Some kids at school thought they knew, like Carrie, but as far as I knew, no one had seen us alone together. Michael and I were just a rumor. Nobody had any proof.

My father stalked over to me, his fists clenched by his side. He was angry but I wasn't afraid he would hurt me. He hadn't spanked me since I was eight, which was about the same time he'd stopped hugging me.

"Tell me," he said.

"He's . . . he's . . ." I stammered, trying to come up with a convincing lie. But while I was okay at small deceptions, I was a terrible outright liar. And I was too wrung out from my day to come up with something. I caved. "He's a teacher at the college."

"A professor! Did he hurt you? Did he threaten you? Force you?"

"No!" I said, wondering why my father always thought the worst of everyone. "It's nothing like that. We've just gone out a few times for coffee."

"You're telling me you're, what? *Dating* him?"

Out of the corner of my eye, I saw my mother take a step back and quietly fold herself into a chair that was along the wall.

"Yes," I said.

My father towered over me, so close that I could smell the dank wool of his coat. "All that stops now. I forbid you to see him again."

"You for*bid* me? You can't forbid me! We like each other a lot!" I said, lifting my chin. "In fact, we're in love."

He snorted. "In love! That's ridiculous. How long have you known him?"

"Five months," I said, even though it had been less.

My father darted a look at my wrist. "Where's your bracelet?"

I looked at my wrist, confused about why he would care right now about my jewelry. "My bracelet?"

"Yes, the 'true love waits' bracelet I gave you for your birthday two or three years ago."

"Two or three? That was six years ago. I was twelve."

"Well, where is it?"

Without thinking, I touched my index finger to my wrist. "It's too small. It cuts off my circulation."

My father's eyes turned into slits. "Are you fornicating?"

"No!" I said, irritated that he always jumped straight to sex, like there wasn't anything worse. "How could you even think that?"

"Because when it comes to the flesh, we're weak,'" he said. He was doing that weird, nervous tugging at his shirt again. "I'm glad it's not too late."

"For what?"

"To have done with it. You know I am a reasonable man, Grace. You may see this man again—but only to break it off. I'm going out of town for a few days. I want it ended by the time I get back."

"We're not doing anything wrong!"

My father leaned toward me and his coat grazed my arm. "There's only one thing a man like that can want with a girl like you, Grace. End it."

He was crowding me, but I didn't step back. I tipped my head away from him to give myself more space. It was because of Michael that I was finally getting somewhere in my life instead of being stuck in neutral. And now my father, thinking I was still Gracie, was telling me to end it.

"I won't," I said.

"You will," he said firmly. "And here's why. Because if you don't, I'll call the president of Corbin College and tell him just what your little professor has been up to. I'm sure he'll do whatever it takes to keep the college's reputation clean." Satisfied that he had made himself clear, he turned to my mother and said, "Yvette, come back to the bedroom and I'll tell you what I'll need for the trip." Then he left.

Stung by my father's threat, I looked to my mother. "Mom? Do you . . . ?"

"Your father knows best," she said grimly, standing up.

I realized I was still holding her knitting. My hands shook as I handed the half-done scarf back to her. "I like this one, Mom. You should finish it this time."

She carefully put the scarf and needles into her knitting bag and closed it. "Maybe sometime I'll finish one," she said, not looking at me. "But not this time."

Eight

"*That bastard!*" I said, fingering the tip of a leaf on my African violet, listening to the familiar scraping sounds of dresser drawers opening and closing as my mom helped my dad pack in the next room.

It wasn't the first time I had thought it about my father, but it was the first time I hadn't swallowed it back. Nice girls didn't think those kinds of things about their fathers and they certainly didn't say them. Liv did, though. She said them as naturally as she said, "Call me later."

I'd tried swearing before, and it always made Liv laugh.

"You're doing it wrong. You say it from your mouth," she says. "To get it right, you have to say it from your gut. You have to mean it."

This time I did mean it. In my mind, I kept going over the fight with my father. I hated his confidence and how he always thought he knew what was best when he didn't even know me anymore. He'd been so smug when he'd said, "You will."

"I won't!" I whispered angrily to my African violet.

When he had said it—"You will!"—his breath had smelled like coffee and stale butterscotch candy, the kind he used to offer me in church when I got restless. Because of his business trip, he must have left early from the office, where he had probably been tallying the profits and losses of his clients or telling them about the latest tax laws.

I couldn't believe I'd ever adored him. When I was little, he and I had taken over one corner of the living room and used it for a never-ending game of Monopoly. He was always the banker and he loved impressing me by doing all the math in his head. Back then, it seemed to me that he solved equations by making the numbers obey him.

As I got older, I saw that numbers either added up or they didn't. I couldn't understand how anyone could even care about them—they were just numbers. But my father had a strong opinion about everything. There were so many dinner "conversations" where he would talk about his clients and their numbers and how they could be more successful if they would only look at the numbers! When he started in on that, I just nodded in all the right places. I learned how from watching my mom.

I took a deep breath and slowly blew it out on the plant, which had been perking up lately, hoping to blow my father out of my head, too.

"There's only one thing a man can want from a girl like you," he had said. *This time, he's wrong,* I thought. *Michael loves me. If he wanted sex, he could get it anywhere.* Probably even with me. Because when it came to making out, my body had been a traitor, sending out all kinds of signals without my permission. Still, Michael hadn't pushed me. But my father didn't know any of that. Couldn't know any of that.

My stomach churned. "End it, or I'll make sure he gets fired," my father had said, standing there, so sure that he'd get his way, not caring that he was shutting down my life. I thought of the way he had blown by my mother almost like she wasn't there, how he always took her for granted. I thought of all the people at church who saw my father as a *good* man, a *kind* man, a *reasonable* man. It made me sick.

"That *bas*tard!" I said again, spitting out the words. And I knew by the feel of it and the sound of it that this time I was doing it right. This time I was saying it from my gut.

* * *

I waited until my father had left on his business trip and my mother was in the bathroom to call Michael.

"What's wrong?" he asked.

"I don't want to talk about it on the phone."

"But is it about this afternoon? Did I come on too strong?"

"No, it's not that. It's . . . it's complicated."

I heard him rustle through some papers on his desk. "I can't get away until 7:00," he said. "Where should I pick you up?"

"The library. I'll be there with Liv," I said, already reaching for my coat and backpack. I couldn't get out of there fast enough. "I'll be waiting."

"All right. I'll see you then, Rabbit."

"Michael, wait." I wished right then that I wasn't so needy. I wished that remembering he had said it just a few hours before would be enough for me, but it wasn't. "Tell me again—tell me what you said this afternoon."

He gave a low, sexy laugh. "I love you," he said. "I need you. I want you."

"You won't forget? Or change your mind?"

"Not a chance."

"I love you, too."

I tapped the off button, not noticing my mother standing there until I turned to set the phone down on the kitchen table. I had been hiding things for so long from my parents that I jumped, feeling I'd been caught.

"Are you going to see him?" she asked.

"In a little while."

"His name is Michael," she said. "I'm sorry. I didn't mean to eavesdrop. I heard it as I was coming into the room."

"Yes, Michael." It was strange to say his name out loud to my mother, and it felt large and unwieldy as I said it.

"Like the archangel who woke the dead."

After years of church and Sunday school and reading the Bible as a family, I knew my Bible pretty well, but not this. "Who?"

"It's at the end of the book of Daniel. Your father would know. Something about Michael taking charge of Daniel's people, 'waking those who sleep in the dust, some to everlasting life and some to shame and everlasting contempt.'" She waved the thought away with her hand. "What's your Michael like?"

I gathered up my hair and pulled it to the front so I could put on my coat without getting it tangled. "He's smart and cute and funny. And confident. He's *such* a good cook . . . He's nice, Mom."

"You love him."

Nodding, I leaned against the kitchen counter and shoved my hands into my coat pockets. "I can't think of anything else. Only him. He's all I *want* to think about."

She tipped her head to the side and looked at me—really looked at me, the way she does when she's trying to figure me out.

"What?" I asked.

"I'm just remembering," she said. "What it was like, not wanting to think about anyone but him."

"Who was it for you?" I asked.

"Your father, of course." She seemed genuinely surprised that I had to ask.

"You felt this way about Dad?"

"Oh, yes," she said. "I fell for him hard. He was handsome and charming. He had the courage of his convictions—and a lot of convictions." She laughed softly. "And he was . . ."

"He was what?"

My mother turned away and straightened the coffee maker on the counter. "He was . . . *very* convincing."

"And then?"

"And then I married him. Until death do us part."

"But—" I stopped, unsure of what I wanted to ask. "But you don't feel that way about him now?"

"It's different after thirty years of marriage."

"That's what I mean. What happened?"

"Oh, Grace, I don't know. I'm not sure that anything happens. It's hard to feel that way forever. If everyone felt that way all the time, nothing would ever get done. We'd just all sit around daydreaming about each other." She picked up a dishrag and began wiping off the table, moving the rag in small circles. "Life happens, I guess, and changes you. Or makes you more . . ."

"More *what?*"

She wiped more slowly. "More what you had been before. Or maybe less what you had been before."

"Well which is it? More or less?" My mother knew and understood me in ways my father never would. But the way she was always so vague made me crazy sometimes. I wished for once she would say something straight out.

"I don't know, Grace. It's not a simple question. Sometimes it makes you more in one way and less in another. Your father became more what he had been before—more adamant. More sure of himself."

Just then the doorbell rang and I could see Liv standing there on the doorstep, talking on her cell phone and motioning to me with her free arm to *come on!* On my way out I gave my mom a quick hug, feeling almost beefy as I wrapped my arms around her bird-like body.

"When will you be back?" she asked, patting the static electricity from my hair.

"I don't know."

"Are you going to his house?"

I turned to go. "I don't know."

My mother put her hand on my sleeve, stopping me. "Grace, you don't have to . . ."

"Don't have to what?" I asked impatiently.

She let her hand fall back to her side. "Nothing. Just don't stay out late."

It wasn't until I closed the door behind me that I realized my mother had never said what I wanted to know most: How had *she* changed since she'd married my dad? What was she more of? Or less of?

* * *

It was still light as Liv and I walked to the library. Liv was talking on her cell phone, rolling her eyes at me like the person on the other end would *not* shut up.

I didn't mind she was on the phone. I was glad for the time to think about what I should do. If I refused to break up with Michael, he would probably lose his job. But if I did what my father wanted, I would lose the only part of my life that felt good and true.

The rhythm of walking and being outside, away from my house, helped me think. The wind changed directions and I suddenly caught a whiff of thawing dirt. It smelled damp and hopeful, like the greenhouse. I took several breaths, breathing more deeply each time, filling myself up with it. I imagined that the air was spring itself and I could almost feel it surging through my body, thawing me, opening me up.

Suddenly I knew I couldn't go back the way my father wanted me to. I was sure that being closed down again, the way my father wanted me to be, would kill me. I couldn't give up Michael. No matter what, I would find a way to be with him for as long as he wanted to be with me.

Liv snapped her cell phone shut. "Sorry," she said. "It was David. He wants to get back together."

"Will you?"

She made a face. "No. He can't do anything for me."

"You mean he *doesn't* do anything for you."

"Yeah, that too," Liv said. "What's going on?"

"You won't believe it. Dad found out about Michael."

Liv gasped and stopped abruptly. "How?"

"He says he saw us. We had a huge fight about it. If I don't break up with him by the time Dad comes home from his trip, he says he is going to call the college and get Michael fired."

"He's not even fighting fair!" Liv exclaimed. "What are you going to do?"

"I don't know. Michael is the best thing that ever happened to me. He's all about *yes* and my dad is all about *no*. I'm so tired of hearing no, and be careful, and watch out!"

Liv made a face. "Death by suffocation."

"Exactly! But Michael has opened everything up for me. I'm completely in love with him—and said he loves me."

"He did? He said that?" she asked, her voice full of awe.

I nodded.

As we fell into step again, I told Liv about going to the college to find Michael and how he told me he loved me in the grove of trees at the edge of campus. And I told her about why I had gone in the first place after overhearing Carrie and Melissa in the girls' bathroom.

"Bitches!" Liv said. "A: They are jealous. You've got something that looks better than what they've got. B: It's none of their G.D. business whether you are or you aren't a virgin. If you want to stay pure because of that paper you signed with your parents, that's up to you." She hiked her backpack up higher on her shoulder. "What was that thing called again? A chastity something?"

"A celibacy contract," I mumbled. I had signed it years before, when I was fourteen or fifteen, still flat-chested, and barely even interested in boys. Apparently, my dad had thought the bracelet wasn't enough. He wanted a backup plan for my virginity.

"You know about the birds and the bees, right?" he'd asked. Terrified that he was going to talk to me about the details of sex, I'd said yes.

But he didn't want to talk about sex itself. He wanted to talk about avoiding it. He explained the contract and talked about how God had intended sex for man and wife and no one else. "Fornicating before marriage is wrong, Grace," he had said, pointing his Cross pen at me. "Signing this means you agree to wait until after you are married. It's a promise, a commitment. Do you understand?" Mortified by the topic and desperate to get away from him, I had taken the pen and signed the paper quickly.

Liv put her arm around my shoulders and squeezed me against her. "Like I said, ignore them," she said. "They're jealous."

"Maybe I can just avoid them."

"Fat chance, unless you quit school or leave town," Liv said, as we came to a busy intersection. She eyed the traffic, calculating the rate of speed of oncoming cars. Liv had made crossing the busy four-lane street with poorly timed traffic lights into an extreme sport. She enjoyed the challenge. "Melissa has never met a club she didn't join. The other day Mr. Katz called her 'effervescent,' which is just a nice way of saying 'too damn chirpy.' And Carrie? David says that her name keeps showing up on the walls of the bathroom."

I put my hand over my mouth and nose to try to filter out the smell of exhaust. "What do the walls say?"

"She's a wench."

Liv stepped out into the street, even though a car was speeding toward us from the right. "What are you waiting for?" she yelled. "We can make it!"

Without waiting to see what I would do, she sprinted diagonally across the street, her long, straight hair streaming out behind her like a black tow rope. I had the impulse to grab hold of it and let her pull me across. The driver laid on the horn, but Liv made it to the other side, like she always did.

I looked left, then right, then left again, before walking across the street at the cross walk and down the sidewalk to where Liv was standing, dabbing at her nose with a Kleenex. The sprint had made her nose run.

She shoved her dirty Kleenex into her coat pocket. "Your problem is you always hesitate. You have to make your own chances crossing there."

I thought about giving her the lecture on safety, which is what I usually did, but I decided not to. I knew what Liv meant. My way was no fun.

* * *

We sat at our usual table in the café section of the library, between the big windows and the bathroom, and just around the corner from the periodicals, where we could talk without getting dirty looks from the librarians.

After I sat down and took off my coat, I crossed my arms on the table and laid my head on them the way I had in kindergarten, when no one got to go out for recess until every student was sitting silent and still. I had always been the first one to have my head down, and my teacher would use me as an example. "Connor, Riley, Julia, look at what a nice job Grace is doing." They'd stick their tongues out at me, but I didn't care; the teacher loved me.

Liv rubbed my back sympathetically. "Maybe you could elope," she said.

"He hasn't asked me to *marry* him," I said, my chin knocking against the table. "He only just now said that he loved me."

"You want to talk about it?"

I rolled my head back and forth. I had thought that I would want to talk about it with Liv, going over every detail of my talk with Michael, reading between the lines, and rehashing the fight with my father, but I didn't. I felt tired, but also tightly wound, like something in me might unexpectedly spring out. I was my own jack-in-the-box. The only problem was that I didn't know what was going to spring out.

Propping myself up on my elbows, I watched Liv brush her hair with long, rhythmic strokes and then lift it away from her high cheekbones with her fingertips. Everything about Liv was angular—her body, her triangle-shaped face with wide-set eyes, even her attitude. When we walked through the mall together, adults were always looking twice at Liv.

Liv pulled a notebook out of her backpack and flipped it open.

"Is that your essay?" I asked.

Liv nodded and put her index finger to the side of her head, cocked her thumb, and pulled the trigger.

"What?"

"I can't do it. It's like I've frozen up."

"Don't put so much pressure on yourself."

"Easy for you to say. I *need* this." The harsh fluorescent light of the library didn't do Liv any favors, and I noticed for the first time gray bags under her eyes.

"I know you do. Why don't you just tell someone about your parents?"

It was an argument we had whenever things got really bad at her house. Normally I got frustrated with Liv, but that night the familiarity of it was reassuring. Even though I couldn't know what would happen with Michael, I did know exactly how Liv's and my conversation about her parents would go. It was almost like we had burned a CD of it and all we had to do whenever the subject came up was to put it in and listen.

Liv rolled her eyes. "What are they going to do, huh, Grace? Suggest *counseling?* They've tried that already. And AA. And separating. They *want* to be this way. They like it. It's the only way that they know how to be." She pulled a book out of her backpack and dropped it carelessly onto the table. "Anyway, I'm almost done with them. Six months and I'll be gone, maybe sooner. If I can just make the judges like what I have to say."

I sat up and bumped my knee gently against hers under the table. "You can do it," I said. "You've always been the best writer in the class." She was, too, but I was the only one who knew it. She got As on all her papers, but that wasn't her best stuff. Her best stuff—the things she wrote in her journal about her life and dreams and feelings, words that seemed to go straight from her heart and onto the page, almost like she'd held her heart in her hands and wrung the words out of it onto the paper—that stuff she never shared with anyone but me, and lately she had been sharing it less and less with me.

"Mrs. Capotosto says that it's not always the best essay that wins, that you need luck—" Liv's eyes shifted up. "Oh! Hello—uh, Professor."

"Hello," he said, nodding at Liv before he turned to me. "'Lo, Rabbit."

"Am I late?" I fumbled with my sleeve, trying to see my watch.

"No, I'm early. My meeting got canceled, and I thought you might already be here. Are you studying hard?"

"We were only just getting started," said Liv.

"Liv's entering The Great Lakes Essay Competition," I explained. "Have you heard of it?"

Michael grinned. "Once or twice. I'm a judge this year."

"Any tips?"

"Just the usual advice. Write as though you're writing to save your life, because that's how good it's going to have to be."

"Thanks, that's so very helpful," said Liv in a monotone, but she looked over at me and I knew what she was thinking: In a way, she really *was* writing to save her life.

Michael raised one eyebrow and said, "Sauciness will get you nowhere with the judges, young lady."

"Is there anything that will?" Liv shot back.

Michael just laughed and picked up my backpack.

"Bye, Liv," I said.

"Don't do anything I wouldn't do," Liv replied, making eyes at me.

"Thanks, you've been so very helpful," I said.

Liv waved me away with a flick of her wrist, like it was nothing. "Hey, that's what friends are for."

Nine

"So tell me," Michael said, as soon as we were in his car. "What's going on?"

"It's my father," I blurted out. "He knows about us. He said I have to stop seeing you. If I don't, he'll make sure you lose your job! I tried to tell him how it is with us, but he wouldn't listen. He thinks I don't know what love is."

I sank into Michael's broad chest and finally let myself cry for a long time. I knew it was making my face bunched up and blotchy, and I didn't want Michael to see me that way, so I stayed against him until I was all cried out and had mopped my face up with the Kleenexes he kept handing me.

"I'm sorry," I said, sniffling. I sat up and stuffed the damp, wadded-up tissues into my coat pocket.

"Don't be," he said, starting the engine. "Let's go to my house. You can tell me everything on the way."

As I talked, he listened, occasionally shaking his head. When I got to the part where my father had said, "You will!" and threatened to call the college, Michael stiffened. "We're both adults," he said. "He can't tell us what to do."

"It's just the way he is," I said. "He's always told me what to do."

"The problem is," Michael said, gunning the engine, "he thinks he still can. I think not." In the bluish light of the dashboard, his cheekbones and chin and nose looked strangely jagged.

Neither of us said anything else until we were all the way upstairs. On the way, we stopped in the kitchen for wine and glasses. Once in his bedroom, he silently poured us each a glass, then disappeared into the walk-in closet to change, while I sat on the bed and drank my wine in small nervous gulps.

I had never seen Michael angry before. When we had been together, just the two of us, he'd always been happy and relaxed. But now the whole room seemed tense. The feeling that it was my fault made me tired.

I lay down on my back on the bed and closed my eyes. All I'd wanted was a real life and real love. It didn't seem like so much to want. Finally, I couldn't stand Michael's silence anymore. "I'm sorry," I said, my voice cracking. There were so many reasons I could lose him right then, and no way to keep him.

His shirt still unbuttoned, Michael walked over and knelt down on the floor beside the bed. He brought his face close to mine and said, "It's not you I'm angry with."

"It's not?"

"Your father is absurd. He's overreacting. Without ever having met me, he thinks the worst of me. He's dismissing me," he said, his voice suddenly bitter, "and I won't be dismissed."

He turned his face away from me for a moment and I had the feeling he was drifting, thinking about something or someone else even though he was talking about my father. But it took him only a heartbeat to come back. "And he doesn't give you enough credit. Look at you—a beautiful young woman who has principles and a good mind that she's learning to use well. I'm outraged by the way he treats you."

He pushed my hair away from my face and sighed. He looked at me steadily for a minute and I wondered again what he was thinking. Finally he said, "'When I glance at you even an instant, I can no longer utter a word. My tongue thickens to a lump, my eyes are blind, my ears fill with humming and in a moment more, I feel I shall die.'"

For that moment, with his deep, quiet voice flowing over me, I believed that somehow things would turn out all right.

"That's beautiful," I whispered.

"The words aren't mine, they are Sappho's. But it doesn't matter because that's the way I feel about you." He took my hand into his and his eyes glistened. "Marry me. Say you'll marry me."

I thought he must be joking, but everything about him told me he was not. "You want to . . . marry me?"

"While I was getting changed, I was thinking about everything. We love each other, so let's get married. If we just stop being clandestine about all this and legitimize our relationship, your father can't hurt us. The college might not totally approve of our relationship, but they won't fire me if you're my fiancée. So let's get married."

"But—"

"Sh-sh-sh," he said. He climbed onto the bed and straddled me. Putting his hands on either side of my head, he bent down over me so that his open shirt made a tent over me. His words came out in a rush. "There's so much I want to introduce you to—people and places and ideas. The things that are out there—great things that you have no idea about, Grace. I want to be the one to show them to you! How can I if we're always worried about your father? I'm ready to do this—more than ready. I want to move on to the next stage of our relationship. Marry me."

For a minute I was too stunned to say anything. A few minutes before, I had been wondering if it would be the last time I would see him. Now he was telling me he wanted to spend the rest of his life with me. The wine, which had slowed my thinking, made it hard for me to string together my words. "Michael, I *do* love you—more than I've loved anyone—but I don't know. Are you sure? I just . . . it's so fast."

I meant I was having a hard time shifting gears and keeping up with his thinking, but Michael misunderstood me. "Everyone thinks that waiting longer is better, but it isn't, Grace," he said. "Something gets lost in the waiting. Something gets drained away and it's never the same."

I concentrated hard on what he was saying, trying to make the fog in my brain lift.

"There are people who watch things happen, people who make things happen, and people who ask, 'What happened?'" he said. "Don't be one of those people who look back with regrets!"

"But my father—"

"Forget your father! Don't you see? If we do this, there's nothing he can do! It's either this or nothing."

"He won't allow it."

Michael sighed. "Okay, for argument's sake, let's say that it does matter what he thinks about our getting married. Why are you so sure he'd be dead set against it? Because I'm older? I can talk to him, make him see that I love you and that there are advantages to my being older, like financial stability and maturity."

"It's more than that. It's because you're one of them—a non-believer. You may as well be the devil himself, as far as he's concerned."

"Isn't there anything that will change his mind?"

"Acts 15:31," I said. "No, wait . . . Acts 16:31."

He frowned. "You're quoting scripture now?"

"I'm telling you what will change his mind. 'Believe in the Lord Jesus Christ and thou shalt be saved, and thy house.'"

"Impossible," he said. "I can't change who I am. I won't change who I am."

"I know," I said miserably.

But Michael wasn't giving up. "What he thinks doesn't matter. We can do it, anyway. You have to choose. Maybe it's good that this happened. To be honest, I don't want to sneak around like a teenager any more. It was fun for a while but it's an inconvenience. I want you immersed in my life, and I want to be in yours."

Every word he said went straight to my heart and blossomed there in the eerie way that roses do in time-lapse photography, seemingly without food or water or the passing of time. *Yes,* I thought. *Yes, I will marry you because you want me so much and I want you so much that it must be right, it has to be right.* But then I remembered.

"My parents," I said.

"He's no match for us. Stop worrying about your father," he said.

I pretended to stretch so I would have an excuse to look away from him for a moment. I tried to clear my head. If I married Michael, my father would shun me, and he would make my mother shun me, too.

If I said no to Michael then everything good in my life—the excitement, the electric current that hummed between us, the *love*—would end. It would go back to the way it was before. Quiet, dull, flat. But if I married Michael, I would be closing the door on my mother, my home, and my childhood. I hadn't been so unhappy before Michael—just a little clueless about how things could be. I didn't want to go back, but I didn't want to leave those parts of me behind, either.

Michael shifted and I felt the weight of his hips pressing against me. I didn't think it was possible to want him more than I had always wanted him before. But now, after the blow-up with my father, after Michael's saying he loved me and wanted to marry me, I craved him. I was tired of fighting it. If I said that I would marry him, wasn't the wedding certificate just a technicality?

I remembered again the night my father had made me promise, how he had been adamant about sex being right only within a marriage. He had said that it was better to marry the wrong person than to have sex before marriage. It didn't make sense. Better to *spend a whole lifetime* with the wrong person?

That's how the idea came to me—how I could get everything I wanted and keep everything I valued. I tried to check myself to make sure it wasn't just the wine that was making me think it was a good idea. But no, it was good. It would work. My father would be outraged for a while at what I was about to do, but eventually he would get over it. He would have to.

I pulled Michael down to me and kissed him.

"We'll get married," he said simply.

"Yes," I said. I lifted my hips and ground them into him. There was a spark of surprise in Michael's eyes.

"Grace," he said. "Stop."

I didn't stop.

His breathing got a beat faster and heavier. "Are you teasing? Because if you start this, there's no going back."

For just a second I thought about going back, not because my plan was bad but because I wasn't sure I could pull it off. After all, I was only Grace and Grace didn't do things like this. Rebecca and other heroines from my romance novels and Liv did things like this—took chances, lived a little recklessly, always on the verge of something. Liv was the one who ran out into traffic and then laughed at me from the other side: *You have to make your own chances, Grace.*

"Are you?" Michael asked insistently.

I looked steadily back at him and undid his belt buckle and his fly and slid my hand into his jeans.

"God, you're serious," he said. His voice was deep and thick.

We undressed each other quickly. I no longer felt awkward, the way I had been at first with Michael. By then I had started to believe that, even if I didn't think I was beautiful, he did, and my modesty had fallen away like a cocoon falls away from a butterfly. That night I didn't think about what I looked like, lying there naked. I thought only of what it would be like, finally, to make love.

Lying on top of me, Michael supported his weight on one arm and reached into the nightstand drawer with his free hand. He fumbled inside the nightstand drawer for a moment before groaning, "Oh, God, Tori."

I jerked away. "Tori?"

"Tori—the woman who cleans here. I know I had a condom in here. She occasionally borrows them. Quinn likes them."

"You mean we can't?"

"No, we still can. It just means that I'll have to pull out instead."

"What? No!" I didn't want him to pull out. I wanted to experience all of it, all of him. And I wanted making love with me to be good for him—as good as it had been with previous lovers. How could it be if he had to pull out?

"Don't worry, Rabbit," he said, settling between my legs. "It always works. It's just not as much fun."

Lifting my hand to his mouth, he kissed the tips of my fingers, my palm, the thin skin on the inside of my wrist. He laid my hand back on the bed and slid his fingers up the underside of my arm, lingering at the soft indent of my elbow. He kissed my shoulder, ran the tip of his tongue up my neck to my ear, pressed himself against my pelvis. And as he moved, he murmured things to me. Soon all of me had become part of the energy between us and I heard the words only as sounds and even they were part of the energy. As the energy surged and carried us with it, I wondered where it would all go and how much intensity I could bear before I split apart.

But I was abruptly torn out of the flow as soon as he came into me, not because it hurt but because he was taking up spaces in me that I never even knew were there, pressing me aside to make room for him. I wanted to be back where we had been a moment before when it was all heat and wonder, but there was no going back. All I could do was think about how strange it felt to have him inside of me, rearranging me. I told myself it was just the first time. I would get used to it. Everyone must get used to it, and eventually I'd be able to stay in the flow even when he was where he was now, lost in what he was doing, doing, doing, still a part of the hum even though I had been jarred out of it, and when it was time, he pulled out and finished and then it was over.

He rolled onto his back beside me and extended his arm so I could rest my head on his chest. "I love you, Rabbit," he said. The words reverberated through me, like an echo in an empty cave.

"I love you, too," I whispered.

He nuzzled the top of my head. "Was it everything you thought it would be?" he asked.

"The earth moved," I said, running my fingers over the swooping scar on his chest.

My ear against his chest, I felt the rumble of his laugh before I heard it. "Mere mortals wept," he said.

It was true that the ground beneath my feet had shifted and that I was different. I was elated, exhausted, and strangely melancholy. Tears sprang to my eyes, taking me by surprise, and I quickly wiped them away, praying that Michael wouldn't open his eyes just then and see them. *Grow up!* I thought fiercely. *It's what you wanted!*

After a few minutes, I could tell that Michael was drifting off to sleep.

"Michael?" I whispered, not wanting to be awake alone.

"It will get better," he mumbled without opening his eyes. "I promise."

I lay there for a long time, thinking. I slid out of bed and put on Michael's shirt. As I was buttoning it up, I steeled myself for what I had to do. I was nervous but determined.

When I was a child, I thought like a child but when I became a man, I gave up my childish ways, I thought. In other words, no turning back.

* * *

In the kitchen, I picked up the phone and tapped in my home number. I was hoping my mother would already be asleep, dead to the world, but when I heard her quiet voice, relief washed over me.

"It's me, Mom," I said, watching my reflection in the floor-to-ceiling windows. Other than wearing only Michael's shirt and having messy hair, it didn't seem like I looked any different. Flatter, maybe, but reflections always are.

"Where are you?" my mom asked.

"With Michael."

"Have you talked to him?"

"Yes."

"Oh, honey."

Hearing the quaver in her voice made me want to crumple to the floor and tell her what had happened and how I felt so alone and adrift somehow. But just then Michael came up behind me, kissed the back of my neck and whispered into my other ear, *"I want you,* Mrs. Irving."

Him standing there shored up my resolve. At the same time, I felt crowded. I smiled tightly to hide my irritation and took a few steps away from him. "I'm okay, Mom."

"When are you coming home?"

I swallowed hard. "I'm not. Not tonight, anyway. I'll be home tomorrow."

"Not coming? Are you going to Liv's, then? Or do you mean you need a ride home?"

"No. I mean I'm not coming home."

"So you'll be staying . . ."

"Here, with Michael."

"Oh, honey," she said again. There was so much sadness in her voice, as though it were she who had just given up something that she couldn't ever get back. The tears pushed at the back of my eyes, but I held them off by looking up at the ceiling. Michael was rummaging around in the fridge, humming.

"Your father will be furious when he finds out."

In a flash I remembered that he had brought all this on himself by being unreasonable. "I don't care," I said. "I can't take him anymore. You know the way he is. I don't want to end up like—like—" I was going to say "you" but I stopped myself just in time. "Like the way I was ending up," I finished lamely.

"He won't stand for it."

Michael had finished eating some cheese and was standing up against my back now, his arms wrapped lightly around me. He smelled salty, and I could feel him growing impatient. I made my voice hard. "He doesn't have any choice."

Michael whispered, "Tell her I've taken care of everything." I broke away from him and covered my free ear to keep him from interrupting again.

"Grace—"

"Mom, I'm *all right.*"

"Honey . . ."

My mother couldn't soothe all this away like she used to soothe away a bad dream by laying her cool hand on my forehead and telling me to find a happiness to think about. She couldn't make it better, and I couldn't take knowing that, on some level, I wished she could.

"I have to go," I said. "I'll explain everything tomorrow." I hung up the phone before she could answer.

* * *

The sound of the front door slamming woke me. "Michael?" I said, squinting at the clock.

"Yeah, right here," he said from the closet. "I overslept. I've got a class that starts in fifteen minutes. Do you want me to drop you at school? Or I can come back in a few hours to get you."

I stretched, then pulled the blankets over my head and groaned. I wasn't the type to skip school or even to be late—at least I hadn't thought I was—but I couldn't imagine being able to concentrate on anything until after I'd had things out with my father. "I'll stay, if it's okay with you."

He stopped by the bed to kiss me on his way out. "Sure, but you might want to put this on," he said. He handed me his grey terrycloth robe.

I looked up at him, not understanding. "Why?"

Just then a girl walked through the door, lugging a vacuum cleaner. "Hey," she said, staring right at us and grinning. Embarrassed, I shrank back, but the girl, who looked a few years older than me, clearly thought it was all very amusing. She didn't even avert her eyes, let alone apologize and get out, which I thought she should be doing.

"That's why," Michael said blandly, shielding me as I wriggled into the robe. Then he turned to the girl. "Tori, didn't anyone ever teach you to knock?"

Tori shrugged. "You're usually gone by now. Besides, it's not like I'm going to see anything I haven't seen before."

Michael rolled his eyes. "Pay no attention to her. She came with the place."

"Yeah," she said. "Because the owners wanted me to keep an eye on you."

Michael smiled in a "Who, me?" way and said, "Grace meet Tori. Tori, this is Grace." He tucked in his shirt and walked to the door. "Sorry I have to leave like this, Rabbit. See you in a little while."

As he left, he said to Tori, "Be nice—and you owe me some condoms!"

"Yeah, yeah, yeah." Tori plugged in the cord and then stared at me. "I gotta strip the bed so . . . do you mind?"

"Oh, sorry." I didn't mean to apologize—*she* was the one who should be apologizing—but it came out automatically. I swung my legs onto the floor, careful to pull the robe tighter around myself and tie the sash. I felt uncomfortable and out of place, like I was in Tori's territory. We'd never had a cleaning lady at home and I was unsure of what I was supposed to be doing. I grabbed a pillow and shook it out of its case. "I'll help."

"Whatever," she said. She threw back the covers and there it was—the rust-red spotting on the sheets from the night before. I could feel my cheeks flame instantly, but there was nothing I could do except hope that Tori would pretend not to see it.

"Well, that would explain why he calls her Rabbit," she said under her breath. I guessed that pretending not to see things wasn't Tori's style. She looked at me and smirked. "First time, huh, Thumper?" she said, picking at her spiked blonde hair. "Look, I don't know how much you know about birth control and all, but let me give you some advice. Pulling out doesn't work that well."

Feeling embarrassed and angry at Michael, who must have known that he was throwing me to the sharks, I yanked the other pillow out of its case. *If you and Quinn would just go buy your own condoms we wouldn't have to!* I thought.

"The reason is that it's up to the guy to do it at the right time," Tori continued, "and since guys are basically brain dead, well, most of the time, but especially during sex, it's pretty risky. You see what I'm saying?"

I hated that Tori already knew way too much about me. Anxious to get past this awkward moment, I silently tugged the fitted sheet off on my side of the bed. Tori didn't seem to be in any hurry, though, and when I looked up to see what was taking her so long, she was giving me the once-over.

"You're not really his type," she said.

Apparently every thought that crossed Tori's mind also came out her mouth. "Excuse me?" I said.

"His old girlfriend was the twiggy type. Straight up and down. Rachelle. Not Rachel. *Rah-shell.* They were together for like a bazillion years or something. Don't worry, though."

"I know all about it. I know all about everything," I said quickly, wanting Tori to know that Michael and I had no secrets. I'd asked Michael one night about past girlfriends and he'd said he was only going to have that conversation once and he wasn't going to go into detail because "I know from experience that therein lies ruination and madness."

I looked across the bed at Tori, determined not to let her intimidate me. "He and Rachelle lived together for a while but they broke up."

"*She* broke up," Tori said. "And left him broken up, so yeah, I guess you could say they broke up. He was pretty devastated."

I was surprised but tried not show it. Michael had told me about Rachelle but he hadn't said how it had ended. "How do you know?"

"Oh, I know. I see stuff—relationship *artifacts*, you know? Old photos in a closet, an old birthday card from her, wine labels he's saved from special nights, that kind of thing."

Not wanting to hear any more from her and desperate to tell her something she didn't already know, I blurted out, "We're getting married. Michael proposed last night."

"Oh, well *that's* rich!" she said with a sarcastic laugh.

I was already feeling tightly wound because of everything that had happened and her know-it-all attitude infuriated me. I stalked over to where she was standing (where she had been doing *nothing* but watching me work), stripped the fitted sheet off that side of the bed, wadded it up, and dumped it at Tori's feet.

"Look," I said. "Do you have some sort of problem with all this? Did you and Michael have a little something going on sometime?"

Tori grinned. "Hey. All right! You do have some carbonation. I was beginning to wonder." She picked up the pile of laundry and held it out to me. Dumbstruck, I took it. "Nah, it's all talk between me and Michael. I just hope you know what you're doing."

"I know exactly what I'm doing."

"Yeah, but I mean beyond the sex." Tori waved her arm over the bare bed. "I know it feels good—getting it on. It feels good, but it isn't love. It's just sex, you know?"

Then she took me by the shoulders and turned me toward the door. "You know where the washer is, right? In the room off the kitchen? Do me a favor and throw those in. Don't forget to put some stain remover on the bottom one. That blood is set, so it's going to be a bitch to get out."

Glad for an excuse to get away from her, I did as I was told. After the sheets were in the washer, I tried to decide the best place to hide out. I listened for Tori, and from the sound of the vacuum figured out that she was still in the master suite, so that was out.

Besides, in spite of my nervous stomach, I was ravenous. I found some leftover pasta alfredo in the fridge and, without bothering to heat it up, ate a plateful and drank two glasses of milk, all while standing over the kitchen sink.

The vacuum shut off and I wondered if Tori was finally finished cleaning the bedroom. I was sure that by now my mother would have called my father, who was probably on his way home to deal with me, and I wanted to get dressed and get the whole thing over with.

Walking past the den, I thought I heard music. The door was ajar and I pushed it open farther. In the darkened den I saw the flicker of the television. "La la la-la, La la la-la, Elmo's song. We've got the music, we've got the words! That's Elmo's song!" The room was empty, and I thought that Michael had accidentally left the TV on. I reached for the remote and clicked the TV off.

On the couch, a little boy popped his head up. "Aww done!" he said. I jumped and the remote flew out of my hand. He climbed off the couch.

"Get it," he said, and then he did. He smiled and handed it to me.

"Thank you," I said. "Who are you?"

He pointed at the TV and said, "Em-O, Em-O."

"Yes, that's Elmo. But what's your name?"

"Kin."

"Hello, Ken."

The floor behind me squeaked. "I see you met Quinn," Tori said.

Quinn barreled across the floor to Tori and threw his arms around her legs. "Up!" he demanded. "Up!"

"*This* is Quinn?"

"Yeah," Tori said. "What of it?"

"Last night, when Michael said Quinn liked the . . . you know. I just thought Quinn was your boyfriend."

Tori laughed. "Oh, the condoms. He plays with the packages because he likes the colors. And sometimes we forget to put them back, don't we Quinnie?" she said, tickling him under the arms. Quinn squealed and ran back to the couch.

"Is he your brother?"

"Nah, he's my kid," said Tori. She motioned for me to give her the clicker.

"Yours?" I repeated stupidly, handing it to her.

"Yeah, mine. Don't look so surprised. It happens, you know? I told you pulling out doesn't always work. Here's the proof." She turned the TV back on. "Mama will be done in three more shows," she said to Quinn. "You want to watch cartoons next?"

"Toons!" Quinn said happily, snuggling down under the blanket she laid over him.

Trying not to be obvious about it, I looked for a wedding ring as she picked up the dust rag. Her ring finger was bare. "And now back to our regularly scheduled programming," she said.

I followed her out of the den. "But what about . . . ?" I knew it was none of my business but felt it was only fair for her to explain, since she knew so much about me and Michael.

"The father?" Tori screwed up her face like she had just smelled something foul. "Pffft," she said. "Didn't need him anyway."

"It's just you don't look old enough to have a kid. You look like you're my age."

Tori thumped the heel of her hand against her forehead, "Well, *duh,*" she said. "I guess that makes both of us old enough to have kids. Scary, isn't it?"

Ten

I let the hot water run until the bathroom mirror steamed up before I gingerly stepped into the gray-tiled shower. The jet propulsion stream showerhead pelted hot beads of water across my shoulders. Wincing, I reached for a black bottle of shampoo. It smelled like Michael—musky but also sweet, like cut hay smells in the summer, after it's been drying in the sun.

The smell reminded me of the time I had run away from home when I was little. My father had found out that I'd lied to him about doing my catechism and had humiliated me by spanking me in front of Liv. Afterwards, I put my stuffed kitten, Mary, a box of Cheerios, and a picture of my mom pushing me on a swing at the park into a bag, and I ran.

Too angry and sure that I'd never go home again to pay attention to landmarks, I just kept going until I didn't know where I was. It all happened so fast, getting lost, but even after I knew I was, I kept going, sure that everything would work out for me somehow.

Eventually, tired and thirsty from all the Cheerios I'd been eating as I walked, I sat down alongside the road in a hayfield. The prickly stubs of hay scratched my legs and I started to miss my mom and wonder what Liv was doing. My father found me there, clutching Mary to my chest and crying. He didn't need to tell me that I'd gone too far, but he did, anyway.

I rinsed my hair and thought about how I'd wear it for the wedding. Michael and I had decided on July because Michael had the house until then, but we'd still have enough time to move back to Amberton before he had to start the new semester. I daydreamed about how we'd walk home from the campus together, cook dinner, and make love. After last night, I felt stretched out and raw inside, but I was sure it would get better. Michael had promised that it would.

He called while I was getting dressed. I could barely understand his words because of the cell phone static. "Rabbit, I'm going to be later than I thought," he said.

"Where are you?"

"I have to . . . ort errand. Have you . . . Liv yet?" I relied on the context to figure out that he was asking about whether I'd called Liv.

"No. She goes to first lunch in a few minutes. I was going to call her then."

". . . parents?"

"No. I just took a shower. I'm going to call them soon."

"You could have . . . there . . . my place." Then ". . . losing you," and his voice was gone. "I love you," I said halfheartedly, knowing that he probably wouldn't hear me anyway.

After blow drying my hair, I pulled it back, away from my face. My lip-gloss was in the bottom of my purse, fortunately, along with an old tube of mascara, which I was happy to find, but it wasn't enough. Today I wanted to look different. It seemed like I should look different, but when I saw myself in the mirror, I still looked like I always had.

The drawers! I thought. Maybe the woman who lived here had left some things behind. Michael's brushes and razors were in the top drawer. Medicine was in the next one down, and I picked up each thing—a box of Band-Aids, Nyquil, Tylenol, and Lamisil, "for athlete's foot." I quickly tossed it back.

In the last drawer, I found some black eyeliner and drew a dark, thin line on each eyelid. The effect was a little dramatic, but right. Farther back in the drawer were a few new, unopened toothbrushes. After using one, I placed it in the holder next to his and kept glancing at it as I filed my nails. Seeing our two toothbrushes side by side gave me a sudden rush of happiness, like the feeling you get going out the doors on the last day of school knowing everything that's any good is stretching out in front of you.

Liv didn't answer her cell phone when I tried to call her a few minutes later, but then I realized that she probably wasn't picking up because she didn't recognize Michael's number on caller ID.

Her voicemail picked up—"Do it," said her voice.

After the beep, I said, "Liv, call me at this number *right away.* I had the most incredible night and, well, call me and I'll tell you."

But then I couldn't hold the news in for one more second and I added, "Michael asked me to marry him! Can you believe it? And now I have to find a maid of honor—somebody who's tall and thin and beautiful but won't steal the show from the woman in the white dress. That's going to be ME, Liv! I'm going to be the one in the white dress. I can hardly breathe I'm so excited. Call me!"

Knowing Liv was on lunch break, I was positive she would listen to the message and would call me right back, so when the phone rang a few minutes later, I didn't bother to check the caller ID. I grabbed it and said, "Isn't it wild?"

There was a pause and then my father said, "It's an abomination—a disgrace. That's what it is. I don't know what you think you're doing over there," he said in a low voice, "or what kind of statement you're trying to make, but it's over. You are to come home now, do you hear me?"

I gasped at the sound of his voice, sucking in more air than I intended and then holding it so that my heart and lungs felt oversized. *And so it begins*, I thought. I let my breath out and said, "I don't have a way home."

"Then I'll come get you."

I started thinking more clearly then. He was right that it was a dis-grace. I was the opposite of Grace, the not-Grace, and it made me feel strong. But he was wrong about coming to get me.

In my head, I calculated how much longer it might be before Michael would be back. I didn't argue with my father; I just gave him directions. When I added a wrong turn in order to buy myself some time, the lie didn't stick in my throat. That one slid out, like I had been lying to him all my life.

Pacing in front of the big windows that overlooked the steep driveway, hoping to catch sight of Michael's car through the bare trees, I thought that in a way, maybe I had been lying to him all my life. I'd been letting him think I was who he wanted me to be.

I tried to call Michael several times but he wasn't picking up. I heard Tori, who I had been avoiding, in the den talking to Quinn as she worked, and I desperately hoped that they would be gone by the time my father arrived. The leftover pasta and milk I'd had before my shower were now burbling around in my stomach. I was about to go into the bathroom, when I saw my father's tan sedan winding up the driveway. I tried once more to reach Michael—where *was* he?—and then opened the door for my father.

He pushed past me into the house. "It's west, Grace, not east," he said derisively. "You have your mother's sense of direction."

"Sorry," I said, feeling smug that my plan had worked. I walked across the room to the fireplace and, taking a deep breath, turned to face him.

He was craning his neck, looking around for Michael. "Where is he?" he asked.

"Out."

"Are you done now? Is everything finished?"

It was, but not the way he meant. I straightened my shoulders. "No," I said quietly. "I didn't end it. I'm not going to end it. Michael and I are getting married."

He snorted. "You're getting *married?* You don't even know how to give directions and you think you're going to get *married?*"

I nodded, waiting for the explosion.

His eyes bulged. "No you most certainly are not! You don't know what you're saying, Grace. This is your whole life we're talking about here."

"I know. It's what I want."

"You're eighteen. You don't know what you want! This foolishness stops here and now." Apparently not caring that he was in someone else's house, he pulled open one drawer after another until he found the phonebook. "I'm calling the college. I hate to have to do it, but it's for your own good," he said, rifling through the pages. "Your professor will cower like a lamb before the lion and then you'll see. Then you'll see what's really important to him."

I cleared my throat. "Dad, wait."

"It's too late," he said, picking up the cordless that was lying on the counter and punching in numbers. "You had your chance and you couldn't handle it. In a way it's my fault because I overestimated you. You're still so young. I should have come with you yesterday. I should have told him myself."

"We had sex."

Index finger poised above the keypad, my father froze. "You *what?*"

I played it the way I had pictured playing it, ever since I had come up with the idea the night before. It wasn't like me to be so calculating, but if I didn't pull this off then my plan would collapse and everything I had done would be for nothing. "I'm sorry. I didn't mean to. I thought I'd be able to stop, but I couldn't," I said. "We just got carried away."

He smacked the phone down. "You don't even realize what you have done! How could you throw away your life? You *promised* me!" he said. Then he whispered it again. "You promised me."

He put both hands on the counter to steady himself and then dropped his chin to his chest and let out a single, raspy sob that shook his shoulders. I had known that my father would be angry and disappointed and I'd been ready for it, but his emotion jarred loose a kernel of little-girl love. I felt a clean pang of regret, remembering how easy we used to be with each other. Once, standing on the church sidewalk after the Christmas Eve service, I held out my hand to catch snowflakes. My father had knelt in the snow in front of me and cupped his hand under mine, so I could rest my hand on his. "Each one is original," he said, looking down at the fat flakes scattered across my blue mitten. "And so are you. You are fearfully and wonderfully made by God. You're our miracle."

I wondered if he still thought that, as I walked across the room and lightly laid my trembling hand on his shoulder. I wanted to take everything back, even to *go* all the way back to that Christmas Eve and to find a way to do all this right, without hurting each other.

Instead I said, "Dad, I'm sorry." This time I said it because it was true. I knew we couldn't go back, but I wanted him to say we could fix things, somehow. To say there was a way to work it out, or at least get past it.

But he didn't. Just that fast, he had already written me off, damned me to hell.

He shrugged my hand off and took a step away from me. "I raised you to know better. You should have known better." He wiped his eyes with his gloves and said in a low, dead voice. "You've always been soft and weak in the spirit. And now you're damaged goods, too. *No one* is going to want you."

His words seared through me. I could feel the anger, thick, hot, and bitter, surge up, but this time I held it so that it cooled and hardened like the wax of a candle after the flame has gone out. I gave up on my father, right then, but I wasn't about to give up my mother.

"It was wrong," I said, forcing the lie out.

"Yes it was. And that's something you'll have to live with. You've made a tremendous mistake—one that you are going to regret forever."

Never, I thought. *I will never regret this. Because you may have found Jesus, but I have found someone who loves me.* As far as I was concerned, it was the best thing I had ever done.

My father gripped the edge of the counter as though it was a pulpit. "The Bible says, 'Be ye not unequally yoked with unbelievers—'"

"'For what fellowship hath righteousness with unrighteousness? And what communion hath light with darkness?'" I finished. "2 Corinthians 6:14." It wasn't a verse I had known by heart, but I'd been pretty sure that he'd bring it up. I'd rummaged through the travel and cooking books until I found a Bible. Luckily it had a concordance.

I saw a flicker of pride cross my father's face, and I pressed my advantage. "Mark 16 tells us to preach the gospel. 'He that believes and is baptized shall be saved.'"

My father grunted. "Don't tell me you think you—"

"I can save him," I said quietly, knowing it wasn't Michael I was saving. I was lying again, acting the part of contrite daughter to give my father a way to save face. "It might take time, but I think he'll come to know God through me."

"You?" he said. "When you're too weak to deny yourself even the pleasures of the body?" But his expression had softened and I could tell that he wanted to believe me. He wanted to believe that I was a better person than I had been.

"You've always said that the Lord works in mysterious ways. Maybe it's through my weakness that Michael—"

"What you have done is not and never will be a good thing."

"I know. But maybe some good could come of it."

My father sighed. "When is this—this wedding?"

"The end of July."

"No," he said, buttoning up his coat. "It's going to be in June. Right after graduation. Because of what you've done, every day you wait further blasphemes the Lord and sullies our family name. God forgives when we make things right. You have to make this right as soon as you can."

"I know," I said meekly, thinking I ought to win an Oscar for this performance. "That's why we're going to get married. We want to make it right."

"See that you do." He pulled his gloves on. "I'll tell your mother you'll be home for dinner."

I stood for another minute, watching him go down the steps to his car. My jaw ached and I realized then that I must have been clenching my teeth most of the time I was talking to him.

As soon as he was gone, my teeth began chattering uncontrollably, as if I had the chills, and I sank into the nearest chair. I closed my eyes in exhaustion and relief. It was finished.

I sat there with my eyes still closed, taking deep breaths and telling myself to relax. Suddenly I got the uneasy feeling that I was being watched. I opened my eyes and Quinn was right in front of me. He popped a sucker out of his mouth, then raced back to Tori, who was getting ready to leave.

"So let me get this straight," she said, like she had been in the room with me and my father all along. "You're getting married because you had sex? Not because you're pregnant but just because you had sex?"

I was too drained to be angry. "No, I'm not pregnant and no, I'm not getting married just because I had sex," I said. "Is there anything you missed? Anything you'd like me to fill you in on?"

"No," Tori said, shoving a bucket of cleaning supplies into the closet. She seemed oblivious to my sarcasm. "I caught the whole thing. I keep a stash of suckers to give to Quinn to keep him quiet so I can hear. You wouldn't believe the stuff I learn about people."

I turned my head away and closed my eyes again, resigned to the fact that, no matter how much I hated it, by the time Tori left, she'd probably know as much about me as I knew about myself.

Even though she didn't say anything else, I knew she hadn't left because I could hear her banging around in the kitchen. After a few minutes I heard her come in and set something on the coffee table with a gentle clink. "I made you a cup of green tea. My feelings won't be hurt or anything if you don't drink it," she said.

I sat still, like an animal playing dead, hoping that the predator would lose interest and leave. I listened as Quinn and Tori zipped up their coats and got on their boots. "Hey, tell Michael I need more Windex," Tori called. Then I heard the door latch click into place.

By the time Michael arrived, I had finished that cup of tea and had made myself a second.

"I'm sorry I was away so long," he said, sitting down on the arm of the chair. "I couldn't wait to get back to you, but there was something I needed to do."

"Where were you?"

"There was a pressing matter I had to attend to." His playful smile told me he wanted me to ask him about it.

I didn't feel especially playful. "Well, while you were out doing your more pressing matter, my dad came to get me."

"Oh, Rabbit. I meant to be with you for all that. I'm sorry!"

"It's okay," I said, realizing that it had been better he wasn't here.

"How did it go?"

"Pretty much the way I thought it would. I've never seen him so angry."

He kissed the top of my head. "People get that way when they know they've lost their power over you."

"You know what the worst thing was? He got all emotional," I said lightly, like it hadn't affected me at all.

"It's natural. He's losing a daughter. And I," he said, hooking his arm around my shoulders and pulling me close, "am gaining a wife." His body angled into mine, forcing my neck into an unnatural position and I cringed. "I'm so proud of you. That took a lot of courage, and you did it."

"He wants us to get married in June."

"June?" Michael said, stepping back. "Well, I guess there's no reason not to."

Because I was already feeling hungover from the emotional cocktail I'd had earlier, the last thing I wanted was a drink. But when Michael brought in a bottle of champagne and two glasses, I set down my cup of tea and moved over to the couch.

"Close your eyes," he instructed. I gave him a puzzled look, but did what he said. I heard the pop of the champagne cork and the fizzing as he filled our glasses, then a curious *plink*. Michael placed the cool glass in my hand. "Keep your eyes closed until I tell you, but let's toast."

"With my eyes closed?"

"Yes, with your eyes closed! To you, Grace. Somehow, you complete me. To you, and all the good things that are ahead of us."

To go from my father damning me to hell to Michael toasting me within a few hours was surreal. "Michael," I said, starting to open my eyes.

"Not yet. First finish the toast."

I lifted the glass to my lips and took a sip. While I could still feel the tingle of it on my tongue, Michael leaned over and kissed me gently on the lips. There was so much in that whisper of a kiss—love and adventure and promise and desire—and I could taste all of it.

"The champagne is a gorgeous color," Michael said. "Open your eyes now so you can see it."

As I held the glass up to the sunlight that was streaming through the windows, something in the bottom of the glass caught my eye. I looked more closely and gasped. "Is it—?" I asked, looking from the glass to Michael, then back to the glass.

"It is," he said. I fished the ring out of the glass with my finger and gave it to him and he slid it, still dripping with champagne, onto my finger. He dabbed at the ring with a napkin. "It's a carat and a half," he said, his eyes bright with pleasure. "It's slightly occluded, but only an expert with a magnifying glass can see the flaws."

"It's stunning," I said, gazing at the Marquise-cut stone. Once, when Liv and I had gone shopping at the mall, we'd window shopped at the jewelry store, comparing favorites. Liv liked the triangle or Marquise rings—ones that always looked a little dangerous to me, with their sharp points. I liked the oval ones, with their long lines and gentle curves. Not too traditional, not too trendy.

But Michael couldn't have known that I preferred ovals, and the stone itself was gorgeous. I took it off and held it up to the sunshine so that the diamond magnified and refracted the sun's rays onto the opposite wall and ceiling. The effect was hypnotic. I had never owned anything so beautiful or expensive. "It's breathtaking," I said, putting the ring back on.

Michael held the ends of my fingers and tipped my hand back and forth, admiring it. "I know." He raised my hand to his lips and playfully kissed it. "I have exquisite taste in rings and in women."

I smiled at Michael's high spirits, but I still felt unsettled. I had never thought of myself as exquisite before. Then again, I had never made a big decision completely on my own, and I had never thought of myself as being impulsive, manipulative, or a liar. And in the last twenty-four hours, I had been all that, and more.

Eleven

I had been like background music all through high school but that changed as soon as everyone heard that Michael and I were engaged.

The girls couldn't keep their eyes off my left hand, which I held at waist level. That made it easy for them to see that no, I wasn't pregnant, which, Liv said, was what everyone immediately thought. The popular guys—very few of whom had talked to me *ever*—kept implying they were disappointed I was unavailable.

Even my teachers treated me differently, taking a new, careful interest in me. I dropped off my paper on the

Crusades to Mr. Tyce after school one day. "Thanks," he said. He put it into his briefcase and then sagged down onto the corner of his desk. "What are your plans for college now?"

"I'm going to the college where Michael teaches," I said, knowing his real question: Was I going to be "one of those"—a smart girl who throws everything away for a guy? The ironic thing was that, in my case, "everything" wasn't much.

Another day, Mrs. Witkowski, my Calculus teacher asked, "He works at the college, doesn't he?" She gave me a thin smile, but raised her eyebrows skeptically. She was in her forties, maybe, and divorced, and she seemed to assume that just because love had gone wrong for her, it would go wrong for me and Michael, too. But we weren't them. We weren't even *like* them.

When they were done pretending they were less interested than they were, my teachers all said the same thing: "Don't ignore your studies." But with a solid GPA less than two months before graduation and a wedding to plan, I was already coasting.

All the other seniors were, too. As the weather got warmer and we could all see our high school years coming to an end, everyone got into the partying mood.

One day at the end of lunch period, when I was easing my history book out of my locker, trying to keep the other books from falling out, Melissa tapped me on the shoulder. "Hey, there."

"Oh, hey," I said, holding the books up with my left hand and looking awkwardly over my right shoulder. For a minute, Melissa, like all the other girls, seemed mesmerized by my ring. I was getting used to it. I pulled the book out of the locker and turned to her. "How's it going?"

"Great!" she chirped.

I looked up and down the hall, expecting to see her Siamese twin coming. "Where's Carrie?"

"We're both working at the candy counter. I'm just taking a break." Melissa looked down at her charm bracelet and began fidgeting with a megaphone charm. "You know," she said slowly, "I just wanted to say I'm sorry for what happened in the bathroom that day." She glanced quickly up at me, and I could tell from the heat in my cheeks that I was blushing just remembering it.

"We didn't know you were there," Melissa said.

"That's kind of beside the point, isn't it?" I asked. "It's like saying you're sorry for getting caught instead of for doing something wrong."

Melissa arched her eyebrows in surprise that I didn't just say it was okay. That's probably what I would have said, before the face-down with my father had given me, as Liv would say, some *cojones*.

When she saw I wasn't going to back down, Melissa tossed her head and sighed with exasperation. "Maybe I didn't say it right, but you know what I mean." She twisted her bracelet around her wrist. She was waiting for me to say something, but when I didn't, she continued.

"I'm, um, throwing a party a week from Saturday, and thought if you weren't doing anything else maybe you'd like to come."

"Maybe," I said, like I didn't care one way or the other.

"It's at my house, starting around 8:00."

"I'll talk to Liv. She's invited too, right?"

Melissa hesitated. "Liv? Well . . . yeah. But your boyfriend—I mean fiancé . . ."

It was weird to think of Michael at a party of high school kids. "I don't know," I said, closing my locker. "I'll ask him."

Melissa's face lit up. "Great! So I'll tell everyone that maybe he—you'll be there."

I shrugged. I knew that Melissa thought that if she could tell everyone that we would be at her party, it would create pre-party buzz. It was just strange to think that someone like Melissa suddenly thought of me as a "party maker," when I was essentially the same person I had been before I had started seeing Michael. For the first time in my life, the fact that the social scene made no sense was working for me. I planned to enjoy it.

* * *

Liv agreed. She smirked with satisfaction when I told her about it on the drive out to Michael's after school. It was cool out, but for the first time since fall we could feel the sun's strengthening rays on our faces. It made us giddy.

We rolled our windows down all the way to let the afternoon in full force. As Liv shifted into third, a gust of wind caught her short, flared skirt and blew it up, exposing her hot-pink underwear. "Liv!" I said, laughing uneasily.

"What?" she said. "It feels good! Out here, who's going to see? You should try it." And she pressed the gas pedal to the floor so the old Subaru hurtled down a long, flat stretch until the wind made the empty McDonald's cups and wadded-up Taco Bell bags rattle in the rear window well.

"You're crazy! And irresponsible!" I shouted over the rattling and the wind.

"Well, *yeah*," Liv retorted, as if there were no other way to be. "I yam what I yam. You should try it!"

I was so happy right then. I felt so full—of Michael, of Liv, of spring, of love itself—too full to hold anything more, even my own happiness. Impulsively, to please Liv, I unbuttoned my shirt, leaned all the way out the window, and put my hands in the air, like I was on a roller coaster, until Liv, screaming in surprise and delight, had to slow for Michael's driveway.

He was walking up the right side of the drive, carrying his mail. When he saw us coming, he grinned and stepped back. Liv stopped the car and he squatted down and rested his arms on the car window frame on my side.

"Well, well. What have we here?" he asked, his face lighting up when he saw my unbuttoned shirt. I fumbled with the most critical buttons. I didn't mind either Liv or Michael seeing me in my bra, but both of them together seeing me that way was too weird for me.

When I was done, I looked up at Michael. He was looking past me, smiling mischievously at Liv, who, it seemed to me, was taking her sweet time putting her skirt down. My good mood evaporated and I frowned at Liv.

"What?" Liv asked innocently.

Disgusted, I ignored her and opened the car door, taking Michael by surprise and throwing him off balance. "Hey!" he said, scrambling to get his footing.

"Tell him about the party," Liv called.

Michael took my backpack and slung it over his shoulder. "Party?"

"It's nothing," I said, wanting to get back at Liv. "Just a group of kids getting together."

"It's nothing?" she said. "That's not what you were saying fifteen minutes ago." She leaned over and propped herself up on the passenger side seat with her elbow so she could see us better. "Michael, it's the best party of the weekend, and if you guys don't go, I can't really go, you know? So even if Grace *says* she doesn't want to go," Liv gave me a pointed look, "which—don't let her fool you—she absolutely does, I want to go. So Michael," she said with a sweet smile, "please say you'll go. Please? I'll never ask you for anything again."

"Yes, uh-huh," Michael tossed back at her. "And where have I heard *that* before?"

There was something about their witty repartee that made my spider senses tingle. I slammed the door, signaling to them, I hoped, that this—whatever little thing Liv thought she had going on with him in this conversation—was *over*.

Michael must have gotten the message, because he curved his free arm around my waist. "Grace and I will talk about it."

"Thanks for the ride," I said to Liv.

"Okay. Call me!" Liv said, sitting up and settling back into her seat. She shifted the car into reverse then waved as she drove away.

"Can you believe her?" I asked, as we walked toward the house.

"She's just young. High-spirited. Gamine," Michael replied.

"On the make is more like it."

"It's spring!"

"And don't defend her!" I snapped.

His eyes widened in surprise and then he laughed a little. "Wait. You're jealous? That's ridiculous."

That just made me angrier. "Don't laugh at me!" I tried to pull out from under his arm, but he tightened it around me. Michael was slender but he ran and lifted weights and I knew from our nights on his bed that under the oxford button-down shirt and black wool jacket, there was a lot of muscle.

"Let go!" I moved to jab my elbow into his abdomen but he felt what I was up to and clutched me so that my elbow was pinned between us.

"No, I won't," he said. "Not until you listen to me." The more I struggled against him, the tighter his grip got. "Liv meant no harm. It was spring fever and that's all. And—*and*," he said insistently, twisting me toward him, "I'm sorry I laughed at you."

My shirt was still cockeyed because I had been sloppy about buttoning it and hadn't bothered to tuck it into my jeans, and he slid his hand onto the bare skin right above the waistband of my jeans and stroked it as though he were trying to calm a spooked horse.

"It's just that, Rabbit," he said, moving his hand up higher, to my rib cage, "what does that piece of carbon on your left hand say to you?" Starting to feel foolish, I relaxed against him. "You know it says I love you, and only you." He slid his hand higher still and I quivered, even though I didn't want to because that made it too easy for him. But I couldn't stop the quiver any more than I could stop my heart from beating.

By the time he pulled me into the woods, down onto a dry mossy spot speckled with sunlight, I knew I'd over-reacted. And, just a few minutes later, when he'd deftly unbuttoned my shirt and unhooked the front clasp of my bra so I could feel both his insistent lips and the sun down the length of my body, I had for the time being forgotten the whole thing.

Afterwards, as I was picking pine needles out of my hair, Michael asked me about the party. I admitted that Liv was right. I did want to go.

"Then we should go," he said simply.

I knew he was probably indulging me, but I let him. Now that everyone at school finally knew I existed, there was a part of me that wanted to hang back for a little while longer, and let them get a really good look.

Twelve

"There it is!" I said, as we rounded the bend on the expressway and the jagged Chicago skyline came into view. "We're finally here. Now you *have* tell me what we're going to do. You promised!"

Michael smiled mischievously. "Technically, we are not in the city limits yet."

I threw my head back against the headrest in exasperation. *"Michael!"*

"You are the most impatient girl I know. Don't you know that the anticipation is half the fun?"

"But I don't even know what I'm anticipating!"

Smiling, he pulled two tickets out of his breast pocket and waved them in the air. "This."

I squealed and threw both my arms around him. "I can't believe it! I'm really going!"

"Steady," he said. "One of us still has to drive, and since I have the wheel and you're delirious with joy, that's me."

I peppered his cheek with kisses, all the way down to the corner of his lips. "How did you get tickets?"

"It wasn't hard."

"Liv said it was sold out."

Michael chuckled. "Liv? What would she know about Puccini?"

"Puccini?" I unwrapped myself from around Michael and slid the tickets out of his hand. I skimmed the bold type on the top ticket. *The Chicago Opera Theatre proudly presents Puccini's* Turandot. Thinking it must be a joke, I flipped to the next ticket. It said the same thing. "The opera?" I said. "We're going to the *opera?*"

"Yes—a matinee," Michael said. "I mentioned opera a few weeks ago and you said it might be fun to go. So I got tickets." He glanced over at me. "Why? What's wrong?"

I let my hair fall like a curtain between us. "Nothing. It's just when I saw the tickets, I thought they were to the We're Skewed concert. That's all."

"Why would you think that?"

"Because, remember? We were in the coffee shop after we first met and you said you'd take me. And I knew there was a concert here this weekend."

Michael put his hand on my leg. "I'm sorry, Grace. I didn't even think of that. You said it might be fun to go to the opera. I thought you'd be happy when I arranged it so quickly."

Sometime, I thought. *What I said is that I'd like to go to the opera sometime.* Like maybe when I was fifty or something, but not now. We were on the stretch of highway where you can see Lake Michigan for a while, so I turned my head and watched a barge crawl across the horizon.

Michael squeezed my leg. "We don't have to go if you don't want to. We could go to the Art Institute of Chicago instead."

Safely behind my veil of hair, I wrinkled my nose. But then I had a thought. "Or the botanical gardens? I remember Lila telling me that they have a lily show in the spring."

"Who's Lila?"

"She owns the greenhouse where I go sometimes."

"I've never heard you talk about going."

"Well, I do go there," I said, frowning. "I just haven't for a while." I tried to remember the last time I'd been there and realized it had been a long time—since before Christmas.

"Is that what you really want to do, then?"

What I really wanted was to go to the concert. But that wasn't going to happen. I stared down at the opera tickets again. It wasn't like I was going to get what I really wanted by making Michael give up what he really wanted.

"Never mind," I said, tucking my hair behind my ear. "Let's just go to this Turn-a-dot thing."

"Tu-ran-dot," he said. "You're really okay with it?"

I nodded, swallowing my disappointment. "I said I wanted to see opera, right?"

"You're going to like it, Grace." Michael said, his eyes sparkling with excitement. "Turandot is a cold-hearted beauty who puts three riddles to any man who wants to marry her. If the man answers the riddle correctly, she will marry him. If he fails, then he's beheaded. It's all about love, and the music is wonderful."

He explained more, but I quickly figured out I didn't have to listen to what he was saying. I knew how to nod in all the right places.

*   *   *

After the opera, I was ravenous. "I know just the place," Michael said, grabbing me by the hand and pulling me after him.

"What about here?" I said, looking longingly into the steamed-up window of a pizza parlor as we walked by. The smell of baking crust wafted over me, making my stomach rumble.

Michael laughed. "Pizza after the opera? That would be a crime."

Finally, he stopped in front of a French-Vietnamese restaurant.

"Here?" I said, not even trying to keep the whine out of my voice.

"Yes, here. Think of it as an adventure."

After we were seated, I skimmed the menu the hostess gave to me and immediately slapped it onto the table. "Why can't anything be in English?" I said. "We just sat through an opera where everything was in Italian and I had to guess at what they were singing and now I have to guess at what I'll be eating?"

"Don't be so provincial." Michael put his arm around my shoulder. I tried to shrug it off but he didn't take the hint. "Relax," he said. "You had subtitles at the opera and there are subtitles here. I'll order for you."

"Great," I said, slouching in my chair.

Michael lifted a finger at the waiter. "My fiancee will have Thit Ga Xao Dam Gung Sa and I'll have Ech Nau Ca-Ri. We'll start with a salad."

"Excellent choices," the waiter said.

"And bread!" I said. "Can you bring some bread?"

I dropped the napkin into my lap. "So what am I getting to eat?"

"Chicken with lemongrass. I'm getting curried frogs' legs. If you stop acting like a petulant child, I'll let you try a bite."

"I'm sorry," I said. "I'm just so hungry that now I feel sick."

"The food will be here soon." He took his arm off my shoulders, finally, and clasped my hands in both of his. "What did you think of *Turandot?* Wasn't it remarkable?"

The only thing remotely remarkable about it was that I had managed to stay awake for the whole thing, even the twenty minutes where nothing happened except that the moon rose and the chorus sang about it rising. I had checked my watch so often that if anyone had been watching me, they would have sworn I had a nervous tic.

The waiter brought over some rolls and I tore off a chunk.

Michael smiled at me encouragingly and tried again. "Wasn't it incredible?"

"I'm not sure I understood it," I said slowly, after I'd swallowed my bite of roll. "Turandot and her boyfriend were both so heartless. I mean, he would have let his own *father* die if that meant he could have Turandot. The only thing he knew about her was that she was beautiful and cruel. So he seemed kind of dumb to me, especially at the end where he says something like 'Tell me my name before morning, and I shall die at dawn.' He'd already solved the riddle, so why does he give her another chance to get away?"

"It's metaphorical," said Michael. "Like all operas are. He doesn't want her to marry him only because he won. He wants her to marry him because she *wants* to."

"But why does he want to marry her when she's such a bitch? And everyone tries to talk him out of pursuing her, but what was it he said? 'I listen to no one.'"

"Because he sees what others don't—that there's more to her. He sees how love can change her."

"But the love isn't true to begin with because it's not based on anything he knows about her other than that she's gorgeous."

Michael's eyes shone and he squeezed my hands. "I knew you'd like it!"

The waiter brought our food then, but suddenly I felt too nauseous to eat any of it. The room closed in around me and I felt like I couldn't breathe. I stood up abruptly. "I need air," I said to Michael, darting behind him. "I have to get out for a minute."

* * *

The queasiness had passed by the time we got to his place a few hours later and when he kissed me first gently along my forehead and eyelids and then more urgently down my cheeks until his lips finally met mine with *May I, will you, can we now?* all of me was already saying yes.

I didn't know about metaphors in opera, exotic food, or fine wine. What I knew was that in the middle of making love, while we were in that secret hothouse—where it felt like tulips and lilies and irises sprouted and then bloomed all at the same time, right at the end—it always seemed like that was enough. Lying beside him, after we were done, I thought, *This is why they make you promise not to do it. Because it's like a drug. It's all you want. It's all you need.*

Thirteen

"Hey, how's it going?" Liv asked, catching a stranger's eye. She was standing with her back to the counter, facing the other customers in line. The man in the brown suit smiled tightly, then pulled out his *Wall Street Journal.*

It was the last day before spring break, and Liv and I were wedding dress shopping downtown. Even though I had eaten only a few hours before, I was hungry again. Positive that I would chew my own arm off if I didn't get something to eat soon, I'd dragged Liv to a Burger King and ordered a Whopper. Unfortunately, the service was slow and Liv was entertaining herself by going against the flow, making people uneasy for sport.

I sidled to the right, trying to put some distance between me and Liv. Usually I admired Liv's rebel streak, but today it was bugging me. Then again, although I was trying not to show it, I had been irritated with Liv ever since she had flirted with Michael in his driveway.

In the line next to us, a guy in a university sweatshirt and his girlfriend were trying to combine their food onto one tray. One of their drinks spilled and Liv quickly grabbed some napkins and helped him mop it up.

"You go to the U of M?" Liv asked, handing him some napkins.

"Yeah," he said.

"I'm thinking about going there," Liv said. "What's your major?"

"Pre-med."

"It's good you're getting a degree because something tells me you wouldn't be so good at waiting tables."

The guy laughed. "Thanks for your help," he said. He carefully picked up the replacement Coke and headed toward a table.

"No problem," Liv replied. Turning back to me, she started to say something but I cut her off.

"Geez, Liv! Exercise a little self-control, why don't you?"

"What are you talking about?"

"You know what—coming on to every guy that crosses your path. He had a girlfriend. Did you happen to notice that?"

"What is your problem?" Liv snapped. "I was just helping him."

"Uh-huh," I said.

Liv crossed her arms. "It was your idea to come in here. We just had lunch and I'm not even hungry. Just ease up, why don't you? Ever since you've gotten engaged you . . ."

"What?"

Liv seemed to lose her bite then. "No. Never mind," she said, walking away. "I'll go find us a table."

By the time I had finally gotten my burger a few minutes later, I regretted blowing up at her. "I'm sorry, Liv," I said, sitting down across from her. "The wedding, school, all the stress at home with my parents—I guess the pressure's getting to me."

Liv shrugged like it had been no big deal. "S'all right." She watched me pick the pickles off my burger, then sighed with exasperation. "You've got to be kidding! You wait ten minutes for that thing and they *still* can't get it right?"

"I know." I held the pickles out to Liv. "Want them?"

"Thanks." Liv took them and holding them high above her head, dropped them one by one onto her outstretched tongue. "Your parents are still pretty ripped about this, huh?" she asked through a mouthful of pickles.

I was trying to be better about not talking with my mouth full—Michael always shot a look at me when I did— so I had a minute to think about her question as I finished chewing my bite of burger.

At first after the fight at Michael's house, I avoided my father, which was easy to do because I knew his routine.

But one Saturday, my timing was off and I walked into the living room while he was there.

He was sitting in his chair, with little stacks of bills balanced on one arm of the chair and a calculator on the other. When he saw me, he winced, like he had seen someone with a deformed face. He struggled up, and held out the checkbook awkwardly, like he needed a reason for being there. Clearing his throat, he said, "I was just leaving. On my way to the bank." The slips of paper fluttered to the floor, but he ignored them.

I abruptly changed directions so that I could pretend I was just passing through. Somehow, we ended up standing right in front of each other. "That's nice. I mean, good."

I took a step to my right at the same moment that he took a step to his left. I was ready to smile, but immediately he took another step to the left and walked by me. "Tell your mother I've gone, would you?"

"Okay." I knelt down and gathered up the bills, one by one, thinking blankly, *He can't even stand to look at me.*

Liv drummed her fingers on the table. "Well?" she said. "Are they still mad or not?"

I swallowed hard. "I think that if he could, my dad would hold up a cross to ward me off. It's like I'm a vampire or a leper or something."

"What about your mom?"

"That's weird, too. When I went home after staying overnight at Michael's, it was just my mom and me. My dad went back to the conference he had been at. She just asked me if this was what I really wanted and I told her yeah, it really is."

"Who wouldn't want it?" Liv said. The pickles had left some mustard on her fingers and she licked it off.

"Then my mom just nodded like she understood—or at least understood that I had decided and there was nothing she could do about it. With her, it's hard to tell." I stirred my pop with my straw to create a whirlpool until I remembered I needed to stop playing with my food. "Ever since then she has been totally into the wedding planning—the church, the reception, the cake, the flowers. We talk about what I want, then she does all the work of getting it."

"It sounds like she's good with it. Maybe she's happy for you."

I couldn't remember the last time I had thought of my mother as happy. "More like resigned. I think she feels bad about what happened with my dad. She can't do anything about that, but she can make sure I have a nice wedding day, you know? So my mom is weirdly energized, and my dad is all quiet and remote. Things are backwards at my house, all because I'm engaged."

"Or all because you stood up to him, maybe."

"Maybe." I folded my burger wrapper in half, then in quarters, flattening it and creasing it each time. Liv and I hadn't really talked in a while, and it felt good to connect again. "Hey," I said, trying to sound casual. "What were you going to say back there at the counter about what I've been like since I got engaged?"

"Oh. Nothing," Liv snatched the wrapper from the table, unfolded it, and balled it up. "It's stupid."

I prodded Liv's foot with mine and grinned. "Come on. Just tell me. It won't be the first time you've said something stupid."

"Or you," she shot back.

"Right, or me."

She looked at me, trying to decide. Finally, she said, "It's like this. Now you have a way out, and it's not fair because I needed it worse than you did. But it's not your fault so I can't even hate you for it."

She threw the wrapper at the nearest trash basket and smiled ruefully when it bounced off the rim. "No way out. The story of my life. Just like when I was a kid, riding in the back seat of the car while my mom was driving drunk. I'd be back there crying—crying so quietly so she couldn't hear me because if she heard me she'd yell at me—I'd be back there crying, looking out the window, wanting to get out of the car. But I was a little kid. What could I do?"

"But now there are things you can do. The scholarship."

"Yeah, well, I'm not good enough to win it."

"You are! I'll help you, if you want."

"Yeah? You think the judges will go for your purple prose?"

That was a sore spot with me and Liv knew it, but I let it go. "I know you're a better writer, I was just saying—"

"I know. Thanks. I may take you up on it. But if I don't win—"

"If you don't win, we can figure out another way."

She shook her head. "No, I'm telling you this is it for me. It's got to happen."

I didn't say anything. Once Liv had made up her mind about something, it was impossible to change it.

Liv stood up and grabbed my hand. "Blah, blah, blah," she said, mocking herself. "That whiner talk is so boring. Let's go *shop*-pin."

*　*　*

As soon as I stepped onto the rose-colored, deep-pile carpeting and I heard the classical music, I knew I was in the wrong place. "It's too ritzy," I whispered to Liv. "Let's go out to that place by the mall."

"No, let's just look here," Liv said, pushing by me.

A salesperson glided up to us. "I'm sorry, we don't carry prom dresses," she said.

Liv snorted and before I could stop her, grabbed my left hand and began waving it in front of the woman. "We're here for a wedding dress," she said. "She's getting married in June."

I pulled my hand back and glared at Liv. Just because I was uncomfortable in the shop didn't mean that I couldn't speak for myself. "We're just looking," I said, backing toward the door.

But Liv's instincts had been right. The diamond trick worked. "It's good that you came in when you did," the woman said warmly, putting her arm around my shoulders and guiding me toward the racks of plastic-wrapped gowns. "But you'll need to make up your mind quickly in order for it to arrive in time. It'll be my pleasure to help you. Call me Maureen."

"You mean we can't just buy one?" Liv asked, looking around the shop. "It looks like you have a ton of them."

"Oh, no," Maureen said. "These are all just samples. You have to order it." She paused between two racks and looked at my face. "Given your coloring, candlelight might be the best color for you."

Liv giggled, then nodded soberly. "It's true, Grace. It's more appropriate, anyway." Maureen knew what she was talking about—white made me look completely washed out—and I knew that my father would think I was rubbing the whole situation in if I wore a white dress. Still, I had been dreaming of my wedding day since I was a little girl, and in those dreams I was always wearing white.

"Can I try both?" I asked.

"Of course," Maureen said. "Now, about style." She gave my body the once-over. "It's a little difficult to tell in those clothes, but you seem to have an hourglass figure."

"Definitely!" Liv exclaimed. "She's built."

"A-line would be lovely on you."

"Would it hide my hips?"

"Pardon me?"

"My hips, well, there seems to be a lot of them," I mumbled.

"It's healthy, not like some of these twigs you see walking around," Maureen said pointedly, looking at Liv. "When it's time to have babies you will thank your lucky stars for those hips."

She began to carefully lift dresses off the rack, showing them to me. When she took the dresses that I wanted to try on into the dressing room for me, Liv, who had been rifling through the racks of dresses on her own, said, *"Maureen*—what a wedding dress Nazi! I mean, like, just give us the chance to *look*, you know? Without hawking over us! It's like she thinks we're going to smear chocolaty hands on them, or shoplift them or something!" Liv stopped her rant abruptly when her hand landed on an ivory satin sheath. "Oh, Grace," she sighed. "Try this one."

"I don't know," I said. It looked all wrong for me.

"Just try it!" Liv said. "Sometimes you can't tell until you try it on."

"That's true," said Maureen, coming out of the dressing room.

"All right. I'll try it."

Maureen selected six others. "I want to give you a taste of our enormous selection," she said.

When I got into the dressing room, it was clear that Maureen was planning to stay and help me try on the dresses. I had a moment of panic, trying to remember whether I had put on ratty or decent underwear. Unzipping my jeans a bit, I caught a glimpse of my panties and sighed with relief. They were a good pair.

Maureen picked a dress at random and slipped it over my head. I looked at Liv's reaction. She pursed her lips and shrugged. I turned toward the mirror.

"Wait a minute," said Maureen. "Not yet." She began buttoning all tiny buttons up the back. "You can't get the full effect without the buttons and a veil." Finished, she held out her hand and helped me onto a pedestal in front of a floor-to-ceiling, three-way mirror.

Worried that I was about to spoil my wedding day fantasy, I looked up slowly. The dress was a champagne-colored, A-line dress of matte satin with an empire waist, a sweetheart neck and sheer cap sleeves. The entire dress had an overlay of delicate floral lace.

Somehow, a long white dress had changed me into a woman—and I was *beautiful.* The dress made my skin look luminous and brought out the highlights in my hair. I fell in love with it immediately.

"We can go home now," I said. "This is the one."

"It does seem to be meant for you." Maureen fluffed the long train of the dress so it billowed out behind me.

"It's pretty, Grace, but kind of ordinary," Liv said. "And you haven't even tried the others."

"I don't need to."

"You'd be surprised how often the first dress a girl tries on is the one she ends up buying," said Maureen. "They try on fifty other dresses but usually end up coming back to that first one." She straightened the veil. "Sometimes I think they fall in love not so much with the dress but with that first vision of themselves in a wedding dress."

Sighing happily, I admired myself in the mirror. The dress fit snuggly over my breasts and hugged my rib cage, then flared just a bit. It was modest but flattering. Best of all, it hid my hips.

"You're going to try on others, aren't you? Humor me," Liv begged.

So I tried on other dresses—silk ones, satin ones, and chiffon ones, some with plunging necklines and others with plunging backs. Several of them made me and Liv laugh so hard that my ribs ached, like one that had a pleated collar— "It makes you look like an accordion," roared Liv—and another with a skirt ringed in feathers. When Maureen went to hang up an armload of dresses, I flapped my arms and stood on my tiptoes. "Look, I'm a bird, flying far, far away!" I said, remembering too late what Liv had said at the restaurant about me getting out. She smiled for a second and nodded, but turned away quickly and sifted through the dresses again.

"I'm tired," I said. "Let's go home."

"Not yet. Look, here's the one I found. Try mine." The dress was draped over both of Liv's arms and she raised it up to me like an offering. "It's the least you can do after calling me a slut," she joked.

I looked at her standing there, holding up that dress, and I was glad I had never accused her of coming on to Michael that day in the driveway. Liv had just been being herself, the same as always. "All right," I said, feeling guilty I'd ever doubted her. "But this is the last one."

It took a bit of tugging to get the dress over my head, but once it was, I could see why Liv had picked it off the rack. It was simple and elegant—an off-the-shoulder, close-fitting chiffon, trimmed at the neckline with delicate pink satin rosebuds. It had sheer bell sleeves that gracefully trailed my arms as I moved them.

"That one has a baroque look," said Maureen.

Liv cupped her hands over her mouth and nose and breathed in sharply. "It's gorgeous! Oh, Grace, you've got to get this one!"

"It is really pretty," I said, fingering the roses. In this dress, my pale shoulders actually looked like an asset. "But look." I bent over at the waist. "I practically fall out of it in front and it's too tight in the back."

"It's sexy!" Liv protested.

Maureen frowned.

"Maybe a larger size?" Liv asked.

"The dress fits her in the waist and across the shoulders, so I don't believe it's a size issue," said Maureen. "It's a style issue." The phone rang then and she went to answer it, leaving us alone.

"I don't know," I said, turning this way and that.

Liv sat back and sighed appreciatively. "It's so romantic. Like right out of the story of King Arthur and Guinevere, you know? It reminds me of the scene in the movie where all the ladies are dancing during the spring festival or whatever it was, with rings of flowers in their hair."

I laughed. "If you keep talking like that, I'll start to think you're a real girl, like Melissa or Carrie."

She flipped me off. "Or you?"

"Yeah. Or me. It sounds like almost anyone, but not like you."

"All I'm saying is that Michael would adore it, I bet," she said, sulking.

"You think?"

"Oh, yeah. You, in this dress? It's an oxymoron, the way it makes you look—sexy and pure at the same time."

I held up my arms, as though I was dancing with an invisible partner. The material of the dress and its sheer bell sleeves did make me look ethereal, almost weightless. For just a second, at a certain angle, I looked like my mother.

I did like the dress. Maybe I just needed to get used to it.

When Maureen returned, she suggested I take pictures of both dresses home and think about it. "But you need to make up your mind soon. It's already so late that we'll have to put a rush on it."

I didn't bother to check myself in the mirror once I had put my jeans and sweater back on. Like Cinderella at midnight, I knew I was back to my real self again, but I didn't mind. Before long, I'd put that glass slipper on again and change for good.

Fourteen

The next day we were hanging out at Liv's house when Michael called and told me that he wouldn't be able to go to the party at Melissa's house after all.

"I have to be at a dinner for a guest lecturer," he said. "It slipped my mind until I ran into the department secretary today. I need to be there. And I want you to be there, too." A knot of stubbornness formed in my chest. "Spouses and significant others are invited. Tonight is an excellent opportunity for me to introduce you to my colleagues."

Tonight is also an excellent opportunity *to be with my friends,* I thought. "But I really wanted to go to Melissa's party. Can't you just go to that thing by yourself?"

"This is important."

"What—and my party isn't?"

"I didn't say that. This is important to our future. Your party is important to you, but it's not just about you. Now there's an *us* to think about."

I sighed. "But you said—"

"I'm sorry. But please try to understand. The entire office will be there and it will look bad if we're not. Also, I want to show you off a bit," he said, trying to tease me out of being mad.

I couldn't stay mad at him. But I desperately wanted to go to an A party once in my life—just to see what it was like—and I was afraid this would be my only chance. "Couldn't I come to that faculty thing late? I could go with Liv to Melissa's party for a little while and then she could bring me there." I looked over at Liv and mouthed, *Can you?*

Liv shrugged. "Sure."

"I think that could work as long as you're there by 9:00."

The knot in my chest tightened again at the thought of having a curfew. But then I thought, *no, it's a compromise.* "I can be there at 9:00."

Michael gave me the address and told me how to get there, then his phone beeped. "I've got to go. I have an incoming call," he said.

"Wait! What should I wear?"

"Something nice," he said. "Just pick out something nice. I'll see you there."

Later, standing in front of my closet back home, I wasn't sure what that meant. "He said to wear something nice," I said to Liv.

"So, like a skirt?"

"I think so." I pulled out a rayon, knee-length butter yellow one that was cut on the bias, paired it with a peasant blouse, and modeled it for Liv. "What do you think?"

"It's overkill for Melissa's," said Liv.

"I know, but that's better than being too casual at the college thing." We decided it would basically work for both, and a little while later headed out to find Melissa's house, which was in a new subdivision—the kind with lots of cul-de-sacs.

"You know, cul-de-sac is just a nice way of saying 'dead end,'" Liv said, as she squinted at the house numbers, trying to figure out if we were headed in the right direction. Melissa had said to look for the big house with a bunch of dormers, but all the houses were big and had dormers. We drove around for fifteen minutes before Liv recognized another friend's car and followed it to the party.

Melissa spotted us as right away and waved cheerfully as she wriggled her way over to us.

"Elbow, elbow, wrist, wrist," Liv said under her breath, mocking Melissa's beauty queen style of waving.

I jabbed my elbow into her ribs. "Behave."

"Hi there!" Melissa said over the music. "There's food in the kitchen," she motioned behind her, "if you can get there, and dancing in the living room," she motioned to her right. Then she leaned in close. "If you want to drink, you'll have to do it in your car because my parents are here," she said, pointing at the ceiling. She looked over their shoulders, through the open door. "Where's . . ."

"Michael?" Liv said.

Melissa nodded.

"Running late," Liv said, before I had time to answer. "He'll be here before you can say 'bikini bottom,' Little 'Lissa." Then Liv pulled me past Melissa and into the kitchen.

"Why did you say that?" I asked, yanking my arm away.

"I don't know. It seemed like the right thing to do at the time. Why not?"

"Maybe because it's a lie?" It seemed to me that Liv's white lies were getting darker all the time.

"A harmless one, though," she said, grinning. "Oh! There's Davis. Be right back."

Some girls from my Calculus class were complaining about the teacher and I hung out with them for a while, listening to them talk about how the last test had been impossible.

"It was like the teacher actually *wanted* us all to flunk," said Lydia.

"I think the teachers are all jealous," said Bethany, who was standing next to me.

"Of what?"

"Of us! We're graduating and moving on but next year they'll be back here."

"Maybe they want to be," said a guy I didn't recognize. "They probably like it here. It's a nice size town with a college, not much crime, a great place to raise kids. You know, teachers are people, too."

The girls all groaned in unison. "Who cares?" Lydia said, scowling.

"My cousin, Will," Bethany said to me, tipping her head toward him.

I smiled and said hello but then made my way to the kitchen island to get a handful of chips. A minute later, Will followed.

"I didn't catch your name," he said.

"Grace," I said, eating a chip carefully so that no crumbs fell onto my shirt. I didn't want to embarrass Michael by showing up at the faculty party with grease stains. "Are you from around here?"

"Montana," he said. "We just moved here."

"Were you this popular at your old school?" I deadpanned, glancing back at the group of girls.

"Oh that," he said. "I was doing a continuation of the 'wet blanket' research project that I started in my psych class back in Montana. I see how people react when I ruin their fun by disagreeing."

"What do they usually do?"

He shoved his hands deep into the pockets of his jeans. "Lots of times kids kind of shred me about it, like just happened there, and then change the subject. Those kids just started talking about prom. Adults usually back off. They say something like, 'That's true,' or 'Good point' and then move on. Either way, people don't much like it."

"So you'll be spending your vacation basically convincing your new classmates that you're a jerk." Smiling innocently, I reached in front of him for another chip.

He balanced his can of pop on the palm of his right hand. "There are worse ways to spend a vacation."

"Neat trick," I said, pointing to the can.

"Thanks. I can also sleep with my eyes open, but we don't know each other well enough for that yet."

"Anything else?"

"I'm working on turning my head 360 degrees, but haven't mastered it."

I chose a perfect bunch of green grapes from the fruit bowl, wondering if the fruit was real. "I meant are you doing anything else over vacation."

"I think we're also going to some indoor garden around here. You know about it?"

"I used to practically live there," I said. "This time of year there's a butterfly exhibit."

Will made a face. "I think it's disgusting the way they pin dead butterflies to a board so people can look at them."

"It's not that kind of exhibit. All the butterflies are alive. Cocoons from all over the world are shipped to the exhibit, and over the next couple of weeks, the butterflies come out of their cocoons and fly around the garden. Go on a sunny day, if you can. That's when the butterflies are the most active."

"Huh," he said, looking at me curiously.

When I started to reach for another bunch of grapes, he moved the entire bowl closer to me. "Thanks," I said. "I used to go once a week, just to see the different stages of the plants and flowers. I thought I might want to study horticulture. It's been months since I've been there."

"Why?"

I wiped my hands with a napkin, then wadded it up. "I don't know. I haven't thought about it, really. I just got busy with other things."

"Hey, maybe we could go together," Will said. "You could show me around."

I shook my head. "I can't. I have a lot to do. I'm planning my wedding."

Will laughed loudly. "I've had girls turn down a date with me before, but none of them ever used that excuse."

I held out my left hand so he could see the ring. "Seriously. I'm getting married in June."

"No shit," he said slowly. "Why would you do a thing like that now?"

I yanked my hand back. "You mean start spending the rest of my life with someone I love?"

"No," he snorted. "I mean narrowize your life like that?"

"What's that supposed to mean, *narrowize?* That's not even a real word!"

"Whoa," he said. "Little Miss Touchy. Methinks she doth protest too much."

"I'm not touchy," I said. *And if I am,* I thought, *it's only because I'm nervous about going to the faculty party.* I took a deep breath and told myself not to be such a bitch. "No, really. I want to know what it means."

"I don't know. Maybe it isn't a real word, but it ought to be. What I mean by narrowize is . . . Here's an example. Back home, the cattle graze on the plain, which is wide open. I mean, you can see for miles. Then they are herded into a big pasture, then a smaller corral, then these tiny individual stations where they can't even turn around. They stand in the same place all day, every day. *That's* narrowization. That's what happened to the teachers we were just talking about."

"But you just said that maybe the teachers wanted to be here."

"That was just for the sake of argument," he said.

I rolled my eyes in frustration. "That's really interesting, but I have to go now."

"Wait. Don't you want to know what happens next?"

I looked past him, scanning the room for Liv. "What happens to who?"

"The cows, after they get put in those tiny stations."

No, I thought. *I don't want to know what happens to some stupid cows.* "Sure," I said.

"They probably think it's a pretty good life for a while," he said. "All they have to do is stand there and eat whatever the farmer feeds them. The cows eat themselves into a stupor."

I gave him a funny look.

"Then they get butchered," he said, popping a cherry tomato into his mouth.

"I'm not a cow," I said, thinking the whole conversation was seriously stupid. "I'm just a girl who fell in love and is getting married."

I saw Melissa's friend Carrie waving to me from the doorway to the den. It was the first time I had ever felt grateful to Carrie for anything. "I really have to go now," I said, squeezing between him and a guy who was telling a dumb blonde joke to a blonde. "Nice meeting you."

"I know you're not a cow," he called after me. "Cows don't have any choice."

Carrie grabbed my arm and pulled me into a circle of girls in the den, who peppered me with questions about the wedding. "What color are the bridesmaids dresses going to be?" (Soft pink.) "Who's standing up with you?" (Liv, of course!) and, everyone's favorite, "Where are you going on your honeymoon?" (France, but I didn't want to ruin the effect by telling them that we wouldn't be able to take it for at least a year because of Michael's teaching schedule.) Not wanting to be late to Michael's department party, I kept my eye on the time.

Liv and I had figured out before the party what time we would have to leave to get me to the faculty party on time, but driving there, we realized we were cutting it close.

Approaching a railroad crossing, we both saw the headlight of the train at the same time. "Shit!" Liv said, pressing her foot to the accelerator. The train was bearing down on us, and the conductor must have known that Liv was thinking she could beat the train, because he laid on the whistle and never let up.

I couldn't believe Liv thought we had time to make it across. "Liv, don't!"

The light from the streetlights flickered over Liv's face as she sped toward the crossing, making her look crazed. "I can make it."

"Stop!" I yelled, flinging my left arm out across Liv's chest and bracing myself against the dashboard with the other.

Liv slammed on the brakes and the car shuddered to a stop. "I could've made it," she complained, as the train roared by. "Now you're going to be late. The last train I was caught behind was ten minutes long."

"It's okay," I said, as much to myself as to Liv. "It's okay. Michael will understand."

Liv shifted the Subaru into neutral. From beneath the seat she pulled a paper bag and shoved it toward me. "You look like you could use a slug," she said.

I looked at the bag, then back at her. "Since when have you started drinking and driving—at the same time?"

"Since last night. We can both use it right about now. You're going to a party and my life is a party," she said sarcastically.

I stared at the bag but didn't move. Smelling like alcohol when I arrived at the faculty party would look bad, but if I refused to drink with Liv, she'd think it was just another way in which I was moving on, when she couldn't.

"Go on," she said, nodding at the bag. "It'll help you relax so you can make a good impression."

"Do you have any mints—besides Altoids?" I asked.

"Are you kidding?" Liv opened the glove compartment so I could see the jumble of breath mints and spearmint gum. She smirked and handed me the bag. We sat watching the train cars, listening to the rhythmic *ka-chunk* as they went over the track, and trading the bottle back and forth between us like we used to share a package of M&Ms in the movie theater when we were kids.

Finally, after I could feel the rum working, I asked, "What happened last night?"

Liv stared straight ahead at the train. "Oh, you know. Just another day at the fun house. The usual screaming scene, but this one ended with a twist." She took a drink from the bottle. "Seems Mom's bored with checking out of her life temporarily by getting drunk. This time she tried to check out permanently."

It took a minute for her words to sink in. "You mean she tried to commit suicide?"

"Yeah, I slept through most of it until my dad stumbled in, looking for a hairpin to unlock the bathroom door. I found one but he was too drunk to get it into the lock, so I had to do it."

"Was she—did she . . . ?"

Liv shook her head. "She hadn't gotten very far. After I bandaged her up, I tucked them both in bed and kissed them goodnight. Then I mopped up as best I could." Liv sighed. "You know, they've picked drinking over me for my whole life, and that's one thing. But this! I mean, my mom would *rather be dead* than be with me?"

As she lifted the bottle again, I put my hand on her arm and stopped her. "You don't have to do this. You once said you'd write your way free of all this."

"That was when I thought I was good enough. But I'm not. It would take a miracle. Unless you helped me."

"I said that I would."

"No offense, but it's going to take a little more firepower than you've got." She paused for a second and then said, "I want you to ask Michael to help me."

I took my hand off her arm. "You mean you want him to help you *cheat?*"

"God, Grace! It's not like I'm killing someone or something. Is it so wrong to want a normal life?"

"No, but—"

"I just need an edge," she said, twisting the bag around the neck of the bottle. "Someone who is pulling for me. I'll let you borrow Fave Jeans."

Liv and I had been friends for a long time and I could let a lot slide, but outright cheating like this—it was crazy of her to even suggest it. "This isn't about Fave Jeans. It's way bigger than Fave Jeans."

Liv smiled a little. "It's always about Fave Jeans."

"Forget about Fave Jeans. Besides, he wouldn't do it."

"How do you know?"

"Because Liv. He wouldn't. He's a college professor."

"Oh, I get it. A college professor—like with a capital C and a capital P. So he's—what? Above this kind of thing? They plagiarize, they cheat, they bang each other's spouses, they stab each other in the back in all kinds of ways," she said, ticking off each thing on her fingers. "They're human—not gods!"

"I don't think he's a god," I said, annoyed. "He just wouldn't do something like that."

"Yeah, well you never know. You never know what someone will or won't do. You think you know them, maybe, and after living with them for your whole life you should know them, but you don't. You don't know shit." She slammed the heel of her hand into the steering wheel, then looked out the driver side window. "Forget it. Just forget it. You can't understand. You with your perfect little life all set for you and your perfect godlike college professor. Never mind." The last of the train cars passed in front of us and the gates slid up. Liv released the brake, shifted into first, and drove across the tracks.

I couldn't stand seeing her that way—sagging and bitter and hopeless. Lately it had seemed like I was standing on one side of a fault line and she was standing on the other, and the crack between us was getting larger, whether we wanted it to or not. And right then, I knew I had to throw her a rope. I didn't think about who would be pulling who to the other side, or if one of us would fall into the crack. Once all my love and loyalty for Liv welled up inside me, there was only one thing I could say.

"I'll do it. I'll talk to him." I took one last swig from Liv's bottle, and then I pitched it out the window.

Fifteen

"You're late," Michael said in a tight voice as he helped me take my coat off. "Camille is waiting for you before she serves dessert. Fortunately she's an accomplished hostess and knows how to smooth things over so no one has noticed."

"I know. I'm sorry! We would have been here on time if it hadn't been for that stupid train." From where we stood in the mahogany and marble entryway, I could hear people talking quietly. Classical music was playing in the background. Going from Melissa's, where the bass rocked the house and everyone was hotwired for a good time, to the subdued atmosphere here was surreal, like I had stepped into some kind of parallel universe.

I was struck by a funny thought. "Where's the body?" I asked, giggling.

"What?"

"Don't you think it's a little like a morgue?"

"No, and I don't see what's so humorous," he snapped.

That just made me giggle harder. I didn't mean to, but I couldn't help it. *"Excuse* me!" I said, hoping to make him smile by imitating the rude woman at coffee shop on our first date.

He glared at me.

I tried again, thinking he'd come around. "No body, no humerous. Like the humerus bone? We learned about it in biology."

He gripped my arm above the elbow and squeezed. "You mean *this* one?"

The shock of it shut me down. "Michael! I'm just a little nervous, okay?"

He relaxed his grip but didn't let go. "There's nothing to be nervous about." He looked at me critically and said, "I thought I told you to wear something nice."

Confused, I looked down at my clothes, thinking maybe I hadn't put on the yellow skirt after all. "But this is nice," I said, wondering what I was missing.

The muscles in his jaw flexed. "It's too late now," he said, steering me toward the dining room. "It will have to do."

When we got to the French doors that led into the dining room, I could see the other guests, who were standing in small groups around the table, chatting. Most of the women were wearing tailored black dresses and the men had on dark or tweed jackets. That's when I understood. By *nice,* Michael had meant *sophisticated.*

I wanted to disappear, sink through the floor, evaporate. Michael still had me by the elbow and he was propelling us both forward and, before I could resist, we were in the dining room. I looked up at him, hoping he'd see in my eyes that I needed to get out, but he was craning his neck, smiling stiffly, searching for someone. Maybe it was just the rum, but everything about him seemed different and stiff.

"I want to introduce you to the chairman of the department," he said. As I made my way with Michael through the crowded room, I overheard bits of conversation—"he lays out a theory of moral efficacy of drama . . . use of vernacular of real people . . . voluminous output"—and I began to feel sick.

"Michael—" I said.

"It'll be fine."

When he introduced me to a man named George Thermopolous, the chairman of the English department and the reason for the party, I shook his hand and smiled. "Nice to meet you, Dr. Thermopolous," I said.

Smiling kindly, he said, "Please, call me George."

It felt strange, wrong, actually, to call someone my father's age by his first name, especially someone who was a teacher, but I did. "Thank you, George."

I glanced at Michael, who looked pleased.

A few others walked up and Michael introduced me to them, too. I waited for the chance to add something to the conversation, but when someone said something about "a contemporary framework for understanding Byron," I decided it was safest to stick with nodding.

I stood there quietly eating the strawberry cheesecake that Camille handed me, thinking how I would have rather had Cheez Whiz on crackers, but this probably wasn't a Cheez Whiz kind of crowd. When the slice of cheesecake was gone, Camille offered me another slice, and since I was hungry and the slices were really just slivers, I took it.

I was halfway through it when I noticed Michael glaring at me.

"What?" I whispered. "It's not like I asked for it. She offered!"

Besides, the more Michael dragged me around the room, the happier I was that I had the dessert. He did all the talking and I stood half a step behind him, pretending to be busy nibbling on the cheesecake.

As we moved to the next cluster of people, he said under his breath, "Stop hiding behind me. And for God's sake, *say* something."

"But I don't—"

"Just make small talk," he said, clipping each syllable. "At the very least you can do that. It's what you and your girlfriends do best."

I was sure Michael would understand if I explained, but just then another person came up.

"Grace, this is Dale," Michael said. "He was on sabbatical last year in England."

Dale, a short professor with long nose hairs, shook my hand limply. "The pleasure is all mine," he said to my chest. He told a long story—something about the terrible service he'd gotten in a pub in the countryside—without ever making eye contact with anything other than my breasts. I tried to take a step back, but Michael was right behind me so the best I could do was slump in the hopes that it would make my breasts less interesting.

Instead, he moved even closer to me. "Excuse me," I said politely, and I bolted for the bathroom.

I hid out there for a while, sitting on the lid of the toilet and paging through back issues of *The New Yorker*, reading the cartoons. I wished I could have stayed in there until it was time to go, but eventually someone knocked and I had to leave my hiding place.

I stopped at a small room that had shelves of books up to the ceiling and a louvered door that led to a den. Through the slats I could see the legs of a few guests who were talking and laughing. I was only half-listening as I scanned the titles on the shelves. Mostly I was trying to avoid being discovered.

"Nobody went to Richard's reading," a woman said. I ran my finger across the books' spines until I realized that there was a coat of dust on them. I looked around for something to wipe my finger on.

"Nobody?" said a man's voice. I spotted a box of Kleenex and quietly pulled a tissue out and wiped off my finger.

"Well, none of us from the department. Except Michael."

"Oh, well, *Michael!*" someone else said, and everyone laughed.

I balled the tissue up in my hand and moved closer to the door.

"Did you know he asked me out?" It was the woman again. "But I said no."

I stood on my tiptoes, trying to get a glimpse of the woman through the slats. *Before or after?* I wondered. *Was that before or after he started seeing me?*

"Why not?"

"When he first got here you could tell he was part of the walking wounded, you know? We'd talked a little and I could tell was struggling to get over his old girlfriend. That was a rebound relationship just waiting to happen. I've done that enough times to know to steer clear of it."

"Too bad his fiancée didn't. Poor thing. She seems so sweet and guileless. He should know better."

Suddenly I felt weak, like I might faint. I quietly took a deep breath and immediately felt better.

"Maybe he's got a Shelley complex."

I remembered from my English classes that Shelley was a poet and I knew that Michael admired his poetry, but I didn't think that meant he had a complex.

"A what?"

The woman laughed. "You know—a Shelley complex. At least, that's what I call it. Remember? Shelley married a young and simple country maiden because he thought he could improve her."

By now I was straining so hard to listen that I almost fell right into the louvered doors.

I heard an older man chuckle. "Don't be too hard on him, my friend. I can understand the appeal of younger women. Their stories are shorter."

Before their laughter died down, I felt a hand on my sleeve.

"Why here you are!" said a woman loudly. I jumped away from the louvered door and held out my balled-up Kleenex. "I was just looking for a wastebasket," I said, hoping that the woman—*Dyan!* I suddenly remembered her name—wouldn't notice I had been eavesdropping.

One look at her, though, and I knew I didn't need to worry. Dyan was holding a drink and seemed to be having trouble focusing. "Come on back and join the party," she said, taking my hand. "We haven't even had a chance to get to know you. Michael has been doing *all* the talking."

I was so relieved I hadn't been caught that I almost didn't mind following Dyan back to the living room where Michael was standing in a large group.

"Here she is! I found her cowering in the library," Dyan announced. I smiled, trying to look unconcerned, but my cheeks were burning. "Apparently we scared her off."

"Grace, dear, we were just talking about Allen's son," said Camille. "He's a student at the college."

"Right," said Allen, another man who looked like he was about the same age as my parents. "So as I was saying, this first-year chem prof gave Tyler a D and told him he was lucky that he didn't flunk him. Now, I'll move heaven and earth before I give one of my students a D—and you all probably would, too—and it shouldn't ever come as a surprise to the student. Most professors agree with that and I bet most students do, too. Am I right, Grace?"

All I wanted to do was to go home, but Michael was looking at me expectantly. In fact, everyone was looking at me. *This is not rocket science,* I said to myself. *Just pretend you're talking to friends.*

"Yes," I said, turning to Allen, trying to picture him thirty years younger and wearing frayed jeans. "I mean, it shouldn't come as a surprise unless, well, unless it's a situation like last year, when a senior cheated and thought he'd gotten away with it, but found out later the teacher caught him and gave him a zero. I think that was a surprise."

I glanced around the circle. People were nodding in agreement and Michael looked relieved. Confident now, I added, "His name was Tyler, too—I know tons of Tylers—but he was black."

The room went cold right then—every person just froze. The woman next to me stopped sipping her wine and the man next to her stopped adjusting his tie. Suddenly I knew what was wrong. I had used the wrong word. At my school, we all used the word *black*, but these people probably didn't. "I mean *African American*," I said, blushing again.

But other than Dale, the short professor who was breast-obsessed, no one was looking at me. They were looking into their drinks or at the floor. My mind was racing. What had I said? Maybe they had misunderstood me—thought I was prejudiced—so I quickly added, "Not that they are the only ones who cheat! I just meant that obviously it wasn't your son."

Allen fixed me with an icy stare. "Tyler was falsely accused," he said. "We cleared that up, but apparently that bit of news wasn't worthy of the secondary school grapevine."

Before it had completely sunk in that the Tyler I was talking about was Allen's son—*adopted, maybe? How stupid could I be?*—Camille swooped in. "Of course he was," she said. "Would you like some more wine, Allen? Oh, Dyan. Tell me, did you find some nice cabernets when you were in Provence last summer? Don't be a wine miser. Tell us what they are!"

As soon as we got into the car, I buried my face in my hands. "I don't fit in," I said, pressing my fingertips into my eyelids to stop myself from crying. When I tried to take a deep breath, it came out a sob and then I couldn't stop myself from crying any more.

Michael drove in silence for a few miles, keeping his eyes on the road ahead, ignoring my quiet sobbing.

"I'll never fit in," I said, my voice breaking.

"Get hold of yourself," Michael said. "You girls are so overemotional!"

"My skirt and then that thing with Tyler—how was I supposed to know?" I cried.

"It was your first time at a party like that," Michael said in a flat voice. "It was partly my fault. I could have coached you a little more."

I remembered the professors in the den. Did Michael want to change me? I picked up the question the way I sometimes picked up shirts that I wasn't really interested in buying while shopping, just to feel the weight of them in my hand.

No, I decided, leaning my head against the smooth window glass. I knew where they got the idea, but they were wrong, just like my teachers were wrong about us. Michael was only trying to help me understand how the world really worked. If my parents had spent less time sheltering me and more time preparing me for this life instead of the next, maybe I wouldn't have embarrassed him at the party.

I wanted to be a good wife and to have a good marriage, but my ideas about it were hazy. Most of the romance novels stopped after the wedding. It was implied that the hero and heroine lived happily ever after, but you never saw how. My parents' marriage was more like a living arrangement than an adventure. There wasn't any passion or even connection, besides me. There was only my father's one-two, one-two rhythm that had kept my mother and me marching in a straight line. And Liv's parents had plenty of passion, but they couldn't control it.

But at the party, I'd caught a glimpse beyond the wedding. When Michael, his face flushed with embarrassment, had walked me out of the room as all the other profs pretended not to watch us, I saw that marriage wasn't going to be him doing his thing and me doing mine. What I said or did or wore mattered to Michael, just like what I did at home mattered to my parents because it reflected on the family name. I thought I was breaking free of all that—of caring about what people thought and of limits like curfews and church. Instead I would just have different limits and rules. Being with Michael was worth it, I just wished I already knew what they were so I could stop blindly bumping up against them.

"I just felt so out of place," I said, as we turned onto my street. I sighed heavily. The whole night, starting with that guy Will's stupid story about the cows, had been a disaster.

"Things will get better," Michael said, handing me another Kleenex. I had the feeling he had to stop himself from adding that things couldn't get any worse. "It's like the first day on a new job."

He pulled into my driveway and, looking relieved the evening was over, threw the car into park. By leaving the car running, he made it clear he didn't want to come in.

"Or the first day of high school," I said lightly, wiping off the mascara that had smudged under my eyes. "Or sex."

He raised his eyebrows and nodded like he wanted to be encouraging. "Exactly. It's uncomfortable at first because you feel like you don't know what you're doing."

Watching him drive away as I stood there in my best shoes, the heels slowly sinking into the soggy spring lawn, I wondered how long it would take before I did.

Sixteen

"She's not good with money," my father told Michael gruffly, folding his arms over his chest.

"Dad!" I said, blushing.

After the big confrontation my father and I had at Michael's, I'd put off introducing Michael to my parents as long as I could, hoping that my father would get used to the idea of my engagement and the meeting would be less tense. So far, though, my father had barely managed to be civil, even though it was a Sunday afternoon, when he was usually most relaxed.

"Better that he knows what he's getting into now instead of finding out later," my father grumbled.

Michael put his hand on my shoulder. "It's all right," he said to my father. "I'm good with money."

"Are you contributing to an IRA?"

"Yes."

"Let me tell you something about that," he said, pointing at Michael. "One hundred thousand in a money-market account and one hundred thousand in an IRA are not the same."

"I know. One has been fully taxed and the other hasn't."

My father scowled. "Car paid for?"

"In a manner of speaking," Michael said coolly.

"And what 'manner of speaking' would that be?"

Michael's jaw tensed. "A manner of speaking that would suggest it's none of your business."

"It's my business if you're marrying my daughter."

My mother pulled a piece of paper out of the wedding planning notebook and waved it timidly in the air. "We really should talk about the guest list. Just come sit down."

"Of course, let's," Michael said. He smiled his most engaging smile, and her cheeks turned pink with pleasure.

My father shooed us with his hands. "You go ahead. I have some things I need to do. Grace, you make sure you empty the trash like I told you."

Just wanting him gone, I nodded.

"Nice meeting you, Dan," Michael said.

"Same here," my father said, already turning to leave.

My mother smiled apologetically at Michael after he sat down on the couch. "We're looking forward to meeting your family at the wedding, Michael," she said. "Is it very large?"

"A few aunts and some cousins. My parents have both died."

"I'm so sorry! Do you have any brothers or sisters?"

"I had an older sister, but she ran away when I was nine. We never learned what happened to her."

My mother gently touched his hand. "That must have been very hard for you."

Michael looked at her and nodded. "Yes, it was," he said slowly. "For a long time, I looked for her wherever I went—especially in crowds—always searching for her face. But the constant hoping just made it harder and eventually I gave up."

"Do you have any pictures of her?"

I shot her a dirty look, worried that he'd think she was prying. Couldn't she see this was hard for him to talk about? And it wasn't any of her business.

Michael saw what I was doing. "It's all right. I don't mind," he said to me. "I do still have one, and it's nice to have an excuse to look at it." I immediately wished I had thought to ask him about a picture back when he first told me about Elise. That it hadn't occurred to me made me feel like I was lacking in some way. It seemed my mother had seen something in Michael that I had missed.

Standing halfway up, he reached into his back pocket for his wallet and rifled through it. "Here it is. She was thirteen then, and I was four, I think."

My mother took it carefully from him, as though it was breakable, and studied it for a moment. "She reminds me of the way Grace looked at that age."

"Let me see," I said, leaning in to get a better look. She tipped the photo in my direction. In the picture, Michael was sitting on Elise's lap, grinning broadly. Elise, her black hair pulled back into a high ponytail and her chin jutting out, was staring straight into the camera like she was daring the person behind it to tell her to smile. "I don't see any resemblance," I said.

"It's the oval-shaped face, I guess, and something about the shape of her mouth," my mother said. She gave the photo back to Michael, who studied it, then shrugged. "I didn't see it before but yes, I think you're right. They do look a bit alike."

After we talked about the guest list for a while, my mother left to get more coffee. Michael stood up and put the picture of Elise back in his wallet.

"Is that why you asked me out?" I asked. "Because I look like Elise?"

"Of course not!" he said. "Don't be absurd. I don't even think you look that much alike. I only said it to be polite."

"But don't you think it's weird—that you think we look even a little alike?"

"A lot of people look alike. I've heard it said that a person will often choose a partner who looks like them. Look at the pictures of couples in the wedding section of the *New York Times* and you'll see it's true. Most of the time, the man and woman look alike."

I made a face. "Still!"

Michael slid over closer to me on the couch. "Come on, Grace. Even if it was what attracted me to you initially—and I'm not saying it was—but even if it was, it's not what made me love you." He slipped his hand under my hair and cupped it around the back of my neck, right at the hairline, and rubbed his thumb up and down my neck. "I fell in love with *you*. Okay?"

The current shot down my spine. "Okay," I said.

While Michael used the bathroom, I pulled the pictures of the wedding dresses out of the notebook. Earlier, I had shown my mom the two pictures of the wedding dresses Liv and I had found at the shop. I rested my chin on her shoulder as she looked first at the satin and lace one—still my favorite—then at the chiffon, before looking again at the satin. She flipped the picture over to read the price the saleslady had neatly printed on the back. $499. Then she looked at the price of the chiffon. I felt her shoulder stiffen when she saw the number there. $1,500. But then my dad had come in so we hadn't had a chance to talk about the dresses.

Michael came back, rubbing his damp hands together and smelling of Dial soap.

"I need to decide on my dress or it won't be here in time for the wedding," I said, spreading the pictures out on the coffee table in front of him. I watched him closely as he looked first at one, then the other, to see if I could tell which one he liked best. His eyes lingered on the Baroque-ish chiffon gown that Liv had predicted he would like.

"I—" he started, but then stopped. "Which one do you prefer? It really is the bride's choice."

"The A-line fits me best, but I wonder if there's too much—"

"That's just what I was thinking! There's a bit too much going on with all the lace. It's a little dowdy. You want something more sophisticated, don't you Rabbit?"

I tucked my hair behind my ear. "Well, yes, but the other is . . . not tight exactly, but kind of revealing."

"Oh, Grace," he said, looping his arm around me and pulling me to him. "You're too modest. What you mean is that it fits."

"That's what Liv said. But I don't know." I studied the picture of the chiffon with its low-cut, rounded neckline. "I'm just not sure it's me."

Michael pursed his lips. "I like them both, but the chiffon one is stunning. It's what a confident woman would wear." He tossed the pictures down on the table like it really didn't matter to him, one way or the other. "But what do you need me for? I'm just the groom. You decide."

My mother came back with Michael's coffee and saw which picture I was holding. "Is that the one you decided on? Are you sure?"

The only thing I was sure of was that I didn't want to make another mistake like I had with my yellow skirt. Michael seemed to think the chiffon was best. "I think so. It's hard to decide."

Right away, her forehead creased. I could tell she didn't want to say anything in front of Michael, but he and I didn't have any secrets. "What, Mom?"

"It's just . . . We can't afford that one, Grace." She said it very quietly, as though she was hoping that Michael might not hear.

I glanced over at Michael, who nodded sympathetically. "I like them both—the satin one, too," he said. "The satin one is great." Secretly I was relieved, but, because I wanted Michael to think I had liked the sophistication of the chiffon, I sighed like I was disappointed.

I felt a twinge of guilt about my fake reaction when my mother said, "I'm sorry. It's just that there's still the flowers and the reception hall and we're already cutting the guest list so we can—but maybe if I . . ."

"Mom, I love the satin. I do!" I said, finally letting some of my excitement show.

"In the scheme of things, the dress isn't important," said Michael. "Grace will look beautiful no matter what she wears."

"All right," my mom said. I could tell my mother thought we were just trying to make her feel better. In truth, I was just relieved the final decision had been made for me.

Liv called later, when I was watering my African violet, which was showing spunk by sprouting two buds. I hadn't called her after the faculty party because I didn't feel like going into everything that had happened that night. She'd probably just tell me I should have flipped the old crones off, but then she had never been great at thinking about consequences. Just getting a ride with Liv had been risky. She was famous for leaving people stranded because she was always thinking of something better to do and leaving without telling them.

"How's your mom doing?" I asked.

"Still likes those sharp, shiny things, but I hid them all." Liv paused for a minute and over the phone, I could hear a door close. "What's going on with you?"

"Michael finally met my mom and dad."

"Did you talk to Michael about my paper?"

I cradled the phone between my shoulder and ear so I could rearrange my plants. "The meeting went well, thanks for asking," I said evenly. "And no, I didn't have a chance."

"You were together all Friday night and this afternoon again and you didn't have the chance?"

"A faculty party isn't exactly conducive to asking Michael to cheat."

"Well, la-di-dah. Listen to you, Miss Highbrow Bigshot. 'A *faculty* party isn't exactly con*duc*ive.' Why do I get the feeling that no time will ever be conducive?"

"Give me a chance, Liv! It hasn't even been 48 hours since you asked me to ask him."

"I know, it's just that—"

"I know," I said, so we wouldn't have to get into the whole thing all over again.

"You can't know. You can't know what it's like."

I stared down at my violet. She was right. I wondered what would let her know that even if I didn't totally understand, I did care.

"Say something!" she demanded.

"What do you want me to say?"

"I don't know. That you haven't forgotten. That you won't let me down."

I shuffled the Boston fern to the other side of the violet, then back again. "Have I ever?"

"Just say it."

"I won't let you down. I just need to find the right time to ask Michael."

"Okay, but don't wait too long," she said. "The deadline is coming up."

I spied some dead leaves on the underside of the violet and picked them off. I wished it would be as obvious what parts of myself weren't needed anymore. "I'll do my best," I said.

"Yeah," she said bitterly. "You do that."

Seventeen

"So what do you and Michael do on dates, anyway, when school's not *in session?*" Tori framed "in session" with air quotes and grinned wickedly.

I gritted my teeth and scrubbed harder on the coffee stain in the sink. "Lots of things," I said.

It was late afternoon midway through our spring break and, tired of hanging out at home, I had borrowed Mom's embarrassingly old car to drive out to Michael's, even though I knew he had to teach class all day and had an evening meeting.

Unfortunately, what I didn't know was that it was Tori's day to clean. I didn't learn that until I unlocked the door with the key Michael had given me, and she opened it from inside.

"Hey," she'd said, as if she'd been expecting me. "Thanks for coming." Then she pointed at the sink with one hand and gave me a sponge with the other. I had been so surprised that I took it. Already I was regretting that I had.

"Like what?" Tori expertly spun a full trash bag and bound the top with a twist-tie.

"We went to the opera."

"Oh, yeah?" said Tori. "You like that kind of stuff, huh? I didn't have you pegged as the classical type."

I silently rinsed the sink and moved on to the counter.

Tori set the trash by the back door. "Your manners could use some work, there," she said. "Don't you know that when someone asks you a question, the polite thing to do is answer them?"

I gave her a dirty look. When it came to good manners, I was, as Liv would say, Emily G.D. Post compared to Tori.

"Well, do you or don't you like opera?" Tori asked, tapping her toe.

"I had fun, *all right?*" I said.

"That's what I thought," Tori said, picking up a bar stool and lugging it out of the kitchen. "You hated it."

I was tired of being grilled. "Where's Quinn?"

"He's at my brother's place. He goes there sometimes."

I squeezed out my sponge in the sink. "Doesn't he ever see his father?"

"Nope," Tori said, pouring ammonia into a bucket.

The strong smell of it made my eyes burn. "Do you care?"

"Care? Hell no. That's the way I wanted it." She held up the bucket. "You about done there? I need to fill this up."

I stepped back from the sink. "Really? How did you know that you wanted it that way?"

"I didn't at first. I was crazy in love with him. And him? He was just plain crazy. A bad boy." Tori shook her head and smiled. "But one night I had a dream about marching in a St. Patrick's Day parade and a green tidal wave that was coming. I was the only one who saw it and I tried to tell the others but they didn't see anything. I froze, you know? I didn't know what to do." She shut off the water and lifted the bucket out of the sink. "When I woke up, I knew."

My jaw dropped. "That's how you decided? You let a dream tell you what to do?"

"What of it? It's the way I work things out, maybe. Better dreams than runaway hormones."

The words were like the sharp pinches Liv loved to give me when I got too serious about stuff. For a minute I couldn't say anything. Finally I said, "We're getting married."

Tori was dipping the mop in and out of the bucket, getting it wet. "So you've said. You think that means you're not ruled by a bad case of the hotties?"

"Now I get it. You're jealous."

She slopped the mop onto the floor and leaned on it. "Let me ask you something. Since you started doing the

Hokey Pokey, how many times have you gone out and *not* ended up in bed?"

"I don't know!" I said. "It's not like I keep track."

"Maybe you should."

Tori, with all her prying questions and knowing smirks, finally pushed me too far. "If you know so much about love and men, then how come you are where you are?" I asked. "Single—with a kid?"

"I don't know so much about men," Tori said, wringing the mop out. "But I know a little about me."

"Right. *You,* and not me. You don't know about me." I tossed the sponge onto the counter. "I'm out of here."

"Good," said Tori. "You were starting to get in my way."

"Then we're even. Because you were starting to get on my nerves."

I stepped around the bucket and slammed the door on my way out. I planned to roar out the driveway, too, but my mother's stupid Saturn station wagon balked. I tried a few more times, but couldn't get it to turn over. I was stuck. With Tori.

I slumped back in the seat, trying to decide what to do. I didn't know anything about cars, but I popped the hood and got out, hoping that, if I fiddled with the wires long enough, I might miraculously fix whatever was wrong. I unscrewed a lid, then screwed it back on more tightly. I pulled on what turned out to be the dipstick and put it back in again.

As I was poking around in the guts of the car, I got grease on my hands, and then on my pants. When I had played with everything, I went back to trying to start the car again. Over and over. *R-ruh, r-ruh, r-ruh.*

"Wishing it'll start won't make it happen," Tori said through the passenger side window, making me jump. I had been so intent on turning the key, watching it, and praying that the car would finally start, that I hadn't noticed Tori walking up. "It's the battery," she added.

"It is?"

"Yeah, I can tell by the sound. If we can find jumper cables, I can give you a jump."

As we walked to the garage, Tori described what jumper cables looked like so I'd know what I was looking for. Once I thought I had found them, but it turned out to be a short extension cord. I expected Tori to laugh at me, but for once she didn't.

While putting the extension cord back on its hook above the workbench, I rested some of my weight on the large garbage container next to the bench. The container slipped out from under me, and I fell onto the floor, taking the garbage can down with me. Loose trash scattered out of it as it hit the floor beside me.

From across the room, Tori laughed. "Can you *get* any dirtier?" she asked, shaking her head.

"Thanks for your concern," I said, getting to my feet and dusting myself off. I tipped the garbage can back up. As I was picking up the pieces of trash, I noticed a white note card with an elegant blue monogram L.R.E.

I hesitated for only a second—*should I or shouldn't I?*—before flipping the card open.

Dearest Michael, the letter began. The words were small and perfectly formed on the page. *How many times and in how many ways can I apologize for the pain and humiliation I've caused you? Your love is such a hard love, Michael. It's a sledgehammer, and I ended up doing that which I should not have done. We need to talk—about everything. Come on Wednesday night, will you?—Rachelle*

"Did you find them yet?" Tori asked, walking over from her side of the garage. "Hey, what've you got?"

Holding the card out stiffly in front of me, I pivoted toward Tori. "Today is Wednesday," I said. My voice sounded flat and far away to me.

"Yeah, Hump Day," Tori said. She plucked the card out of my hand like she was choosing a card for a card trick, and skimmed the note. "What a wench," she said, looking at me hard as she gave the note back to me. "You think he's falling for her little cry for attention."

"No," I said, squatting to pick up an orange juice carton. "No pulp," the label said. I liked at least some pulp and I wondered if someday we'd fight about how much pulp was too much. "Michael has a meeting tonight. He said so this morning. He has a meeting."

Tori shrugged. "Maybe."

"I know he wouldn't lie to me."

"You 'know' he loves you. You 'know' he wants to marry you. You 'know' he would never tear one off with an ex just for auld lang syne," Tori said, using those air quotes again every time she said the word "know." "Seems like there's a lot you know for not knowing him very long."

It was the air quotes that set me off. I grabbed her arm and pulled her through the door and into the house. "I'll prove it."

"Don't do it for my benefit," said Tori, tripping on the landing. "It's your life."

My watch showed that it was already after 6:00. He'd be on his way to the meeting. I dialed his cell phone number and listened to it ring three, four, five times and then it went to his voicemail.

Tori looked at me skeptically. "Does he know you're here?"

"We talked earlier. I told him I might come. Why?"

"Caller ID. He knows you're trying to reach him and that's why he's not picking up. He doesn't want to be found."

I crossed my arms. "You're just like my dad—you always assume the worst about people! He's probably already in his meeting and he can't pick up."

"Or he's giving Rachelle some of his—what did she call it?—hard love."

I didn't understand how she could be so cold and unfeeling. Did she really hate me so much that she wanted to make me feel worse? Or was she just clueless about what she was doing? "Shut up," I said. "If you had the tiniest bit of heart, you'd just shut up."

Unfazed, Tori held out her cell phone. "Try mine," she said. "He won't recognize the number."

I kept my arms where they were and looked away.

"I get it," Tori said. "You got a good story going on in your head. I'm not sure I'd want to spoil it, either, if I was you. It must be nice to be so sure of someone. But what if he's just marrying you to stick it to this Rachelle because she dumped him? Have you thought of that?"

I exploded. "That's stupid! Nobody would do that!" *Especially not Michael,* I said to myself.

"Right. Nobody *ever* does stupid things," Tori said with a wry smile. "Especially not the man of your dreams."

When I pulled into my parents' driveway an hour later, I was still a wreck. I hated Tori's smugness, hated that Tori had known what was wrong with the car, hated that I had needed Tori to give my car a jump. Most of all, I hated myself for not taking Tori up on her offer to use her cell phone to call Michael.

Why, when he had thrown the note away, did I worry that he was with Rachelle? I knew he loved me but I couldn't convince my stomach to stop twisting itself into knots.

Through the kitchen window, I saw my mother lifting a loaf of bread out of the bread machine. Lately she had been eating more and her pale face had a new pinkish tone. Planning my wedding had given her something to do and all the activity had been like some sort of pleasure injection or something. Or maybe it was because my father had been gone so much that she had been able to take more breaks from being a prop for his life. Whatever it was, she had been more relaxed and less . . . strange. It was only now, when she had gotten a little better, that I could see how bad she had been before.

Walking through the door, I was suddenly grateful for my mom in the same way I had been grateful for my own bed as a kid when I came home from a week away at camp, and I impulsively gave her a quick hug before sitting down at the kitchen table. The smell of the bread, one of my favorite things to eat, made my stomach lurch. That's how upset I was about everything.

"The bread won't be cool for a while yet," my mom said, sitting down. The head of broccoli she put in front of her still had beads of water clinging to it. "I'm making pasta primavera to go with it."

My stomach churned and pitched. "I'm not hungry," I said. It was too bad I was losing my appetite just when she was learning to cook. Over the last week, she had made salmon with dill and stuffed pork tenderloin—and the recipes had actually turned out. This was as much a miracle to me as Jesus raising Lazarus from the dead.

"It's not like you to not be hungry," she said. "I bought another jar of Cheez Whiz. How about some of that on toast?"

I made a pained face and shook my head. Liv and I had made chips and Cheez Whiz the week before and I could have sworn the Whiz had gone sour.

"Cheez Whiz doesn't go bad," Liv said, through a mouthful of chips. "There's nothing real in it." I still couldn't eat it. Liv just shrugged and said, "More for me!" Then she ate the entire plate of chips.

My mom looked worried. "No to that, too?" She reached out and put the back of her hand on my forehead. "Are you feeling sick? You look peaked."

"I have an upset stomach is all. Where's Dad?"

"He left for Columbus just this afternoon. Another meeting."

I rubbed at my engagement ring with my thumb. I still wasn't used to the weight of it on my finger. "Do you miss him when he's gone?"

"Sure I do, honey. Why?" She put the broccoli on a plastic cutting board and began cutting it up. She cut the stalks at an angle and held one up for me to see. "Isn't it amazing how much prettier something can look when you do something as simple as cutting it differently?"

"Yes," I said, pretending to admire the broccoli stalk. "It just seems like your life is easier when Dad's not around."

"I guess it is in some ways."

I thought about how much my dad had been gone recently. My parents didn't have the kind of marriage I wanted, but I bet that my mom never doubted my dad's faithfulness. He was strict, but he would never cheat.

My mom reached up again, this time laying the back of her hand on my cheek. "Are you sure you're all right?" Her touch was so familiar and gentle and, unlike Michael's touch, it didn't want anything from me. There in the kitchen, just the two of us without Michael or my father to pull us away from each other, I wanted to confide in her, to tell her about Rachelle's note and about how I was worried that Michael might be with her, like I had been worried when he had flirted with Liv, and even when he had sighed in my ear while we were making love and the sigh had sounded like "Anna."

I was ready to tell her everything, and I started to. "It's just there's something I'm not sure about. You know, the wedding—sometimes it's so overwhelming. And spending your—"

"Oh, honey," my mother said, putting down the paring knife. "It's the dress, isn't it? You wanted the one we couldn't afford."

I started to say no, that it was about me worrying about Michael's cheating and was that normal or was it a sign that maybe I shouldn't be getting married to him after all and if I *maybe* wanted to change my mind—which would never actually happen because I really did love him and he was the one thing that was good in my life—but if I ever did want to, was it too late to go back? But right when all those words were lining up, ready to come marching out of my mouth, my mother's eyes lit up with excitement, and she held up a finger and pressed it against her own lip, and I stopped myself.

"I was going to wait until it came to tell you," she said, "but I'll tell you now." She leaned forward and laughed, and it was the tinkling laugh that I remembered from when I was small and every week we went to a park and waded in the cold stream and she always laughed that laugh when we first put our toes in. I remembered that I always thought her laugh sounded like the water looked—fresh and sparkly. It was a laugh I hadn't heard in a long time.

"I bought you the dress you really wanted—the chiffon sheath. It was all Liv's idea, and you know Liv! She can be so persuasive. She thought you should have the dress you really wanted, so she went to the library and got onto the Internet and she found it for just $100 more than the other one. I shaved a little money off the flower budget so we could afford it. It's arriving next week. We can't return it, but Liv knew it was what you really wanted and she even knew your size."

For a minute I thought I was going to pass out, but I was able to stop myself by pinching the skin in the crook of my arm, just the way Liv did.

"It was what you wanted, right?" My mother's smile was so wide that I could tell she thought the tears I was working so hard to blink back were tears of happiness. Instead of answering her, I reached across the table and hugged her. I didn't want her to see that I wasn't sure what I wanted anymore.

Eighteen

Tough as it was to wait and agonize about it—was he cheating? Wasn't he? If he was, *why* was he?—I figured it was better to wait to confront Michael until the next night, when I could talk to him in person.

"No, of course I wasn't with Rachelle," he said impatiently. He was sitting on the couch, drinking a glass of wine, looking up at me.

"But it's right here—in the note." I flicked at the note card with my finger so that it made a sharp snap. I had planned to be cool but my emotions were already taking the express elevator to the top floor, the way they sometimes did right before I got my period. "Why did you ask me to marry you? If you want to play around, why don't you do it without dragging me along? All those women!"

"What are you talking about?"

"Rachelle!" I shouted. "Anna—whoever the hell she is!"

"I don't know what you're talking about," he said. His expression was impossible to read, like he had pulled down a curtain.

That he could be calm when I was livid made me even angrier. "And then there's Liv. Hitting on my own best friend, Michael? How low is that?"

A flicker of irritation or recognition or maybe frustration crossed his face right then.

"You're generalizing. Let's just back up." He pointed to the note. "Yes, that is a note. Yes, Rachelle asked me to come. But I declined." His voice was the way I had wanted mine to be. Steady, reasonable, adult. "If I was going to see her, do you think I'd leave the note lying around?"

"You didn't leave it lying around, did you? Did you?" My voice was high and thin, almost shrill.

"No, I threw it away. That's what I do with all my trash." He reached for my hand and tried to pull me down onto the couch next to him. "What's the matter with you? This isn't like you at all."

I jerked my hand away. "I just want you to tell me the truth about where you were."

"I told you—I was at a meeting."

"With who? What did you talk about? Where was it held?"

Michael paused. "It was a guest lecturer at the college," he said. "We talked about postmodern existentialism. We met at a restaurant."

Michael was everything to me. I needed him and I desperately wanted to believe him. Besides, the dress was bought and the invitations were ready to go. And I didn't want my father to be right about Michael.

But the doubt I had felt since spending the afternoon with Tori was like a pop-up ad that kept coming up, no matter how many times I tried to close it out on my screen. I was so tired of closing it, closing it, closing it. I wanted someone to tell me how much doubt was too much. I wanted someone to tell me what I should do.

"Why didn't you pick up the phone?" I said, blinking to keep back my tears. "You could have at least picked up when I called."

Michael stood up, put his arms around me, and cradled the back of my head with his hands. "Oh, Rabbit. Think about it. I didn't know that you were at the other end of the line making up this—this outlandish scenario in your head. I had no idea. While you were seeing fantastic visions of me being randy, I was in a meeting—that's all. Don't ruin things by being this way. You're letting your insecurities show."

The tears dribbled down my cheeks to my chin. In his arms, smelling the familiar mixture of leather and after-shave and a hint of smoke, I wanted more than anything to believe him, but him saying it didn't mean it was true. I thought of Thomas, who had to touch the nail marks in Jesus's hand after the resurrection in order to believe. "Prove it," I said, swiping at my tears with the back of my hand. "Let me call whoever you met with."

I expected that he would be angry but he hesitated, like I did sometimes when I wanted to make sure I said just the right thing. Then he reached into his pocket and pulled out his cell phone. "I can do better than that. Call Rachelle. Ask her yourself."

Even though the phone was as light as a calculator, when I took it in my hand it weighed me down. A voice my head whispered, *Don't be stupid. He's working some angle.* It sounded a little like Tori's.

I knew from my romance novels that if he was guilty, he'd look down or away—it's what all the men did when they betray the heroine—but Michael just looked at me steadily, like he was sure I would come around. I tried to think clearly, but my head hurt. I went back through everything. What if he had thrown away the note, maybe even forgotten about it, and really had gone to his meeting like he said? What if he had done everything right, and now I was driving myself crazy over something that he had not done? If that's the way it was, then right now he was probably thinking, *I don't need someone like this.*

Suddenly I knew he wasn't working an angle. I just knew it. And he wasn't lying about not being with Rachelle.

I shook my head. "No, I don't need to call her. I know you're telling the truth."

Michael cupped his hands around mine. I was still holding the little phone, which was cool and hard. I had the urge to place it against my hot cheek. "Please do it," he said. "I don't want anything to come between us, especially mistrust. Not now. Not ever."

The whole thing was backwards, like we had switched places. It was all too weird for me, especially the thought of talking to his ex. "No. I believe you."

My diamond cut into the fleshy part of my finger when he squeezed my hands in his. "We can take care of it once and for all right here," he said. "Just make the call. Even if you don't want to do it for yourself, then do it for me."

I would have done anything right then to get out of calling her, but I was embarrassed that I'd been so wrong. I wanted to make things right again before he changed his mind about us.

"Okay," I said.

He told me the number and I tapped it in, but as soon as Rachelle picked up on the other end of the line, I was sorry. What was I supposed to say—*Hello, you don't know me, but did you sleep with my fiancé last night?* I probably would have just hung up without saying anything, but Michael was standing right there watching me. The best I could do was to get it over quickly.

Rachelle must have recognized his number on her caller ID because when she picked up the first thing she said was "Michael?" She sounded eager and breathless, like she'd run for the phone.

I swallowed hard. "Ah, no. You don't know me—my name is Grace—I'm just borrowing Michael's cell. Well, it's not just that I'm borrowing his cell. There's more to it than that, but . . ."

I stopped, not knowing what or how much to say. I tried to pull myself together. "I know this is a strange question, but was Michael with you last night?"

I could almost hear Rachelle on the other end trying to make sense of the conversation. *"Who* did you say this is?"

"My name is Grace. I-I'm . . . Michael's girlfriend," I stammered.

"Oh, God," Rachelle said. "God. Is he there? He's there, isn't he?"

I hesitated, watching Michael who was mouthing something at me. "Yes," I finally said into the phone. I shrugged at Michael to show him I still didn't understand what he was saying. He picked up my left hand and pointed to the ring.

I couldn't see what difference it made whether I was his girlfriend or fiancée, but I automatically said, "I mean, I'm his fiancée."

I heard Rachelle suck in her breath. "Oh, Michael's getting married?"

"It all happened so fast, we haven't been together that long," I said awkwardly. "I know it's strange, but if you could just tell me if he was there last night?"

"I see," Rachelle said. "No, he wasn't here. I asked him but he didn't come. I should apologize to you. I didn't realize he was involved with someone."

A wave of relief washed over me. I had been worrying about nothing. It was just like he said, just like I thought.

He hadn't been with her. "No, no. It's okay," I said. "Thanks. Sorry to bother you."

I started to say "goodbye" but Rachelle interrupted me.

"It's none of my business," she said quietly. "But it could be that you're asking the wrong question."

I already had what I wanted from her, and I was eager to get off the phone. "Thanks, really," I said. "Goodbye."

I didn't notice until I gave Michael his phone back that my hands were shaking. "I'm sorry," I said. "I don't know what's wrong with me. Pre-wedding jitters, I guess. I was making myself crazy."

Michael enveloped me in his arms. "It's okay," he said. He pressed his mouth against my head, right above my ear. "But let's not go through that again. From now on, know that I love you. *Know* it, Grace. It hurt me to think you'd think so little of me—that you'd think I'd do something like that! I *love* you. Don't you know what that means, what that means for us?"

When I realized Michael was hurt but not angry, I let out a sob of relief. He loved me and he wasn't going to break up with me, even though I'd been a neurotic.

"I'm sorry! I know you wouldn't. It was just once I saw the note, it was like, I don't know, I lost my mind for a day. And when I couldn't reach you . . . And Rachelle—she sounds so sophisticated and why wouldn't you want to be with her and not me?"

"Shhh," he said softly, stroking my back.

"All of it was making me crazy! And then Tori—"

Michael nodded. "She likes to cause trouble. She's had an unhappy life, and misery loves company. Don't misunderstand me—I like her. But she doesn't have great judgment, in my opinion."

I followed him into the living room, glad to talk about something that we agreed on. "Did you know she decided to raise her son alone because of a *dream?*"

"It figures," he said, sitting down on the couch. "Let's just forget about all this."

We sat together for a few minutes and then he reached for a box on the coffee table. Inside was a lighter and a pack of cigarettes, which he slipped into his pocket.

I raised my eyebrows. "I thought you were a pack a semester kind of smoker."

"Whenever I get stressed," he said, putting the lid back on the box. "I need to relieve the tension." He walked out the sliding glass doors onto the dark deck. From the couch, I watched the ember on the tip of the cigarette grow brighter every time he inhaled, wondering why he was stressed when the fight was over and everything was okay between us.

Maybe I should take up smoking, I mused, *so I could relieve the tension I felt about Liv.*

Everything was definitely not okay between her and me. She had been reminding me almost every day to ask Michael about helping her win the competition, and lately she had gotten almost bitchy about it. "Ever since you got yours," she had said, slamming her locker, "you don't seem to care much about me getting mine."

"My what?" I asked.

"Your gig, your thing," she had said, pointing at my ring. "Your future. You're not reneging on me, are you?"

"No," I said. "I'll get to it."

She was right that I had been putting it off, but not because I didn't care. Whenever I thought about it, I felt trapped between two things that felt wrong—asking Michael to help Liv cheat and going back on my word—so I hadn't done either of them. Lost in a hall of mirrors, it seemed safest to just stand where I was, hoping I wouldn't get even more disoriented.

When Michael lit up another cigarette, I went out to him.

"That's a lot of tension," I said. "I know another way to relieve it." Letting me take the cigarette out of his fingers, he turned his head and blew the last of the smoke away from me.

I put the cigarette out by tapping it on the deck railing, the way I'd seen it done in the movies. Lacing my hands behind his back, I formed my body to his so our bodies were touching from my shoulders to my thighs. I had only come out to the deck because I wanted to be with him, even if we didn't talk, but when Michael's hands slipped under my shirt and skimmed along my back, I could feel the low thrumming start in my body. On his way to unhooking the front clasp, he grazed my breasts, and I winced. The tenderness made me realize I'd be getting my period soon. Now I knew why my emotions had been all over the place.

Michael shifted his hips and held me tightly to him. "Make-up sex," he said into my hair. "There are worse ways to end the day."

Afterwards, we lingered in each other's arms in the dark living room. I nestled into the dip where his shoulder met his chest and sank into a fog of contentment. *This is it,* I thought. *This is what I've been missing all along.* I tried to synch up our heartbeats by holding my breath, but gave up when the sound of his steady, strong heartbeat drowned out my own. I thought of how this connection would be the constant in my life now—he would be the constant, my soulmate.

The connection I felt with Michael transcended anything I'd ever known. I'd never felt so embraced and understood—not by Liv, who was always teasing me about how boring I was, or my mother, who for a long time hadn't seemed like she was "there" even when she was standing right next to me, and certainly not by my father. To him, I was some kind of project, on loan from God to see what my father could make of me. But Michael's love was different. It filled me and enveloped me. He was my alpha and omega, my beginning and my end.

I shifted my weight and lifted my head so I could watch Michael, who was on the verge of drifting off. He must have thought I was going to get up because he started to pull his arm out from underneath me.

"I'm not going anywhere," I said.

He smiled lazily without opening his eyes. "I never said you were."

I sat all the way up and admired his long, lean body. Stretched out naked on the leather couch, he had a casualness about him that reminded me of a tiger, comfortable in his own skin because of the power that lies beneath it. "Michael?"

"Mmm?"

I opened my mouth to ask him about Liv and the contest, but changed my mind at the last minute. "What was Rachelle talking about in the note—the thing that she wished she hadn't done?"

He sighed heavily. "Grace, let's not do this—talk about the lovers in our past."

"I won't, I promise. I just want to know that one thing." I held the palm of my hand an inch above his chest, over his heart. If he wouldn't tell me, then maybe I could divine an answer.

He finally opened his eyes and looked past me, to the ceiling. "Just this one thing?"

"Yes."

"All right. She had an abortion."

I yanked my hand away, pretending that I needed to get something out of my eye.

"It was a long time ago," he said quietly. "We were both in graduate school. We agreed it was the right thing to do. Later she decided we'd made a mistake. After that she couldn't live with herself—or with me."

A shiver went up my spine and I pulled a throw that was hanging over the back of the couch around my shoulders. "Are you sorry?"

"I don't think about it. What's done is done." He sat on the edge of the couch, flipped on the recessed lights, and pulled his khakis on. "All you can do is move on." The bulb in one of the recessed lights had burned out, so the shadows in the room were different. They made him look strange and unknowable.

"You disapprove," he said.

"I'm surprised, I guess," I said, like it was no big deal. "You never told me."

"There was nothing to tell."

The words jumped out of me before I could stop them. "You think that's nothing?"

Michael ran his fingers through his hair. "I suppose you believe all that Right to Life propaganda. Am I right?" He didn't wait for me to answer. "It's not your fault. That's probably the only thing you've ever been exposed to. Just remember there are two sides to every issue and you have to know both sides before you can think for yourself."

"But they're babies—"

Michael picked up his shirt from the floor and snapped it, trying to get the wrinkles out. "See? Right there! That's the Right to Life mentality that I'm talking about. For a long time, they *aren't* babies. They are just zygotes. They aren't babies until they are viable—until they can live on their own, which is somewhere around five months. Rachelle did what we had to do long before that."

I watched him button up his shirt and remembered when I had gone with my father while he stood outside an abortion clinic. He'd given me a sign to hold that said, "Wanted, loved, cherished." I was old enough to read it and young enough to believe it, so I carried the sign proudly. I made friends with another girl whose sign said, "If you wouldn't dream of killing me, then don't think of killing them."

My father's sign said, "Thou shalt not kill." Even then I knew that it was the commandment that came after "honor thy father and thy mother" and before "thou shalt not commit adultery" but that was before I knew what adultery was. I didn't remember much else, except that the other girl got the last apple donut when I had wanted it. And I remembered a teenager, head down and face hidden behind her sheet of long blond hair, darting into the clinic.

I pulled my knees up to my face and pretended to be looking at a scab so Michael wouldn't know he had guessed right: I didn't really know what I thought about abortion.

Michael tucked in his shirt. "Think about it. Would it have been better for us to have a baby neither of us wanted? What kind of parent can you be when you don't even want the baby to begin with?"

"I don't know. Maybe there was something else you could have done," I said, picking at the scab.

He walked over to the couch and batted my hand away from my knee. "Come on, Grace. *How* old are you? Don't pick at it," he said. "It'll get infected."

He stood looking at me with a funny expression on his face. I got the feeling he was trying to figure out if I would ever come around, like I had stood looking at my African violet, wondering if it was worth taking on or if it was beyond hope and I should just leave it there in the school hallway.

After a minute he said, "You're young yet. In a few years, you'll see things differently."

With the throw wrapped around me, I had gotten hot, and the tops of my thighs were sticking to my stomach, which felt a little bloated. Suddenly I had a thought. "What if I got pregnant now?" I asked.

"We'd have it, I suppose. I want kids, don't you? We'd already be married. You could stay home with the baby so it wouldn't affect my job."

"But if I wanted to go to college?" I asked.

"You could go later."

"But if I wanted to go now?"

"I don't know, Grace!" Michael said, throwing up his hands impatiently. "This is a hypothetical situation we're taking about, right?"

I was suddenly conscious of my stomach. Was it bloated—or was it swollen? Exactly how long ago had I had my last period? "Right," I said.

"So let's not argue about it. You're worse than Rachelle! Maybe I *should* have gone to see her last night."

Mentally, I kicked myself for pushing him too hard—and just when we had recovered from the Rachelle thing. I wanted to get back to that place where he thought only of his love for me, not of how I compared to Rachelle. I stood up and let the blanket fall to the floor.

Pretending to be my old modest self, I half covered my breasts with my hands. "I'm sorry," I said, smiling shyly as I walked over to him.

The anger in Michael's eyes faded. I waited for it to be replaced by the intense look of desire, but instead the look in his eyes softened. He wrapped his arms around me and drew me close. "I'm sorry, too," he said, sighing. He rested his cheek against my head and rubbed my back tenderly. "It's just I wish all that had turned out differently. Talking about it is hard for me. And talking to you about it is something I didn't want to have to do."

I tried to pull away from him. I wanted to see his face so I could read his expression, but he held me fast.

"Because," he said into my hair, his voice quavering, "because you're my fresh start and this taints it—taints me. Then again, maybe it's tainted anyway."

Hearing the emotion in his voice sent a surge of love through me. Slowly, I shook my head. "No," I said. "It's not. I'll never believe that."

He didn't say anything, just squeezed me tightly to him, but that was enough to let me know we were okay again.

I had stopped talking to God a long time ago, but, as I stood there, pressed against him, breathing in the smell of his salt and sweat and faint musky aftershave, I sent up a prayer of thanks. Everything I ever wanted had almost slipped away from me just now, but somehow I had managed to hang onto it. Michael's love was still mine.

Nineteen

By the end of the following week, the invitations were finally ready to go out in the mail. The Emily Post book said we should have sent them earlier, but my mother had some weird idea about how I should address all the invitations myself.

"It's the way it's done in our family," she had said. To make her happy, I'd said I would do it. And I had meant to, but somehow I always ended up putting it off. Getting married and being with Michael was what I wanted; other than my closest friends and my mom, who ended up coming didn't matter very much to me.

But the Rachelle thing had put me on edge. The fallout from that night was that I started watching for signs he was losing interest. One evening when we'd planned to go to an art opening, he called.

"Would you mind so much if we didn't go tonight?" he asked.

"Not at all," I said, trying to keep the relief out of my voice. We'd gone to an exhibit on American Impression once and I'd yawned all the way through it, until Michael glared at me. As the curator explained how the American artists had traveled abroad and had their eyes opened to the possibilities of light and color, I tried to listen, but in truth it made my own eyes heavy. "What should we do instead?"

"I think I just want to go home. I'm feeling like a cold's coming on and I want to fight it off, if I can."

"I could come over and we could just hang out and talk."

"That's very thoughtful, but I really just want to go to bed—alone," he added, like he knew what I'd say next.

The whole conversation made me uneasy. Later, I called him. When he didn't pick up at home or on his cell, I grabbed a can of soup from the cupboard and headed out. His house was dark when I let myself in with the key. "Michael," I called, slipping my keys into my coat pocket. "Michael?"

I walked back to the bedroom, where I found him, cradling a box of Kleenex, watching TV from bed. He was propped up on three pillows, channel surfing.

"Hey," I said, sitting down on the foot of the bed. "How are you?"

"I've felt better," he said, muting the TV. "What are you doing here?"

I held the can up high, then gracefully swept my other hand in front of it, like I was a game show host. "I brought you this."

"Campbell's chicken noodle," he said, turning his attention back to the TV.

"Yes, the finest soup in the land. If you showed a little appreciation, I might even warm it up for you."

He turned up the volume.

I tossed the can onto the bed. "I guess you can just do it yourself."

"Don't get mad. I didn't ask you to come. In fact, as I recall, I said don't." He blew his nose and dropped it onto the floor on a mound of others. "When I'm feeling lousy, I get extremely irritable. So I'd just rather be by myself."

How quickly would he go from not wanting to be with me then to not wanting to be with me at all? As I drove home, I put another check mark in the "wants out" column I was keeping about Michael in my head. Back at my own house, I immediately sat down in front of the TV with the stack of invitations and the guest list. I didn't get up again until after midnight, when I finally finished with them.

I was going to drop them at the post office the next morning before I left on the senior class trip, but because I had been up so late the night before, I overslept. By the time I'd taken a shower and gotten dressed, there wasn't time. I left them stacked by the back door. I figured one more day wouldn't make that big of a difference.

Mom came into my room while I was frantically pulling back my hair, trying to get out the door in time so I wouldn't miss the field trip bus. She was still in her bathrobe, but her hair was brushed and she was holding a cup of coffee. "I toasted you a bagel," she said.

I looked at my watch. "I am *so* late!"

"I'll wrap it up. You can take it with you."

"Thanks."

"Which museum are you going to again?"

"Science and Industry." I rummaged through the heap of shoes on the floor of my closet. Why did the ones I wanted always, *always* have to be at the bottom of the pile? "Have you seen my brown shoes? The ones with the—"

"They're by the couch."

I sprang up. "Okay, where are the—Oh! There." I picked up the jade earrings that Michael had given me. "What are you doing today?" I asked, poking both earrings through my earlobes at the same time.

"Taking down all the drapes and washing them. I haven't done them for years. With you and your father both in Chicago, today is a good day to do it."

"He's there, too, huh?" I asked, automatically. I didn't care where he was, as long as it wasn't near me.

"Yes, at a conference, I think, at the University of Chicago. I have an idea! The two of you could ride home together tonight! You could call him on his cell."

I rolled my eyes. I couldn't believe that after everything that had happened between me and my father, my mother would think that either of us would want to spend three hours together in a car. "It's the senior class trip, Mom. I'm not going to ride home with Dad."

"He loves you, in his own way," she said quietly.

I knew she was hoping to fix things between me and my dad, but I didn't want to get into it. "I have to go or I'm going to miss the bus." Taking one last look in the mirror, I lifted my chin so I could admire the earrings.

"They bring out the highlights in your hair," my mom said.

"Yeah, they do," I said. "Michael has really good taste."

My mom nodded. "You can tell that just by the company he keeps."

I pivoted around. "Why? Who did you see him with?" I asked.

She smiled like she couldn't figure me out. "No one, honey. I'm talking about *you.*"

* * *

I had to run all the way to school, where the tour bus was waiting to take all the seniors to Chicago. Last year's seniors had gotten to stay overnight, but because of budget cuts, we were going to the same place we'd gone in sixth grade, the Museum of Science and Industry. All the kids complained about it, but even a trip to the museum was better than spending all day in class.

The bus driver pulled away from the curb as soon as I was in the door of the bus. "Glad you could make it on time," sniped one of the parent chaperones.

"Sorry," I said.

I stood there for a minute, holding onto the pole at the front of the bus, looking around for Liv. I spotted her toward the back, sitting with Cory, a football player she had always wanted to go out with. She waved happily but looked a little guilty, which was unusual. Liv never felt guilty for doing whatever she wanted.

Although in a way I was relieved that I wouldn't have to sit with Liv—I still hadn't talked to Michael about helping her cheat—I wished I hadn't been so late. Now I'd have to spend the whole bus ride sitting next to . . . I swiveled my head, checking out my options. A few rows back was a seat next to Regina, who was nice and everything but had terrible BO. Just behind her was Emily, who I knew from Calculus class and liked. I stumbled to that seat, but right before I got there, a boy named Devon slid in beside Emily. "Had to take a leak," he mumbled at the floor.

The bus lurched. "Find a seat," yelled the driver. "I don't want nobody getting hurt on my watch."

"Then learn how to drive," I said under my breath, making my way down the aisle. To my right I heard a quick laugh, followed by "Good one." Will, the weird kid who had been doing "wet blanket" research at Melissa's party, slid over to make room for me. I sat down beside him, figuring it was the best I was going to do.

"Hey, Miss Engaged," he said.

"Hi." Other than saying "hi" to him in the halls, I hadn't spoken to Will since the party. He seemed like he was kind of a loner, but he never had that pathetic look that most new kids have. "How's it going for you? Are you getting used to the school and everything?"

"It's going all right." He had a new crew cut and I noticed for the first time that he had dimples. He reminded me of the kid who played Opie on the *Andy Griffith Show* reruns I had watched the night before while doing the invitations.

He craned his neck so he could see my left hand and didn't try to hide it. At least I didn't have to guess what he was thinking. "Dang," he said. "Still engaged."

"Sorry," I said. "The invitations go out tomorrow."

His face lit up. "Not until tomorrow? I've got plenty of time, then."

I smirked. "Very funny."

He raised his eyebrows in mock surprise. "You don't think I'm serious? Listen, I've changed girls' minds before."

"Girls who were engaged?"

"Well, no," he said, running his hand across the top of his bristly head. "It's true that this would set a new reference point for me. But I think I'm up to it."

I despised long bus rides and I was already bored, so I decided to play along. I made a sweeping motion with my arm. "Be my guest."

Will flashed another smile. "Okay. Let's start with this guy's assets. From what I've heard—and let me tell you, I've heard a lot! The kids here live to gossip—Anyway, from what I've heard, he's a college professor, so he's probably smart, and he's good looking. Since he has a career, he probably has money. He's what my parents would call *established*." He looked at me and pursed his lips. "Anything I'm missing?"

"He loves me."

Will smacked his forehead with his hand. "Of course. He loves you. And he's great in the sack."

My cheeks felt like they were flaming. "Will!"

Will looked apologetic. "Sorry. I didn't mean to get personal."

"Is that something you heard around?"

"Not exactly. Not how good he is, anyway."

I took my time unzipping and taking off my spring jacket so I wouldn't have to look at him.

"Look," Will continued. "I'm not saying you're, you know, *doing it*. All I meant was that we have to assume he is good, since he's older and probably more experienced than the average high school senior who, say, has never had sex. Do you think that's a fair assumption to make?"

The way Will was so blunt and personal reminded me of Tori, and suddenly I felt irritable. "Reference point. Assets. Assumptions. What's next—hypotheses?"

"That comes later," he said. Either he didn't notice I was mocking him or he didn't care. "First we'll do liabilities. One: He's old! When you're forty, he'll be in his fifties. When you're sixty, he'll be headed for dead."

I rolled my eyes. "Like I haven't thought of that before."

That didn't slow him down. "Two: Did you know that women reach their sexual peak when they are thirty, but men," Will spread his arms wide and ducked his head modestly, "well, you're looking at a man at his sexual peak. Three—and this one is the clincher. He is not fun."

"Who said?"

"Nobody—including you. When we were listing his assets, I was specifically listening for that one, because it was the only one I was worried about. If you had said he's fun, I would have admitted defeat and sent you best wishes for a full and happy life. But you did not say 'He's fun.'"

"He's fun!"

He had an "I win!" look in his eye. "Nope. Fun is a major asset, and if he had it, you definitely would have said it right away. Does he make you laugh?"

"Just last week," I said, even though I couldn't remember the last time. He had made me laugh at the beginning. But lately everything had been so hard between us.

"Last week? Last *week*?" Will said, raising his eyebrows. "Oh, that's just plain sad. He should make you laugh every day. Me? I could make you laugh every day."

"Then do it," I said, wondering why annoying people seemed to be attracted to me.

Without missing a beat, Will pushed his upper lip up into his gums until it stuck there. It made his teeth look absurdly long. It made him look a little like a squirrel.

"It might take me a minute," he said through his squirrel teeth. I couldn't not grin.

"What? What?" he asked, looking around, pretending that there was nothing unusual about his face. "Hey, have you seen my nuts? I'm kind of attached to them."

Even after I was laughing, Will pretended to be clueless, which made me laugh harder. I doubled over until my head was pressed against the seat in front of us. "You see them down there?" he asked.

I straightened up and gave him a sorrowful look. "Nope, not there."

His upper lip still folded up into his gums, Will smiled. "Dang, you're easy."

I shook my head. "And you are strange."

* * *

When we got to the museum, Mr. Graebill split us up into two groups, using the aisle as the dividing line.

"Listen up, students," he called. "Blue group is going to the Omnimax first, while Red group goes through the coal mine."

Our side of the bus, the Red group, groaned. Mr. Graebill waited until we were finished then said, "Then we'll switch. After that, you're free to wander. Just remember to meet back in front of the Zephyr—that's the big train on the first floor—by 3:00."

In a way, it was lucky for me. Liv was across the aisle, which meant we wouldn't be in the same group and maybe I could avoid her for another day and then talk to Michael that night. I tried to hide my relief when I caught Liv's eye. She sighed dramatically, but it seemed like she was doing it for my benefit.

When we reached the Rotunda, Will hung back. "You like the coal mine?"

"It's okay," I said. Everyone else was crowding into the elevator that would take them down to the exhibit.

He stepped to the side, putting one of the big structural columns between him and everyone else. "This is my first time here," he said. "Let's not waste time on 'okay.' Show me spectacular." He leaned against the column, waiting for me to decide.

"Spectacular?" I had been to the museum so many times, I wasn't sure that anything was spectacular to me anymore.

Will grinned. "I made you laugh, now it's your turn. Show me miraculous. Fill me with wonder."

When I heard him say that—*fill me with wonder*—I knew exactly what I wanted to show him. I looked one last time at the elevator to make sure no one had missed us and then I grabbed his hand. "This way to wonder," I said.

We cut through the red staircase to get to the genetics exhibit. "Oh, yeah," Will said, looking at the double helix banners. "Genetics is amazing."

"No," I said, still pulling him along, veering right and weaving through another group of high school students. "Not yet."

I heard what I was looking for before we saw it—the high-pitched squeaks and the "oh, look"s and "Look at this one!"s of the little kids already there.

As we got closer, I had second thoughts. Most of the guys I knew would laugh at the chick hatchery. It wasn't too late to cruise on by, to pretend that I had planned all along to go to the Virtual Reality exhibit but had gotten turned around. Then again, most of the guys I knew—except Michael, of course—wouldn't even use a word like *miraculous,* let alone ask to see it.

Like always, chicks were pecking their way out of their shells, some with more success than others. I waited for a minute before I tried to explain. "It was wondrous to me as a kid—you know, the way they use an egg tooth and have to be strong enough to get out on their own. I guess I just never outgrew it."

"New life definitely qualifies." He put his hand on the glass and watched the struggling chicks. "Only it's kind of ironic that they peck their way out of one container only to find themselves in another."

I had been so impressed by their drive to break free of the shell that I had never noticed. But it was true. Once the chicks, some of which were so exhausted by getting out of the shell that they looked dead for a while, recovered enough to pick their heads up, what did they see? That their world had gotten only slightly larger.

I jabbed him with my elbow. "Way to ruin it for me!"

"Sorry," he said, looking remorseful. "Sometimes I don't think before I say something."

"That's okay. At least with you, I don't have to guess."

Will stared down at the chicks again. "You know what, though? They probably don't even notice. The glass is clear. Everything looks different. To them, it *is* a whole new world."

I was immediately suspicious. I didn't know Will very well, but the cheerful "whole new world" thing didn't seem to fit. I put my hands on my hips. "Are you just saying that to make me feel better?"

He grinned. "Yeah, I am. It won't be long before they bump up against it, then they'll know."

We watched for a while longer, then took the blue stairway down one floor so we could watch the giant pendulum hanging there swing this way and that, as the earth turned. Somehow, after that, we both just kind of assumed we'd hang out together for the day. We wandered through the exhibits, sometimes drifting apart for a while so we could look more closely at something one of us especially liked— he made a face when I said I wanted to see the Fairy Castle, and moved on—but then we'd always meet up again in the same general area before we went to the next section.

We ended up in the balcony late in the day. At first, it didn't look like there was anything I wanted to see, and I remembered why I usually skipped that floor. Except now that I was there, I knew there had been something intriguing. What was it? Will stopped at a physics exhibit, but I kept walking. I found what I was looking for at the very back of the hall. It was the "bottled babies" exhibit—babies at different stages of pregnancy.

I had always thought they were just plastic dolls, until middle school, when Liv had insisted they were real dead babies. I didn't believe her until she dragged me back to the beginning of the exhibit and pointed at the sign that read, "To the best of our knowledge, the survival of the fetuses was prevented by natural causes or accident."

I stopped in front of the first bottle, thinking about what Michael had said about fetuses not being babies for five months. The thing inside looked like the tadpoles I caught as a kid at Camp Tomanda. My parents thought that the second the sperm wormed its way into the egg—BOOM! Life!

Life? Really? Right then? I couldn't quite accept it. *But if it not then, when?*

I read the plaques below each bottle. "At twenty-six days, the heart has begun to beat." *Is it when the heart begins to beat?* I walked on, dragging my finger along the cool glass wall that separated visitors from the babies entombed in their bottles. *Or when the fetus responds to touch? That happens at seven weeks. Just six days after that, the sex glands start to form. Is that when life begins—when it becomes a girl or a boy?*

A large family came up behind me, forcing me to keep moving along the narrow walkway in front of the exhibit. I stopped short, though, when I came to the baby with a frown frozen on its face. I leaned my forehead against the glass to get a closer look and block out the people all around me.

A kid in a ratty White Sox cap bumped my elbow trying to get in front of me, but I couldn't tear myself away from the glass. He scuttled around me, giving me a dirty look. I checked the plaque beneath the baby. For sure by now it was a baby, even if it wasn't "viable," as Michael had said. Why was the baby frowning? *Had it hurt—whatever had happened to him? Had he felt the pain?*

A little girl behind me yelled, "Coming through! Coming through!"

I started moving again along the row of babies. Each was bigger than the last and I couldn't stop thinking about how they ended up there, in those bottles, for everybody to see. Whose baby boy was this or this or this? And did his mother get to hold him before they took him away? Did she run her fingertips along the smooth curve of his cheek and try to forget all the images she'd already had of him splashing in the lake or falling asleep in her arms? Did she lift his feather-light body to her lips and kiss his forehead? Had he known he was loved—*wanted?*

My stomach pitched and rolled and I felt a burning at the back of my throat. I clenched the muscles of my throat to keep from throwing up right then. I didn't want to see any more dead babies in bottles or wonder if they were babies or fetuses, or think about how they had ended up forever floating in those bottles.

I turned abruptly and plowed into the woman behind me. "Are you all right?" she asked. I nodded and pushed past her. I was wobbling toward an exit sign when Will caught up with me. "Are you all right? You look awful," he said.

"I need to get out," I said. Will nodded and held out his arm to me. I took it and held on until we got to the bathroom. Pressing my arms to my stomach, I sprinted inside and heaved all that was in me into the nearest toilet.

Twenty

By the time I'd cleaned myself up, it was almost 3:00, when we were supposed to meet up with everyone else at the Zephyr, so we headed downstairs. No one else was there, yet, so we sat down outside the gift shop and watched a guy demonstrating a cardboard airplane that was for sale in the shop.

We hadn't said anything since I had come out of the bathroom. I hadn't told Will that I had thrown up because I didn't want him asking a lot of questions. He asked a lot of questions, anyway.

"What were you doing back there before I found you?"

"Just looking at the exhibit," I said, trying to sound casual. If I told him about the sad dead babies in bottles then I'd dissolve into tears. And if I cried, he'd put his arm around me or say something nice. And if he did anything like that, I would blurt out what I had only just admitted to myself—that it was not totally out of the question that I could be, might be, probably was in trouble. I shoved the real word for it down deep and mentally put a cement block on it to keep it there. I was afraid that if I even thought of the real word, it would explode like an airbag and smother me.

Will looked at me hard. "And thinking. You were looking at it, but also thinking. I was watching you."

I concentrated on the guy throwing the plane. He was really good. He threw the plane, it did a loop-d-loop and flew right back to his hand, over and over again. He never even had to take a step to catch it. He made it look easy.

"Anybody who can look at dead babies and not think is heartless," I finally said.

"Touché," he said. "Can I ask you something? I'll give you an outsie."

Another word of Will's that I didn't know. It was like he made new ones up every day. "An outsie?"

"Yeah. It means you don't have to answer it if you don't want to."

"All right."

"Have you had one—an abortion? Is that why you were thinking so hard back there?"

From Melissa's party, I knew that Will was a little different. He didn't care about what you should and shouldn't do or say. He just put things he was thinking right out there. Still, I hadn't expected him to ask that. I was so shocked that my first reaction was to laugh. "Will! No!"

"Why do you think it's funny?"

"It's not funny."

"Then why did you laugh?"

"I don't know. Because if you knew me at all, you wouldn't even ask me that."

But he just kept looking at me, like he was waiting for more. "No, I don't think I ever could," I said.

"Because you think it's wrong?"

My head felt unbelievably heavy right then, and there was a metal taste in my mouth left over from throwing up. I pretended to be busy watching the plane guy, who was showing two boys how to throw the plane so it would come back to them. They tried to throw it the way he showed them, but their planes kept doing nosedives onto the marble floor. The boys were stomping their feet because they couldn't get it right. "You just need to practice," the guy said. As the boys shuffled past us, the taller one said, "What a rip-off."

Will poked me in the arm. "Because you think it's wrong?" he asked again.

"I'm so tired," I said.

"I won't ask you anything else, just this." He held up two fingers. "Scout's honor."

I sighed. Will would never just let something drop, at least not when he was really interested. "No . . . well, I guess

I don't know for sure," I said. "I understand why other people do it. I just don't think I could do it myself."

"Maybe it's one of those things where you don't know what you're capable of doing until you're in that situation," he said. "Like when that plane crashed in a remote place and the survivors had to decide between eating a guy who died and dying of hunger themselves."

I wrinkled my nose.

"I know," he said. "I think it's disgusting, too. But that's what I'm talking about. They didn't know what they were capable of."

"I guess." I sat there watching the plane make its perfect loops. I wondered if the guy ever got bored standing in the same spot, throwing that plane and catching it over and over. I knew what Will was saying, and in a way I was an example of it. A few months ago, I didn't know that I could stand up to my father the way I had. If I hadn't met Michael when I had been so angry with my dad, I probably wouldn't have flirted with him. We never would have hooked up. I'd still be the good girl my parents had thought I was—that *I* had thought I was—going to church, planning to be a teacher. I'd be like the guy with the plane, standing in the same spot throwing the plane and catching it, time after time, not knowing that things could be different. That I could be different.

But I had hooked up with Michael, and everything had felt a little dangerous and thrilling since then, like I was rushing headlong toward the edge of the Grand Canyon. But maybe that's how true love feels, and how you can tell you're really living with a full and open heart. Maybe when you're in love, you get to the rim and gather all your muscles underneath you and just *leap*. And then you soar.

Will pulled out his wallet. "It's human nature," he said, looking for some money.

"What is?"

"Not to think about that stuff ahead of time—the hard things. I mean, no one wants to believe that they'd scramble up the intestines of someone they'd shared peanuts with on the plane, right?"

"Did you have to put that picture in my head?" I asked.

"But, see, I think they should think about it ahead of time. Because I think you have to go in knowing what you think and believe. Otherwise you'll just do what's easiest."

"But maybe you can't know what you believe way deep down until you're tested," I said, thinking about how I'd crossed a new line when I'd told Liv I'd help her cheat.

"So you think it's one of those chicken and egg questions? You don't know what comes first?"

"I guess I think it's both. It's better if you know what you think before the plane ever crashes. But if it does, then maybe you learn what you really think. Before you—you know." I swished my fingers back and forth in front of him.

Will grinned. "Scramble the intestines?"

"Yeah."

He asked me to come with him into the gift shop then, but I told him I'd just wait for him. I had some hard things to sort out. I could almost hear Tori mocking me, saying, "Ha! Thumper finally gets a clue!"

What I wanted to know was, how do you get from having a clue to knowing what you should do?

* * *

On the ride home, we got stuck in road construction almost right away. Then, because the bus driver was in the wrong lane, he had to take a wrong turn. We ended up riding through a part of Chicago I didn't recognize.

Will and I were sitting together again. He had stopped talking just like he'd promised, right after he gave me his wadded-up sweatshirt and told me to use it as a pillow. He was looking at the map of Chicago that he'd bought at the last minute in the gift shop.

I was kneading his sweatshirt into just the right position up against the window when I saw them out my window, standing in front of a hotel. The wind had blown the gray-and-blue tie I had given him for his birthday over his shoulder, and he was squinting into the sun, talking. The woman gazed up at him, hand resting on his forearm, listening to whatever he was saying.

Later, when I replayed it in my head, I would freeze-frame that second when the woman laughed, so I could study every detail. It was that moment that surprised me the most; it seemed impossible he could still make a woman's eyes crinkle up with happiness, the way he had hers.

A delivery truck pulled up to the curb and blocked my view of them. The light changed, and the bus rolled ahead.

I jumped up and pressed my cheek to the glass to try to see them again, but it was useless.

"It's okay," said Will.

I slumped back into my seat. "What's okay?"

"I figured out where we are. It looks like our trusty bus driver is heading in the right direction, finally." He held up the map and pointed to a section on it. "We're right here."

I looked at the map without focusing. I was afraid it would erase what I had just seen. When I didn't say anything, Will looked at me.

"You look pasty again." He offered me his bottle of water, and watched me take a couple of sips. "No offense or anything," he said, "but I'm starting to think you're what we'd call 'delicate' back where I come from."

"I'm not, usually," I said, then stopped, afraid I had given myself away. "I just saw someone. Someone I know."

"On the street?"

"With another woman." I covered my face with his sweatshirt. It smelled fresh and practical.

"Oh," Will said. After a second, he slapped the map down to his lap. "*Oh!* You just saw him with another woman. You mean, like *with* another woman or just with another woman?"

"I don't know!" I said, my voice muffled by the heavy material.

"Okay, just tell me exactly what you saw. Describe it. Be as objective as you can. Pretend you're a reporter."

I lowered the sweatshirt and told him everything. When I was finished, he asked, "Did you know he was going to be here?"

"I knew he was in Chicago for work. He comes here a lot to see customers. Here and Columbus."

"Hold up. I thought you said he was a professor."

"Who?"

"Aren't we talking about your boyfriend?"

I had a second of panic, and my heart skipped a beat. "Michael? No. It was my father."

"Oh, your *father.*" Will leaned back against the seat and took a deep breath. "Okay, let's think about this. You said *her* hand was on *his* arm. Maybe she was just flirting with him. There's nothing he could do about that. I mean, he has to at least be friendly, right? He can't really say, 'Take your hand off my arm, you miserable wench, or I'll summon the police!' because that kind of talk probably isn't going to get his firm any more business, right?"

"Right," I said, because he was trying so hard to make me feel better.

I turned towards the window and watched the city go by. Will could be right, but there had been something in the woman's smile—something in the way her body had tilted into my father—that suggested more. If it was more, then I didn't know him at all. None of us really knew him. The "pillar of the community" was a fake.

My stomach churned again, as I remembered what he'd said about Michael: "There's only one thing *a man like that* wants." And now it looked like my father was a man like that. *John something: something, Dad*, I thought. *He that is without sin among you, let him first cast a stone.*

Should I tell my mom what I had seen? I tried to imagine the conversation: "No, Mom, really. I know it sounds like it was nothing, but you should have seen them. That woman was *smiling*." She'd look at me like she was concerned—about *me*—and say, "Well, of course she was. Your father is very good with his clients. They all love him."

Maybe she already knew. No, she couldn't know. Even my mother, devoted as she was, wouldn't stay if she knew that about him. Would she?

"Hey," Will said softly.

"Hey what?"

"They were just standing together. That's all you saw. That's what you described."

"I can read between the lines. I know what I saw."

"Maybe, but I read about this study once where people had to study a list then put it away and write down all the words from the list they could remember. They were words like candy, sugar, bitter, good, taste, and a bunch of other words."

"Does this have anything to do with anything?"

Will ignored my sarcasm. "Later, when the people had to remember the words, like ninety percent of them wrote down 'sweet' even though it wasn't on the list. They swore the test giver was wrong, because they remembered it so vividly."

"So?"

"So your memory can play tricks on you. Maybe you didn't see what you think you saw."

I grabbed two fistfuls of my hair, scrunching it up until it hurt. "I can't stand to think of him cheating on my mother," I said. "He's such a hypocrite. He comes off like he's so much better than everyone else, especially Michael. But Michael would never do to me what my dad is doing to my mom."

"That's a good thing to know about someone before you marry them. If you are in fact going to marry him." He gave me a hopeful look. "Are you, still? Going to marry him?"

I nodded. "I'm so tired. So tired of thinking about it."

He patted his own shoulder. "You can lean against me, if you want. I mean, if it would be more comfortable than the window."

I did, and in spite of the noise on the bus and what I now thought I knew about my father, and what I suspected about myself, I immediately fell dead asleep.

*　*　*

When I woke up, my stomach had settled and my head was clear. I knew I needed to talk to Liv and make at least one thing right with myself.

I found her toward the back of the bus, sitting next to Cory—lying across him, actually. She was leaning against the window and had her legs stretched across his lap. Her feet dangled out over the aisle.

"I need to talk to Liv," I said to Cory.

"So talk," he said, looking up at me as he tapped her kneecap. It was clear that he wasn't planning on moving anytime soon.

"Alone," I said.

Liv pouted like I was ruining her fun, but then said to Cory, "Go ask David where everyone is going after the bus gets back." As Cory squeezed past, she said to me, "We kept missing each other today. You kind of got stuck with Will, huh? That's the problem, Grace. You're too nice."

I swatted her legs off the seat and sat down. "I didn't mind. The day went fast." I twisted my engagement ring, dreading saying what I had to say. "Liv, you know I love you, and I'd do just about anything for you."

"Yeah, just about." She pulled her foot up onto the seat and rested her chin on her knee so she could see her toenail polish. "Do you think this Bermuda Pink makes my toes look fat?"

"No," I said. I wondered why she wasn't asking me what was up or why I wanted to talk to her. It was almost like she was afraid of what I was going to say. "You know how I said I'd ask Michael to help you with your essay?"

"Yeah?" Chin still on her knee, she looked up at me.

"I can't."

"I knew it," she said, her voice full of disgust.

"I'm sorry. If I did, it would be like I was saying it's okay with me, and it's not."

"Forget it. I'm not the sharpest knife in the drawer, but eventually I got the message, you know? So I figured it out for myself. It's all taken care of."

"You could ask Mrs. Richards to help you make it better. She's always liked you and it's not against the rules because she's your English teacher—"

"I *said* I figured it out." She was looking past me, maybe hoping that Cory would come back. "I figured it out so that you don't have to get your lily-white hands dirty."

I knew Liv would be mad, but it wasn't like her to be mean. "How?"

"You really want me to answer that?" Her voice was steely, the way it got when she talked about her parents' drinking.

"Why wouldn't I?"

"I asked Michael myself. He said he would."

My jaw dropped. "You asked . . . Michael? And he said—"

"Yeah, that he would. That's what he said."

"But—when?" I asked. What I really wanted to know, though, was *why* had he said yes to Liv? I had been so sure that if I'd asked him, he would have laughed and said something like, "You know I can't do that."

Liv lifted her chin, the way she had when she had gotten caught shoplifting lip gloss at the drug store in fifth grade, and said defiantly, "It doesn't matter. You're clear of it. You're out of it, just like you wanted to be." She pulled out her water bottle and tugged on the opening.

She was mad, but she was something else, too. I had known Liv since we were five, when she saw me in my one-piece swimsuit with the frill at the waist running through the sprinkler and asked if she could play, too. Before I could even answer, she had stripped off all her clothes and was running around me naked, teasing me about my frilly suit. I didn't know that she was making fun of it because she wanted it. But I knew Liv a lot better now and I could tell there was still something she wasn't telling me.

"Anything else I should know?" I said. "I know there is, so you might as well just tell me."

Liv hugged her knee to her chest. "Sometimes I think I hate you."

I looked at her steadily.

"All right!" she finally said. "It's the ring. I helped Michael pick out your stupid engagement ring. He called and asked me to. He wanted to pick out something you'd like and he asked me to help him."

I stared at Liv, then down at my ring. "But—but—you didn't even pick out something I would like. This is what *you* like! You like diamond-shaped. I like oval rings, Liv. Don't you remember?"

"Don't be such a baby. Oval, Marquise—they're basically the same shape! It's a diamond, Grace, a big one that comes with a man who is taking you away from here! What more do you want? You don't get it and you never will, so just get out. Get out of my seat." Liv leaned back against the window, put her bare feet against my thighs and shoved me out of the seat.

As I stumbled into the aisle, I grabbed the seat back so I wouldn't fall. "Cut it out!" I said. "I'm not really mad about it. I'm just surprised."

"Good," she said, scowling. "Great. I'm glad that's over with so we can go back to being best friends and helping each other out, *especially when things get tough.*"

It wasn't really over with, but when Cory bumped against me as he slid into the seat next to Liv and asked, "You about done with girl talk?" she crossed her arms over her chest and muttered, "Totally done."

* * *

Back in the school parking lot, Will and I got off the bus and stood around for a few minutes not saying much, just watching the other kids.

Finally I said, "About my dad . . ."

"Oh, that," he said. "Don't worry about it. I won't say anything. If there's even anything to say, which you don't know for sure yet, right?"

"Right." I folded up his sweatshirt and handed it to him.

"You didn't drool on it, did you?"

"Maybe a little," I said. "I had fun today."

"Me, too. Best senior class trip I've ever been on."

I looked across the parking lot in the direction of home. "Well, I guess I'd better . . ."

"Yeah, I suppose the Prof will be waiting for you." Will scratched the back of his neck and looked at the ground. "All I want to know is, what's your hurry, you know? You've hung out this long with your parents, what's another year? Couldn't you just postpone the part where you say, 'I do'?"

I shrugged.

"I know, I know. You *love* him. You think he's perfect for you. You want to get started on forever now—like that commercial for diamonds says. Haven't you ever heard that love is blind?"

It had been dark for a while and the cool spring breeze was turning cold. I pulled my jacket tighter around myself. "Give it up, Will."

"Nev-ah!" he said, with a dramatic sweep of his arm. "Not until you're at the church, at the altar, saying the words that will chain you *forev-ah!*"

Right then, Will reminded me of Conrad, the hero in my romance novel, when he was trying to convince Rebecca to break things off with Devon, and in spite of all the lousy things that happened on the field trip, I laughed.

I clasped my hands together and put them over my heart. "Why?" I pleaded, batting my eyelashes at him. "Why torment yourself so? Release me! Free me to do what I must!"

Will grinned, then said somberly, "Nay, that I cannot do. He's as wrong for thee as . . . as . . . as milk is for pizza. He would giveth thee a life-long stomachache."

When we were done laughing at ourselves, and I was walking away, he called, "Seriously, it's not too late."

I didn't say anything. Without looking back, I waved and kept walking toward home, thinking that, yeah, it probably really was too late to change my mind now. In my case, love wasn't blind, but I was starting to think that, with Michael, it was a little blinding.

Twenty-one

"I thought you'd be pleased that I was going to help Liv," Michael said.

Even though it was after 9:00 by the time I got home, Michael had wanted to come over, and he'd brought lemon sorbet with him. He couldn't have known I didn't like lemon sorbet, but it irritated me that he didn't. Will would say you should definitely know what kind of sorbet someone likes before marrying them.

"Liv said you were going to ask me yourself but hadn't gotten around to it yet," he added.

Sitting beside Michael on the couch, I smashed the sorbet with the back of my spoon, hoping he'd get the impression I was eating it.

"It doesn't feel right," I said. "It's not fair to everyone else."

He carved a chunk out of the perfect scoop in his bowl. "It's the way things get done sometimes in academia. It's almost assumed."

"So you don't think it's wrong."

"I guess it's all where you draw the line."

I swirled the soupy sorbet around in the bowl. "I shouldn't have told Liv I'd talk to you, but I felt sorry for her. And you should have told me that Liv helped pick out my ring—and that she asked you to help her cheat. When did she ask, anyway?"

Michael's thigh, which was touching mine, tensed. I kept mixing the sorbet. "Would you just please *stop that*," he said.

A few nights ago I would have apologized, but after everything I had been through that day, I didn't much care what he thought about me playing with my food. I tossed the spoon onto the coffee table and it clattered to the edge. "There! Are you happy?"

"I don't know why you're so angry."

I slammed the bowl down, too, and some sorbet slopped out. *Because I'm not sure of anything or anyone anymore and because everything has spiraled out of control and gone too far, way beyond what I can handle, and because even if I want to stop it all I don't know how.* But I only said, "I was so sure you'd say no. I even told her that professors don't do things like that!"

He laughed. "If you only knew!" he said, reaching for the spoon and putting it back in my bowl. "But if it bothers you so much, I'll tell her I changed my mind."

"That's not the point!"

He put his arm around me, but high, so his index finger was on the bottom edge of my bra, right at my ribs. I flicked it away with my other hand and slid down the couch, away from him. "Don't," I said.

"What's wrong?

"I don't know. You and I are just different, I guess. Maybe too different."

He looked worried, like he was afraid I was going to do something stupid. "You're overreacting again and taking everything too literally, Rabbit. Please—let's not do all this again. It's like you enjoy making trouble where there isn't any, like you like to stir things up for fun. All you need to know is I want to marry you."

The funny thing is, for once I didn't have any doubts about that—he *did* want to get married. And it was like once I really knew it was what he wanted, the fog of love lifted, and I could move on to the next question: Did *I* really want to?

Michael was still looking at me, holding me there with his gaze as if he could tell I was drifting. "As you get a little older, you'll get more savvy to the world. You'll see the way that things are. The differences between us that you worry about now will all smooth out."

I stood up and picked up the bowls. "I'm really tired, and I'm not feeling well, so . . ."

"You're right," he said. "It's senseless to have this kind of discussion this late." He tried to kiss me long and deep, but I pulled away. His eyes told me I'd hurt him.

"I'm just tired," I said, walking him to the door. "That's all."

After he left and I had put the dishes in the dishwasher, I shut off all the lights and headed to my room. On my way down the hall, I saw that my mother's light was still on. I slowly pushed the door open a bit and saw my mom sitting up in bed, reading a book. She smiled when she saw me, and for an instant she looked radiant.

She had been lovely, once. When her mother died, Mom had brought home a box of old photographs I had never seen before. There was one of her when she was about my age, standing on top of a dune overlooking Lake Michigan, which stretched out in front of her all the way to the horizon. She wasn't pretty in a flashy way—in fact, her long, loose hair was all tangled because of the wind and her nose was sunburned—but you could see that she was happy and at ease, somehow, and pretty in a deep way.

She didn't look like that anymore, not usually. Maybe living with my father had drained all of the loveliness out of her. But right then, standing in her bedroom doorway, I saw a flash of it again, and it made me sad, knowing what I did about my father. When she saw the look on my face, her smile faded.

"What is it? What's happened?" she asked.

I wanted tell her about everything that had happened and maybe even tell her what might be happening, and I wanted to talk about what I should do.

"It's—oh everything! It's Michael, and it's Liv and—" but before I could say the rest, something in me crumpled and the tears started streaming down my face. Still unable to speak, I raised my arms helplessly.

My mother slid over on the bed and held back the blankets. I did what I had done as a kid when a clap of thunder had woken me so suddenly that I was sure it was Judgement Day. I tumbled into my mother's bed and put my head in her lap. She smelled like lavender, sweet and light, the way she always smelled if I just got close enough to smell her.

She laid her arms across my shaking shoulders, holding me loosely while I sobbed against her. Eventually, when I was all cried out and breathing almost normally again, she said, "So what about Michael and Liv?" The way she paired the names made it sound like Michael and Liv were a couple.

"Nothing, we just had a fight," I said. Sitting up, I remembered Michael had said he'd been going to tell me about agreeing to help Liv. What had he been waiting for?

"You don't want to talk about it?"

"Not really." It seemed like I'd cried out all the words I'd had in me and I no longer wanted to tell my mom everything. There wasn't anything she could do about any of it. *And if I am pregnant*, I thought, forcing myself to use the real word, *then nothing will matter, anyway.*

"How was your day?" I asked.

She smiled shyly. "Well, I was down at the floral shop, just doing a final check on the flowers that you decided on, and they were in the middle of a rush because one of their people had called in sick and they had a funeral—you knew Mr. Sletta, the elementary school teacher, died, right? Cancer, and so quickly, too." I nodded, even though I hadn't known. "Well, I know Mary Jane who works there at the counter and they were so harried that I felt sorry for them and it wasn't like I had anything better to do, what with your father out of town, except wash curtains, and I can do that any old time. So I offered to help them in a pinch and I even did a little arranging and, well, at the end of the day," she said, her cheeks flushing with pleasure, "they offered me a job. They said I have an artistic eye."

My mom wasn't very good with houseplants, but I could understand how arranging flowers was different. She didn't have to make them grow. She just had to make them look nice together. I gave her a quick hug. "Oh, Mom! I can see where you'd be good at that. Only, I didn't know you wanted a job."

"I didn't, but it started me thinking that it might be nice. And even if I don't take it, it was nice to be asked—that they liked my work well enough to ask me." She fluffed up the blanket, looking pleased with herself. "It's all just talk, anyway. Your father would never agree to it."

I couldn't hold back a snort when she mentioned my father.

"I know he's not perfect, and you two have been at sixes and sevens," she said. "But he's a good man."

"So he says," I said, not trying very hard to keep the bitterness out of my voice.

"Of course he is! He's a wonderful provider and an upstanding member of the community. People respect him, and no amount of money can buy that."

I wondered then whether she really thought that, or if she had just repeated it so often that she had forgotten it wasn't true. Suddenly feeling like I had to know, I said, "And he would never do anything wrong, like have an affair."

As soon as I said the word *affair*, I regretted it. My mother looked shocked for a moment but then all the emotion went out of her face, until she looked like a plaster mask of herself. "No, of course not," she said. Her voice was soft but curt. She knew.

"I know he wouldn't," I said. I wished she could be honest with me, but in a way I understood. She had already lost so much. She shouldn't have to lose face, too. "It's just . . . even though he's a good man, he can be such an ogre. You know—demanding and unreasonable, like not wanting you to get a job because then you wouldn't be around for him. I don't know how you can stand it."

She leaned forward and rearranged the pillow behind her. "It shouldn't be such a mystery to you," she said, moving the pillow higher. "When I married him I made a promise, and I did not make it lightly."

"But does that mean you have to be unhappy for your whole life?" I asked. It seemed so unfair. How could she have known what he was really like when she married him? Or what he would become?

"I don't think of myself as unhappy," she said. "I loved your father back when I married him, and if life has changed him, well, loving someone means staying. And when you finally came to us Grace, oh! Then I was deliriously happy. I fell in love all over again."

"But he's che—" I started, before I remembered that we were pretending not to know about my father. "It's just, how can you *stay?*"

She reached out and wrapped my hands in her own and looked at me, her eyes clear and bright. "Like I said, when you were born, I fell in love all over again—but it was with *you*, Grace. Loving you the way I do, how could I go?"

"You could have taken me."

"I know it's hard for you to believe, but your father loves you, too, as much as I do. He wouldn't have allowed it. He would have fought it and it would have been ugly and he could have won. I would never take the risk. As long as I can be with you and I know that you're happy, well, that's all I need. Like now, helping you with the wedding. You're in love and I'm happy to be a part of it. Someday, when you and Michael have children of your own, you will understand."

I laced my fingers through hers and shook my head. "I don't think so." *But it might not be long before I find out for sure.*

"Yes, you will. Besides, your marriage will be different. Michael is not so hard, like your father."

I frowned, remembering what Rachelle had written to Michael. *You have such a hard love,* the note had said, *like a sledgehammer.*

My mother was still looking at me intently. "You love him, right? He treats you well. He'll take care of you." Something inside me twisted up when she said that. Is that what marriage came down to—being taken care of?

"You're overtired," she said. "I can see it in your eyes. You always get emotional when you're overtired and you've been under a lot of stress. A good night of sleep, that's what you need."

I nodded and slipped out of her bed. Too bad that being overtired was the least of my problems.

"Honey," she said, as I walked to the door. "You're not having second thoughts, are you?" For a second, I thought about turning around and telling her I was, but then she said, "Because I saw the invitations by the back door, all ready to go, so I mailed them. I hope that was all right."

"Sure, Mom," I said. "Thanks."

In my own room, I took off my clothes and looked at myself in the full-length mirror that hung on the back of my door. Maybe it was my imagination, but it looked like my stomach was pooching out a little more than it usually did. I counted the weeks on my calendar. I couldn't remember exactly, but it had probably been five or six weeks since my last period. I had been that late before. Maybe I wasn't pregnant.

Even if I was, Michael and I would be married by the time I really started showing. Until then, people could just think I had gotten fat. Michael had said he wanted kids. I had thought we'd wait until I finished college, at least, to start having kids, but we'd just do it sooner, that's all. It wasn't a big deal. Not at all.

Twenty-two

Squatting over the toilet, gingerly holding the tiny stick between my legs, I didn't think about what the pregnancy test would show or what it would mean or the wedding or Michael or anything. As I concentrated on peeing on the stick, I had only one thought: *This is so gross.*

I had bought the test at one of those megastores, figuring that it was less likely anyone would recognize me, and then shoved it in my purse and waited until I knew I would be by myself at Michael's. I didn't want to tell him I thought I might be pregnant because I wanted time to think things through for myself.

If only Liv were with me, she would've found a way to lighten things up, but she still wasn't speaking to me. I wasn't too worried. This was typical for her when she was feeling left out. Plus, to her I had been the worst kind of friend—someone who had let her down after I had promised her that I'd come through. I understood why she was mad, but I hoped she'd get over it soon.

I carefully laid the stick on the counter and looked at my watch. *Wait five minutes,* the directions had said. I washed my hands and sat down on the rim of the bathtub to wait.

How could Michael have let this happen? He was the one who had all the experience with sex! I thought he knew what he was doing. I had believed him when he said pulling out would work. When a condom was close by, we used it. But on the warm day that Liv had dropped me off in Michael's driveway and Michael had pulled me into the woods, insisting he couldn't wait to have me . . .

I wanted to hate him for taking a chance, but even if he had warned me, I probably wouldn't have stopped. Once the current got going between me and Michael, there was only one thing I cared about. When we were together that way, nothing else mattered. Nothing else even existed. It was like we had fallen into a velvety, black hole. The miracle was that we ever climbed back out of it at all. That's the way it had been between us.

But since the field trip to Chicago, when I learned more than I wanted to know about my father and mother and Michael and babies with expressions on their faces even before they were born—since then, that other place didn't have the same hold on me.

I checked my watch. Three minutes had gone by. Two to go. On the back of the toilet was a bowl of pine potpourri. I took a deep breath, hoping the smell would relax me, but it smelled fake, like pine spray instead of like real pine.

The front door slammed. "Hello!" a voice yelled. "Hell-oooo. Grace?"

Tori. Why did she have to come now? I propped my elbows up on my knees and put my head in my hands. Well, whatever. I couldn't hide a pregnancy test when I was right in the middle of it.

"I'm in here," I said.

"What'd you say?"

I lifted my head from my hands and yelled, "I'm in here!"

Tori stopped at the bathroom door, which I had left open. "Oh, hey. What're you—" She stopped when she saw the pregnancy kit on the counter. "Shit. Don't tell me."

I held up my left wrist so she could see my watch. "In exactly one more minute we'll both know," I said. "Join the party."

"Quinn left his blanket here earlier, so we had to come back. I'll go as soon as we find it. He's looking for it now." She shoved her hands into the back pockets of her faded jeans and leaned against the door jamb. I waited for her to start in on me, but she just stood there.

"Aren't you going to say anything?" I asked.

"Like?"

"Like I told you so."

Her knees buckled as she pretended to be hurt. "God, you must think I'm Cruella or something. I wouldn't wish this on my worst enemy."

I straightened out the shower curtain and tried to look unconcerned. "It doesn't matter, either way. It's not like I'd have to do this on my own."

"It looks to me like you already *are* on your own. Where's Lover Boy?"

"I didn't want to tell him until I was sure."

"You want some company? I can stay."

"Why not," I said, surprising myself. Tori was no Liv, but she was better than no one at all. "What does the stick say?"

Tori glanced at the stick. "There's just one line. This one's different than the one I used. Does that mean you're pregnant or not?"

I slumped over in relief. "Not. Two lines and I'm pregnant."

"How late are you?"

"I don't know, exactly. A little over a week or two."

Tori picked at her spiked hair. "It might be too early, still. You might not be making enough of the pregnancy hormone yet to show up. Wait a few days and try it again."

"Great," I said, standing up. "That's just great that I still don't know." I picked up the wastebasket and, holding it next to the counter, angrily swept the test and its box into it. But I was in too much of a hurry and the sharp corner of the countertop gashed my arm. "Shit," I said. I grabbed a Kleenex and held it against my arm. "This is all I need!"

Tori opened the medicine cabinet door. "I'll look for a band-aid," she said.

"Don't!"

"Geez, relax. I'm just trying to help," Tori said.

"That's just it!" I cried, angrily. "You can't help me! You can't help me with—" I waved my arm over the wastebasket, "all this!"

Still dabbing at my scrape, I awkwardly pulled the liner out of the basket. I didn't want Michael to see the empty box or the test, even though it was negative. In a few more days, it might not be. At the thought of that, I wanted to cry. I was angry with myself for even being in this situation and furious with God for jerking me around. *Don't cry!* I told myself. *Do not cry in front of Tori.* But I couldn't help it. The best I could do was to hide behind my hair.

"I don't know what you're so upset about," Tori said, following me into the kitchen. "I thought you said it didn't matter, either way. You love him?"

I used the bloody Kleenex to wipe my nose. It was all I had. "Yes," I said in exasperation. "I still love him."

"You're getting married?"

"Yes!" I heard the TV come on in the den and then Quinn laughing.

"So what's the big deal if you're pregnant? Are you afraid it's going to ruin your perfect 36-24-36?"

I dropped the bag of trash on the kitchen floor. "No, it's not that!"

"Then what?"

"I don't know!" I said, throwing up my hands in frustration. "If I'm pregnant, that will be like, like . . . I don't know. Like jumping off the diving board and *then* realizing you don't know how to swim—but there's no way to get back to the board. You're already in the air."

Tori rolled her eyes. "God, Quinnie explains stuff better than you and he can barely talk. Just say what you mean."

"Why can't you leave me alone? You're always in my face!"

Tori crossed her arms over her chest, covering the "What's in it for ME?" slogan on her T-shirt. "And why can't *you* finish a simple sentence, like 'If I'm pregnant then'? If you're going to be a professor's wife, you should at least be able to do that."

Tori had finally pushed me too far. "Shut up!" I shouted. "Just shut up! You don't understand *any*thing!"

"Oh, like I've never had a bun in the oven after the chef left the kitchen?" she said sarcastically. "Get a grip, Thumper. I understand everything."

"No, you don't." I leaned over and put a twist-tie on the trash bag, then straightened back up. "I'm not like you, okay? All independent and—and, and handling a kid and a job on your own. I'm not! If I'm pregnant—"

She took a step forward so that her face was just inches from mine. "Then what?" she said. *"What?"*

"I won't be able to change my mind!" I pushed her away and kicked the bag of trash as hard as I could. It skidded across the floor and slumped against the back door.

"If I'm pregnant, *if I'm pregnant*," I cried, "I'll have to go through with it!"

Tori slouched down on the bar stool behind her, even though I was the one who was shaking. For a long minute, we both just stared at each other, stunned.

"Wow," she finally said. "I didn't know you were thinking about *not* going through with it."

I took a deep breath. "Neither did I," I said quietly, wiping my fingertips under my eyes. "At least not seriously. I had some little doubts, I guess. But that's normal. And how could I *not* want to marry Michael? Before I met him, my life was so, I don't know, not terrible or anything. Just narrow and not very interesting, but I didn't even know it. He cracked my whole world open."

Tori pulled out the barstool next to her so I could sit down. "So what?" she said. "That world he showed you—now that you know it's there, it won't disappear if you don't marry him."

"It's not just that. He *wants* me. He loves me like no one ever has. What if no one ever loves me like this again? What if this is it, the real deal, true love, and I'm throwing it all away?"

Tori snorted. "You're . . . what? Eighteen? Of course he loves you like no one ever has before. Plus you did it for the first time with him, so yeah, in that way it is special. It won't ever be quite like that again."

I rested my arms on the cool marble countertop and looked out the window over the sink. It was late afternoon, and the sunlight was streaming down through the trees.

The leaves on all the trees were completely open now. They looked fragile to me, like they couldn't hold up to strong winds. Before long, they would turn a deeper green, but at first they are always a bright, techno green, because they don't have much chlorophyll in them yet.

"He thinks I have potential," I said. "He says he can already see the woman I'll become."

Tori slapped one of her palms down on the counter. "That's a nice story you've got going in your head. What if the woman he sees is the woman he wants you to be? What if that's not who *you* want to be?"

I looked at her. "But what if it's never like this again? Can you promise me that someone else will make me feel the way that Michael does?"

"I can't *promise* you anything. No one can!" she said angrily. "Plus, are you sure you want to feel the way Michael makes you feel—not just the tingly stuff, because that's easy to get, believe me. I'm talking about all the rest. Insecure. Not quite good enough. Grateful to have him. It might be nice to marry someone who feels grateful to have you, you know?"

Tori's words were like a line of upright dominoes. I had to wait for them all to fall, then go back and set each word up again, one at time, before I could understand them. But once I did, something finally settled inside me. I was tired of always feeling worried about what he thought about me. I was tired of trying to be as mature as he was.

When I didn't say anything, Tori threw her hands into the air in frustration and went to check on Quinn. In a minute, she came back and sat down next to me.

"Look," she said. "You're making this harder than it has to be. What is it that you want?"

"What?"

"It's just a simple question. What. Do. You. Want. Do you want Michael? Because if you want great sex or to see the world or to be an adult—you can have all those things without him. He's not the only guy who can show you all those things. He's just the only one you've gone out with. You have to decide what you want, just like I did. But then you have to be okay with giving some things up, too, because you can't have everything."

"What did you want?"

Tori leaned back and clasped her hands behind her head. From where I was sitting, her arms looked a little like wings. I hadn't ever noticed her arms before, but now I could see that they were strong but not in a hard, stringy way. Her biceps had a pretty curve, like they had been sculpted by an artist. "Freedom," Tori said. "I wanted to be able to call the shots."

"And what did you give up?"

Tori shrugged. "Nothing much. Fame, fortune, a live-in maid."

My shoulders sagged in disappointment. "Just when it looked like you might actually say something helpful," I said. "I thought we were having a serious conversation, here, but that must be too much to ask."

"I am being serious, at least about the fortune part. My last name is Winters. My first name is actually Victoria, but I hate it."

"Winters? As in . . . The Winters Performing Arts Center? And the Robert J. Winters Expressway?"

Tori pretended to shudder. "Yeah, everyone's gone overboard on the naming thing, if you ask me."

I looked at Tori, in her faded jeans and T-shirt. What she was saying didn't make any sense. "But—you clean houses."

"That's right. When I told my parents I was pregnant, they gave me an ultimatum. Get rid of the baby or lose my inheritance. I told them what they could do with their ultimatum and their inheritance."

"So you don't get any money?"

"They wouldn't let me starve or anything, but no, no money. That's okay with me. I like it this way."

Quinn laughed again and Tori and I both looked toward the den, where he was still watching TV. Then she said, "Me and Quinn are more of a family than my family ever was with its nannies and maids and gardeners. My parents hire people to do everything—even raise their kids. So believe me, it's no great loss."

I tried to imagine her making that decision to do everything by herself—no family and no boyfriend. And it wasn't just herself she would have to take care of. It was also a baby. "You wanted a baby that much?"

She laughed. "At first it was probably more like I wanted to irritate my parents that much. But yeah, I wanted him that much."

"Wow. I couldn't do it on my own."

"You sure? You might be able to do it like me. And you run a mean vacuum, so maybe we could be a team—Maids on the Verge. No, wait! *Virgins* on the Verge, and then we'd bring our kids along. It would be worth it just to see people's faces when they opened the door and saw us standing there holding a bucket in one arm and a kid in the other. You should think about it, if you decide not to get married."

"Yeah, it would be funny," I said ruefully, standing up. But I couldn't imagine it. I picked up the bag of trash.

"Let me help you with that," Tori said, sliding off the barstool.

"That's okay. It's my trash. I'll take care of it."

She snorted. "As if!" she said. "I meant I'll get the *door*." She opened the door for me. "What are you going to do?"

"I don't know," I said, holding the trash out in front of me so it wouldn't hit anything. "I might not have a choice."

"There's always a choice. You just have to be able to live with the consequences."

She closed the door behind me, and through it I heard her yell for Quinn.

Twenty-three

Coralei drew her cloak more tightly around her shoulders and rapped sharply on the heavy wooden door. The mansion was dark and silent, but she had no doubt Trig was lurking in the bowels of the house, sharpening his knife, whether to use on her or on her brother, she could not tell.

Desperate, she threw all her weight against the door and pounded on it with her fist. "Open the door," she groaned. "I beg of you. Now that I know all, don't deny me the chance to explain all!"

The door swung open and she—

". . . hurled the book against the wall," I said, throwing *A Season of Obsession* onto the floor next to my bed. Tori had called me to see how I was doing and I'd told her I couldn't stand not knowing. I was going to buy another pregnancy test.

"Don't waste your money. Wait a few more days," she'd reminded me. "Either you are or you aren't, and pissing on the stick any sooner won't change it one way or the other."

I was hoping to make the time go faster by escaping into a good romance, which I hadn't done for a while, but the story wasn't holding my attention.

I looked around for something I could do to bring on my period. I'd already gone jogging that day and punished my body by doing three sets of fifty sit-ups. I'd taken a bath in scalding water. And I'd prayed long, earnest but intentionally vague prayers in which I swore I'd do better, I'd be better, if God would just give me one more chance. It was the way I was spending my days, now. Waiting for my period. Waiting on the Lord.

Michael called every day, wanting to see me, but I made up excuses not to. I complained about the heavy load of end-of-the-year homework. I pretended to be sick. I told him I had responsibilities to take care of at home, I was taking care of wedding details, my father was acting weird about everything again and the best thing Michael could do was to fade into the background for awhile. I told him whatever I had to so I wouldn't have to see him for a few days.

"I miss you," he said, and I knew from his low voice the way he missed me most. The desire in it still set me off, sent that current racing through me. I wondered if it came from being wanted or from the real deal—from the power of love. Because in spite of everything, I was still in love with him.

If only everything had stayed as simple as it had been at the beginning—just me and Michael, completely into each other. But after we'd gotten engaged, what we had together had gotten all tangled up with other things. It was like what happens when necklaces in a jewelry box get intertwined. Pulling on the chains of one of the necklaces just makes them knot up worse, so you have to coax them loose, one at a time, even though it's hard to tell which necklace you're working on untangling, especially when all the chains look alike.

Feeling sorry for myself, I listlessly punched my pillow.

"Is something going on?"

I looked up from my bed to see my mother standing in the doorway to my room. "What do you mean?"

"You haven't been out with Michael."

"Oh, that," I said, easily. "He's busy with end-of-the-year stuff—grading papers, writing exams. Stuff like that."

She nodded thoughtfully. "You don't look very well. I know you want to be in shape for the wedding, but you've been running too much. You're low on iron. You shouldn't have bags like that under your eyes when you're only eighteen."

"Gee thanks, Mom. That's just what I want to hear right before I get married." She shifted the books she was holding to one side and leaned against the door jamb, waiting for me to say more. "I guess I'm overwhelmed by the wedding details, and graduation, and trying to pack up for the move to Michael's."

"What can I do to help?"

I sat up and reached for the wedding notebook at the foot of my bed and flipped through a few pages, looking for something to distract her. "Can you call the caterers and tell them I want centerpieces with candles? And if you could box up my shelf of books in the living room, that would help."

"I will after I run these to the library. And take one of my iron supplements. They're up in the medicine cabinet in my bathroom."

"Thanks, Mom," I said, thinking I'd better start wearing concealer. It was also clear I was going to have to keep Mom busy with wedding details.

My father was home again briefly over Memorial Day weekend, but I could barely look at him, knowing what I did about him. By then we had become so good at avoiding each other that he didn't even notice I couldn't stand to look at him. *That would be the one good thing about being pregnant and having to go ahead with the wedding*, I thought. *At least I wouldn't have to live with my father.*

He left for Chicago late in the afternoon on Monday. When I said goodbye, I thought about hinting I knew what he was up to there. It was only because my mom was in the room that I didn't. I wouldn't have been able to stick it to him without also hurting her.

After my mom and I had dinner—salmon wrapped in phyllo dough, sprinkled with parsley—I went out to sit on the front step where I could watch the sun set and think.

I put my feet on the step right below the one I was sitting on and played with the shoelaces of my ratty tennis shoes. If I didn't get my period by tomorrow, I decided, then I'd buy another pregnancy test. I was tired of the "what if/if only" tape that had been playing in my head over and over, and I was tired of hanging out at the edge of two futures without knowing which would be mine. Either way, I knew it would be tough, and I just wanted to get on with it, whatever *it* was.

When Liv's Subaru screeched to a stop right in front of me, and Liv threw open the passenger side door, and said, "Get in," I was glad, even though I could tell she was still mad and primed for a fight. Anything was better than spending more time in my head.

I yelled to my mother that I was going with Liv, then got into the Subaru. Liv hit the gas and the car leapt forward, throwing me off balance and against the door. "Wait!" I said. "I don't even have my seatbelt on."

Liv's eyes were red and watery. "Yeah, well, join the club, Cupcake."

She rocketed the car around a corner so we were heading west out of town, toward the farms where we had gone on hayrides in middle school. The road was flat and deserted; I could still make out the muted colors of the barns and outbuildings, but I knew in a few minutes they'd be silhouettes against the mauvey gray sky.

"Liv, I shouldn't have—"

"You're right. You shouldn't have." She lifted the fast food cup she'd been holding between her legs and took a sip. "You're so lame for a friend."

Even though I had known that our first time talking before making up would be like that, the words snapped against me. I was surprised by how much they stung. "You don't need to cheat," I said. "You can win without it. That's what I thought."

"No, what you were thinking about was *you*. You were thinking about what you would and wouldn't do, because in your charmed life you can afford to be all moral and ethical and everything, but you know what? I don't have that luxury. And it all would have been *fine*, you know? Because I was *on* to you. I had it all under control," she said. She pressed her foot all the way to the floor and the Subaru shuddered.

I shifted a little so Liv wouldn't be able to see that I was gripping the door handle. She was going too fast, but telling her that when she was like this would only make her wilder.

"We could have come up with other ways," I said, peering into the dusk. I wished Liv would turn the headlights on.

"I didn't need other ways. Michael and I—we understood each other. But then after the senior trip, you had to go whining to him and he reneged, just like you. God, you two deserve each other!"

She took another sip. I held out my hand for her cup. I wanted to find out what she was drinking.

"Oh, fine. Now you want my drink, too," Liv snapped, but she gave me the cup. I took a sip. It burned all the way down my throat. Rum and Coke. Mostly rum.

"I didn't tell him not to," I said, keeping my voice even. "I just told him I was surprised that he would." Liv was looking off to her left, and the car followed her gaze, drifting over the centerline.

"Liv!" I yelped.

She pulled the car back into the lane, as if it was no big deal. "He's done a lot of things that would surprise you," she said.

Thinking she was talking about Rachelle's abortion, I said, "I know more than you think I do."

Liv lifted her hands off the steering wheel so she could flip off the universe with both middle fingers.

"That son of a bitch!" she said. "I knew he felt guilty, but I never thought he'd—But I'm glad. I'm glad it's out in the open." She waved both hands in front of her. She must have had a lot to drink before she picked me up, because she was getting drunker by the minute. "Let's clear the . . . you know, the murk. The thing is, I was just flirting, just thinking that I'd, you know, loosen things up a little, so he'd want to help me with the essay."

I was concentrating on keeping my eyes on the road in case I needed to keep Liv on course, but when Liv's words sank in, I shot her a look. "I was keeping it light with him, you know?" she said, punching the air with her fist. "Cas-u-al. But then . . ."

"Then what?"

In the fading light, I could see that Liv's face was twisted, but I couldn't tell if it was from the rum or regret. "We kissed and I didn't mean, didn't think he would—"

Later, I would remember that it was only because I couldn't stand to watch Liv reveal any more that I looked away from her in time to see the dim, massive outline of the back of an old hay wagon rushing up at our windshield, the muddied reflective warning triangle barely visible.

"Liv!" I grabbed the steering wheel and yanked it. The car veered to the right, skimmed over the shoulder of the road as though it were made of ice, then hit something and rose into the evening sky.

As we cartwheeled through the air, I saw the whole thing in slow motion, like it was a movie. *This must be when your life flashes before your eyes,* I thought. *There's so much more time than I thought there would be.* But I didn't see anything from my life. Instead, I watched as Liv's white cup rotated gracefully through the air and hit the windshield before disappearing into her long hair, which spread like a great black web around her. *It's all so lovely and beautiful, like a dream,* I thought.

But then the movie stopped abruptly and my personal theater went black.

* * *

The first thing I noticed when I came to was to the sweet, heavy smell of alfalfa. It made me think of Daphne, the heroine from my favorite romance novel, and how she had fallen asleep in a barn after she had broken things off with Lord Kensington and awakened to find flames all around her. I was irritated I couldn't remember how she had gotten out of the burning barn. It had been something to do with a wagon—no, a wheelbarrow. But as soon as I felt I was getting close to the answer, it slipped away from me.

Suddenly I was aware of someone talking above me. I tried to open my eyes but my eyelashes were too heavy.

"Yeah, wait," the voice said. "Her eyes are fluttering. Yup, okay. I won't move her. I'll just sit tight." I heard a snap, like a cell phone closing. "All right, there, miss. Hang on. I don't think you're hurt too badly, but I'm no doctor. The ambulance is on its way."

He leaned over me just as I managed to finally open my eyes. Slowly his face came into focus. It was dark out, but there was a light coming from somewhere, and I could see that he had a crew cut, like Will, and kind eyes.

"Aren't cell phones the darndest things?" he said. "My wife makes me carry one in case of an emergency, she says. Well, let me tell you. Her idea of an emergency is that she forgot to get the dry cleaning. Or she'll call and ask me do I want burgers or stew for dinner, or ask me should we invite the Dinels or the Rastens to go to a show with us. Then she'll call and ask me what show do I think we should go see! I've had the phone for, oh, about six months, I guess, and I was just starting to think about getting rid of the dang thing just so I wouldn't have to make so many decisions every day. Your stunt pretty much takes care of that idea."

I didn't know what to say. "Sorry," I whispered. I slowly turned my head, looking for the car. "Liv?" I said.

The man reached down and lightly touched my shoulder. "No, no! Don't move. They said not to move."

"Where's Liv?"

"Is that your friend? She high-tailed it out of here. She was already running by the time I got back here, and when I saw there was still somebody in the car, I let her go. By the smell of you, I'd say you were having a good time right up until you went airborne. I yelled after her, but she was hell-bent on making things worse for herself."

He shook his head slowly, as though nothing surprised him anymore. "A bad mistake followed by a worse one," he said, scratching the back of his neck. "She should've cut her losses."

Twenty-four

Michael and my mother were waiting at the emergency room. "Internal bruises and a broken leg," the doctor said, after checking me over. "That's always the way it happens. The one who's been drinking stays relaxed during an accident. That's why they are able to walk away. But you saw it coming and braced yourself." He checked his watch. "It's late. I'll set your leg and then how about we keep you overnight for observation?"

Once I was settled in my hospital room, my mother hovered, straightening the sheets and talking about how upset my father had been when she'd called him.

"He'll be here first thing in the morning," she said. "He probably shouldn't even be driving. He was beside himself—a wreck. But he'll be here."

I turned my head to the wall, wondering whether his girlfriend had been in the room while he talked to my mother. I could picture the two of them together, him telling her about me. I wished I'd never seen his girlfriend's face.

Michael started to say something, but I closed my eyes and shook my head. I didn't want him to start asking questions about what happened. I was too weak to get into the whole Liv thing now. What I really wanted was to be left alone.

The doctor had promised that the painkiller would give me the best night of sleep of my life. Already I was drifting into it.

In a fading voice my mother said, "We'll be back in the morning." She sounded very far away.

*　*　*

The rhythmic squeak of a nurse's shoes past my door woke me early the next morning. Someone was sitting in the chair next to my head, holding my hand. His head was bowed.

"Michael?" I said, trying to focus.

"No, honey. It's Daddy." He moved so I could see him better.

Daddy—the word little girls use when they still believe their fathers are perfect and wonderful. "When did you get here?"

"Late. Early. Is there anything I can get you?"

I sat up carefully. My leg was throbbing under the cast. "Water, I guess."

He reached for it, never letting go of my hand. "I was so worried. I prayed all the way here."

"I'm okay. It's just a broken leg." I touched my hand to my forehead and winced. I hadn't seen my face since the accident. "Is my travel bag here?"

He found it in the bathroom; my mother must have thought to bring it the night before. I took out a little mirror and, after using the corner of my sheet to wipe the smudges off it, looked at myself.

Deep bruises lined the right side of my face, like fruit on a kitchen counter. Right below my hairline there was a lump the size and shape of a lemon. The area around my eye was swollen and purple—a plum. A strawberry welt was on my cheekbone. The lower part of my cheek was covered with a gauze bandage; I couldn't even guess what was under there.

Another bandage covered my eyebrow, which had been slashed down the middle during the accident. I vaguely remembered the doctor, when he stitched it together again, saying how lucky I was that it was my eyebrow and not my eye. An inch lower and my vision in that eye would have been permanently damaged, he said.

My hair was lank and looked darker than usual because of the oiliness. I shoved my travel bag back at my father.

"Here," I said, blinking back my tears. "I'm done."

He made a big deal out of clearing a spot on the nightstand for the bag. "It will all heal," he said. "You'll be back to your old self before you know it."

I threw my arms out in frustration and then yelped at the pain that shot along my shoulders. "Look at me!" I cried. "I'm the bride of Frankenstein."

"You're *alive!*" he said angrily. "Be thankful. I'm filled with gratitude at God's goodness—that he was watching over you. You've been a good friend to Liv all these years, but somewhere along the line the devil got his hooks in that girl."

I reached for the TV remote control. It had been a long time since my father and I had tried to have a conversation about anything, even the weather, and everything on my mind—the wedding, Michael, Liv, a baby, my mom—was a landmine, waiting to blow up if we touched on it.

I flipped through the channels until I found a daily devotion show on the Christ Channel. I didn't care. I'd watch anything to keep from talking to him. I needed some space to put together what had happened the night before and think about if it changed anything for me.

So we sat, him listening to scripture and me pretending to. Everything from the night before was murky and my brain was still foggy from the painkiller. I wasn't sure I was remembering things right. Liv and Michael had kissed—is that what she had told me? Maybe they'd done more. Or maybe I'd misunderstood everything.

When the show was over, my father shut the TV off. I glanced at the door, hoping Michael or Mom would appear and save me from having to talk to him. Neither one did.

"Have you talked to your mom?" he asked.

"Not yet. It must still be too early."

"I meant since the accident."

"Oh. Yes, last night. She was here waiting for me."

He sighed. "She's got this idea that she's getting a job."

It hadn't occurred to me that my father might not be paying attention to the TV show, either. I wondered what he'd been thinking about besides Mom. His girlfriend?

His hand had been pinning mine to the bed for the last hour. I shifted some of my weight to my palm, pressing down on the bed and creating some space between my hand and his. "Are you going to let her take it?" I asked, wriggling my hand free.

"You know how I feel about that. Your mother's place is at home."

Where's your girlfriend's place? I thought, bitterly. *In the bedroom? Does she do everything for you there the way Mom does everything for you at home?* I resented it that he was able to have respectability and an affair, but he wouldn't give my mother room to stretch a little. He had it both ways, but my mother had nothing. In fact, if she knew about his affair like I thought, then she had less than nothing. My father probably didn't even know she knew. It wasn't like my mother to confront or question.

He stood up and paced beside my bed. I knew he was just getting going. "Ephesians says, 'Wives be subject to your husbands, as to the Lord.'"

"Also from Ephesians, 'Husbands love your wives as Christ loved the church,'" I shot back. "Is that the way you love Mom?" I hadn't wanted to talk about any of this, but he was bringing it right to me.

"Of course it is."

Things had gone so wrong with Liv, and I hadn't been able to help her, and they had gone wrong with me and Michael, but right then I had a crazy idea for making things go right for my mom.

"I think you should let her decide for herself about the job. Give her the choice."

My father stopped pacing and gave me a queer look. "I'm not going to change my mind about this."

Quickly, before I lost my nerve, I said, "I saw you. I saw you with that woman in Chicago. I know what's going on. If you don't let Mom take the job, I'll tell her. And I'll tell Pastor Mark."

My father picked compulsively at the front of his shirt, pulling it away from his body over and over. "Those drugs they gave you must have done something to your brain," he said. "What you're saying doesn't make any sense!"

I hesitated. What if I was wrong? What if I had seen things that weren't there? If I just told what happened, like Will said to, then that woman standing there on the street in Chicago had simply smiled and put her hand my father's arm. So what?

And what if I had wrongly interpreted my mother's reaction to my question about my father? Anybody would be surprised if someone just blurted out "Does your husband sleep around?" I hadn't said those exact words, but almost.

There in the hospital, I was winging it. There were too many things on my mind to think through any one of them completely. I had been reading between the lines—I *had* to read between them if I wanted to make sense of everything. What if I had read wrong?

Then my father lifted his tie and I saw the tip of it quiver. His hands were trembling. If there wasn't anything going on, he wouldn't be afraid. He would be cool, factual, the way he was with his columns of numbers.

"You're such a hypocrite," I said. "If Jesus loved the church the way you love Mom, then the church would be totally screwed." I knew it would make him angry. I wanted it to. I didn't understand much about him, but rage I understood and somehow his anger put us on equal footing.

He dropped his arms to his side and clenched his fists. "How dare you blaspheme God that way?"

"Me? *Me?* You blaspheme him every time you and your girlfriend get it on!"

"That has nothing to do with God!"

My hand flew to my mouth. He had as good as admitted he was guilty. Instead of feeling satisfied, though, I felt completely alone, an island separated from everyone by a vast ocean. I realized with a start that I had wanted to be wrong about everything. If I had been wrong about this, then maybe I would have been wrong about Liv and Michael, too, and maybe everything would still be okay.

"How can *you* say that it has nothing to do with God?" I said. "With you, everything is about God. Your whole life is about God!" I held up my hand and angrily ticked off on my fingers what I had heard so many times from him. "God, family, self—in that order. Isn't that what you've always said? *Isn't it?*"

He raised both his arms, like he was going to give the benediction, and then he did something odd. He sat down beside me on my bed and lowered his hands until they were resting on either side of me. Then laid his cheek on the top of my head. If Liv had been there, she would have called it a faux hug.

"I tried," he said, his voice breaking. "I tried to be that righteous man for you and your mother, but I was too weak. All men—all men sin . . . and fall short . . . of the . . . glory of God."

He was shaking and kind of dry heaving so hard he couldn't say any more. Or maybe he didn't have anything else to say. He just kept heaving and gasping like he was all broken on the inside.

He deserves it, I thought. *He's a jerk, a hypocrite, a fake.* But even in the middle of all that, he was still my dad, and that's why I reminded him of the second part of the passage he'd started. "'. . . And are justified by his grace as a gift.'"

We sat like that for a few minutes. I held my body stiff, waiting until he had pulled himself together enough to stand up and move away from the bed. He had his back to me, but I could tell he was wiping his nose and face with a Kleenex.

"I didn't even want a perfect father," I said quietly. "I just wanted one who loved me the way I was."

He turned in surprise. "I've done *nothing* but love you! If I didn't, then I wouldn't have tried to prepare you for eternal life."

302

"But all I want is to be loved in this one! Why is that so hard?"

Before he could reply, my mother tiptoed into the room, carrying a basket. I knew from the smell of cinnamon that it was a coffee cake like the one she'd made the week before. My father turned toward her quickly, as though he'd been caught doing something wrong.

"Oh, you're already here!" she said. "Our girl looks good, doesn't she?"

"She does," he said, looking relieved to see her. He knew I wouldn't keep talking about it with Mom there.

"I look awful," I moaned.

My mother sat on the edge of the bed next to me, exactly where my father had been just a few minutes before. "Let me take a closer look." As she pushed my hair back from my face, I watched my father over my mother's shoulder. He was gazing out the window, jingling some change in his pocket.

My mother touched a tender spot. "Ouch!" I said, jerking away. "Do you have to touch it?"

"I'm sorry. I just wanted to check the swelling." She stood up. "I'm sure the worst of it will be gone by the wedding. And what's not gone, we can cover with pancake makeup."

"I don't own any."

My mother pretended not to notice my mood. "The good news is that your dress will cover your broken leg."

For the first time, I pictured myself on crutches hobbling down the aisle. It wasn't exactly how I'd imagined my wedding after Michael proposed. Now everything felt wrong. Everything had been ruined.

My mother looked up at my father. "What time did you get here?"

"Around 3:00. There wasn't any traffic, so I made good time." He rocked forward on his toes a bit, so he towered over her. "We were just talking about that job you mentioned."

"Oh, that," she said, pulling napkins out of her purse.

"You know how I feel. I think the family needs you at home, and that's where God intended women to be. However, if you feel like this time you need to put yourself first, so be it."

I glared at my father. By talking about the job like she'd be going against God's will, he was trying to make sure she wouldn't even think of taking the job. He would be able to say he had done what I asked, and he'd still get what he wanted. It was his idea of "free will"—him twisting her arm.

He looked at her, waiting to see what she'd say. She had begun cutting the coffee cake into large pieces. The smell of cinnamon briefly hung in the air before the antiseptic smell of the hospital overpowered it. My mother offered me the first piece of cake.

"Did you hear what I just said?" my father asked impatiently, as she handed him a slice on a napkin.

I wanted to jump up and run out of the room. I would have rather been anywhere but there, waiting for her to do what she had always done, what she would always do—cave in to him.

Taking a bite of her coffee cake, she nodded. She chewed slowly, looking down at the cake in her hand. After she swallowed, she said, "I was just thinking about the parable of the talents, and how God approved of the men—"

"Who used their talents," my father said, trying to rush her.

"But they didn't just use their talents," she said. "They expanded on them. God gave me the talent of homemaking, but maybe he gave me another one, too. My family doesn't need me so much any more. Grace is getting married and you . . ." She stopped what she was doing to look right at him. "You're hardly ever home now." He looked away, then, out the window.

"I can bring joy to people through my flower arrangements," she said. "I think God would permit me that."

I sucked in my breath at how she had shifted everything, just that quickly. When I was little, even if my mom sat on my side of the teeter-totter, we didn't weigh enough to put my dad in the air, but we could make her toes touch the ground. And that's what had just happened. In a way, her toes were touching the ground.

My father stood there, jingling his keys, pretending it was nothing. "I'm going home to shower and change," he said. "They'll be discharging you soon, Grace. I'll be back then, to drive you home."

After he left, I said, "You just said no to Dad."

She put the plastic wrap back over the coffee cake, expertly pulling it across the top and wrapping it over the plate's edge, so the plastic didn't have any wrinkles.

"It felt more like I was saying yes to myself, like you did, when you decided to . . ." She fumbled with the words. "You know—stand up to him that way, when it came to Michael. I didn't approve of what you did, but still, I saw you stand up to him. I think that until then I had forgotten that I could, too."

"That was months ago. What took you so long?"

"I had to mull it over, I guess, and find the courage," she said, placing the plate back in the basket. "Yesterday I found it in Second Timothy: 'For God hath not given us the spirit of fear, but of power, and of love, and of a sound mind.'" She scanned the room, like she wanted to make sure she hadn't left a mess for anyone else to clean up.

I thought about how messed up things were for me, all because of the things I had done. I was happy my mother was hopeful; at the same time, it made my own situation seem more hopeless. What if I was headed into what she was just digging her way out of?

When you've screwed up your life so badly that it's one giant knot, how do you begin to unknot it? My fear and disappointment all gathered thickly at the back of my throat so that when I tried to talk, my voice came out like a little bleat. I stared up at the ceiling to keep the tears from forming.

My mom knelt down next to the bed and stroked my cheek and then there was nothing I could do to hold back the tears. They spilled out, rolled over my cheeks, and down my neck. "Oh, honey," she said, softly. "This, too, will pass."

But she still didn't know what "this" was—that it wasn't just the car accident, or the bruised face or broken leg, or even what Liv had done that I was crying about—and it wouldn't do any good to tell her. I already knew what I had to do. And that's what I was crying about.

She stood up. "I'm going to see what time they expect the doctor to come by. I'll be right back."

While waiting for her, I thought about what she said about saying yes to herself as much as saying no to my father. In a way, I had said yes when I first slept with Michael. I had wanted him. But looking back I could see that it had also been about saying no to my father—about drawing a line between him and me so firm and dark that we'd all know I was my own person. But it hadn't been quite that easy. What was it the man at the accident had said about Liv? *A bad mistake followed by a worse one. She should have cut her losses.*

I knew for sure what I'd do, if all I had to think about was myself. But it might be that I would have to think about not just myself but also a baby, and that changed my answer completely.

Looking up at the ceiling, I prayed, *Please don't make me think for two when I haven't even learned to think for one.* I hoped for once God didn't have better things to do. I hoped for once he was listening to me.

A few minutes later, after I'd made my way to the bathroom, I discovered that he had been. Either that, or I had just gotten very, very lucky.

Twenty-five

I took my time stumping along the wooded path on my crutches. Since the accident, I'd taken my time about everything because if I hurried, I usually tripped or bumped into something, and I didn't want to do anything that might make me fall.

"Here we go," Michael said, guiding me over to the bench beside the lake and helping me sit down. "Just what the doctor ordered—rest and recuperation."

He set the crutches against the bench and then sat beside me. With my back pressed against his shoulder, I had enough room to swing my bad leg up on the bench and keep it elevated.

He pulled out the bottle of white wine and held it up to me with a questioning look. "An after-dinner drink?"

I shook my head. Drinking while on crutches seemed like a bad idea.

He poured two glasses anyway and handed me one. "Just in case you change your mind," he said.

Leaning over awkwardly, I set it on the ground, while he opened a book of poems. Maybe because the sun was setting, he picked one called "Darkness" by Lord Byron. The first line was something about a dream that wasn't a dream. After that, I wasn't really listening, and from the few words I did hear—dead mistresses, and ships rotting in the sea—I knew I wasn't missing much.

Yawning, I played with my engagement ring, working it over my knuckle and off my finger. The sunlight was filtering through the trees, but we were sitting in the shade. Out of the light, the ring looked like an ordinary chunk of glass. I slipped the ring back on again. I didn't want to be impulsive, the way I had been at the beginning of everything. Even though I was pretty sure about what I wanted and what I had to do, I hadn't done it yet.

"It's about the year without summer," Michael said, closing the book.

"Hmmm?" I said, idly sliding my ring back and forth along my finger.

"That's what the poem is about. In the early 1800s, a volcano in Indonesia erupted and the eruption changed the weather. The summer was cold and grey, so the crops failed, which led to disease and a shortage of food. People revolted."

"Oh," I said.

If anyone saw us, they would think the whole scene was romantic—two lovers at a lake reading poetry and drinking wine—but it just wasn't working for me. I'd never liked poetry, and even though I'd tried to like it for months, because Michael did, listening to it still practically put me into a coma.

Michael reached over my shoulder and laid his hand on mine. "Can you just stop that please?" he said. "Can you just, *for once*, not fidget."

At the moment he'd put his hand over mine, the ring was already mostly off. I turned his hand over and put the ring into it.

"I'm sorry," I said. I carefully swung my leg off the bench and ducked out from under his arm so I could face him.

Puzzled, he looked at the ring and then at me. "About what?" His eyes were large and soft, and I felt a pang in my heart. *Am I crazy to think that I can live without him, without this?*

"I can't marry you." My voice sounded small and the words were light, like they would waft away if someone just blew on them.

"You don't want to get married?"

"No, I don't."

Michael gave a quick laugh, like he was waiting for me to tell him it was a joke. "But, the invitations have gone out. All my friends and colleagues are practically on their way. We can't change plans now just because of pre-wedding nerves."

"I know it won't be easy."

"That's an understatement," he said, tucking some loose strands of hair behind my ear. "Look, you've been through a lot the last couple of days with Liv and the accident. You feel overwhelmed, is that it?"

"Not anymore," I said. He looked at me, waiting for me to explain. "Before we crashed, Liv told me what you and she did. That's where you were on that Wednesday night, the night I thought you were with Rachelle. You were with Liv."

He let his hand fall away from my face. "What did she tell you?"

"That you were together."

"Together how?"

It made me angry that he was trying to see how much I knew, like he could play me. "Michael! Don't be stupid! Together making out."

"Don't be absurd!" he said, laughing like he couldn't believe I'd been fooled. "You know how desperate and unstable she is right now. And desperate people say and do desperate things. She wanted me to help her cheat, so she came on to me."

It didn't really matter anymore, but I still couldn't help asking the question. "How far did you go, exactly?"

He turned toward me again, resting his arm on the top of the bench so that his fingers grazed my upper arm. "Not as far as she wanted to. She kissed me, and I pushed her away."

I had always sensed an undercurrent of something between Liv and Michael. And knowing both Liv and Michael, I doubted they would stop after one kiss. But even if they had, it didn't change anything for me.

"It's not just that. I think we might be too different to spend a whole life together," I said, wishing that it could be different—wishing, in a way, that I could be different.

"I can't believe you're still angry about my agreeing to help Liv at first," Michael said. "What do you want? First I tell her I'll help her, and I do that for you. Then you ask me *not* to do it, so then I tell her I won't do it."

"That's what I mean. You did it for me, not because you think it's wrong. I *believe* it's wrong."

Michael stood up abruptly. "That's a bit self-righteous, don't you think?"

"What's that supposed to mean?"

"That you thought premarital sex was wrong, too—until it worked to your advantage. Maybe if you were in Liv's situation, you wouldn't see things quite the same way."

"Stop turning everything around! I'm not the one who cheated!"

He shook his head slowly and said in a patronizing voice, "You're naïve if you think life is black and white. It's more complicated than that."

Since the sun had gone down, the evening had turned cool, but my face was hot. "Wait! Now you're trying to tell me that sleeping with someone else isn't wrong?"

"Your problem is you don't know a good thing when you see it. What we have is a good thing, Grace. I've made some mistakes, but everyone does. Is that the kind of person you are? You just give up when things aren't perfect? Is this what you really want?"

I was going to say yes, just flat out yes. I meant to say it, but I hesitated. What did I really know about love or relationships? Was all this just a normal part of being a couple? When my parents heard about people they knew divorcing, they often said that the couple had taken the easy way out by running from their problems instead of working them out. Was I being a quitter?

Sensing my hesitation, Michael knelt in front of me. He gently took my left hand, kissed it, then put the ring on my finger.

"This is where it belongs," he said. "Just like you belong with me." Still kneeling in front of me, he carefully put his arms around my waist. "Rabbit, let's not do this. I love you. You're the one I want to be with. I can explain everything about Liv. After I do, you'll see that you're overreacting."

He leaned forward and kissed me. It was a long, tender kiss and it held the promise that he really could explain it all away. Maybe I was overreacting. Maybe I did expect too much. When we had finished kissing, I put my arms around his shoulders, where they now fit naturally, and looked down at him. He seemed so sincere, and sincerity isn't easy to fake.

I sighed. It would be so much easier to go ahead with the wedding than to cancel it. It made me tired to think about all the calls I would have to make—how many times I would have to say, "No, we're not getting married" to people, how many times I'd have to watch them smile smugly, thinking that I was only a fling for Michael and not anything serious, after all. If I went ahead with the wedding, there was a good chance—wasn't there?—that in a few years Michael and I would look back and laugh about how I had almost ruined everything. "You were young," he would say. "You couldn't possibly know how things would work out. Fortunately, I did know, and you listened to me."

Michael stroked my cheek. "This is just a lover's quarrel," he said. "Someday we'll tell our kids about how we almost didn't get married. And they'll ask us what the fight was over, and we won't be able to remember." He squeezed my hand. "I'll take care of you, Grace, if you just let me."

It was tempting, just like it was always tempting to stay out on the beach too long. Liv and I, lulled into a stupor by the warm sun and the sound of the waves, always felt like we should stay just a little longer to make it worth the hassle of packing the cooler and dragging it, plus the towels, beach chairs, beach bag, and Frisbee across the hot sand. Liv managed just fine, but I always ended up burned.

Neither of us said anything for a while. He could tell I was thinking, I guess. I'm sure he was hoping that I wouldn't end it, like Rachelle had less than a year before. And, listening to the call of the red-winged black birds and the chorus of frogs, I doubted myself again, doubted that the decision to end it was any better than the decision to start it had been.

Michael was right—how could I know what was a good thing when this was my first serious relationship? Michael, who'd had a lot more experience, thought it was a good thing. If I broke up with him, I might always regret it. That time I'd called Rachelle, I thought I'd heard something like regret in her voice, before it had turned cold.

Michael squeezed my hand again, like he could press an answer out of me. But he couldn't know the answer that would come out of me. Right then, neither could I. I felt like a chameleon that turned gray when it was on a gray rock and green when it was on moss. Tori made me believe I didn't want to marry Michael. But when I was with Michael, I wasn't sure. And then I started to wonder about chameleons. What color were they, really? I mean, does a chameleon even *have* its own color, apart from its surrounding? And what color was I?

Next to the bench was an old-fashioned bug zapper that came on automatically every night at dusk. I listened to its hum as it warmed up, then heard the "zzzt . . . zzzt" as one insect after another flung itself into it.

I turned my head to watch. "Why do you think they do that?" I asked.

Michael followed my gaze. "Maybe they don't know any better," he said.

Zzzzt. Zzzzt. Zzzzt.

He could have been right. Or maybe they did know, but even with knowing they couldn't help themselves. It was a compulsion. They got near the blue light and they had to throw themselves into it. Listening to that zzzt, zzzt, zzzt, I suddenly knew there was only one thing I could say to Michael. The insects couldn't help themselves, but I could.

I pulled the ring off my finger for the last time and held it out to him. I looked him dead in the eye and said, "It's over." I said it from my gut, just like Liv had told me I should say swear words. This time, my words felt solid and heavy.

He took the ring and examined it for a minute. When he looked up again, his expression was set. "I can't believe that you—you!—are breaking up with me. People warned me it was a mistake to get involved with someone so young," he said. "They said at eighteen you can't know what you want. I thought they were wrong. I thought you did know."

"So did I."

"The problem is, you'll never know," he said, derisively. "The way you were raised makes you incapable of knowing. You're stunted. We all have it in us to create something better, if we just open ourselves up to the universe." And then he said the words he had to know would cut me the deepest. "You're just like your father. You're all clamped down and clenched up. You're incapable of opening yourself up in any real way."

The funny thing was, right then I did feel open—more open to the universe than I ever had. And I felt eighteen again.

I was angry I hadn't seen it all sooner, but at the same time, I was so relieved that I had finally seen it. That I was doing something about it. It was strange to feel so glad on the inside right then, but I was. I was glad he was bitter and spiteful, and that he was hurting me and making me angry and spiteful, too. It was so much easier to walk away from him than if he had held me close and whispered in my ear about how much he loved me. If he had done that . . . I don't know. I like to think I still would have walked away, but I can't say for sure that I would have. But he didn't hold me close. Instead, he had sliced the knife in and then twisted it.

But I could do that, too. "You know what you're really mad about?" I said. "You're mad because I know what I *don't* want. I don't want you."

It was close to dark by then, so I only saw a glint of silver in the air before the cell phone that Michael threw at me glanced off my shoulder. "If you're so fucking brilliant," he said, "find your own way home."

Twenty-six

Tori didn't sound surprised when I called her and told her I needed help getting out of the woods. "He's humiliated and he's making you pay," she said, tipping the flashlight so it would throw light on the next step of the path so I could see where to set down the tips of my crutches. "It's not that he's so brokenhearted over losing you. He's thinking about what his friends are going to say."

"Gee, that makes me feel so much better," I said, but I didn't put any bite into the words. I was thinking how, even when you know it's the right thing to do, breaking up makes you feel like crap.

"I just didn't know if you'd really changed the story you had going in your head about Michael," she said.

"Pretty much. By the way, I'm not pregnant," I said, stopping to rest. The path was uneven and covered with pine needles, and it was hard going.

She flicked the light of the flashlight far ahead of us, checking to see how far we still had to go. "I figured."

We went the rest of the way in silence, me concentrating on not falling and her trying to help me as best she could. The house was dark when we walked past, and Michael's car was gone.

"What do you want to do with his phone?" Tori asked. "I'll break it for you, if you want. Tell him it was an accident."

"You'd do that for me?"

"Sure," Tori said, holding her car door open and taking the crutches from me so I could sit down.

Thinking about it made me smile, but it wasn't in me to break other people's things. "Just leave it on the kitchen counter."

She shrugged. "If that's what you really want." She slid the crutches onto the floor in the back seat, where Quinn was sleeping in his car seat, then jogged up the steps. She was back by the time I had figured out that I needed to wedge my body hard against the seat back in order to create enough room for what Tori had started referring to as "leg-in-a-cast," like it was a new item on some fast food menu.

"Where to?" she asked, turning the key in the ignition.

"I don't know." Out of habit, I ran my thumb around the base of my ring finger, where my engagement ring had been just a few hours before. "Can we just drive around for a while?"

"Why not?" Glancing over her shoulder at Quinn, who was drooling in his sleep, Tori braked gently, then eased the car out onto the road.

All the windows were rolled down, and I let my arm hang out so I could feel the night air. The dank smell of the woods gave way to the sweet smell of the meadows and alfalfa fields, and I closed my eyes and let the evening pass through me.

Tori hummed a little bit, took the corners slow, didn't ask me to make any decisions. She didn't seem to be in any hurry, and she didn't even mind when I asked her to stop at a Gas Mart because I had a sudden craving for Cheez Whiz.

After that she drove us around for a little longer, while I put Cheez Whiz on crackers and handed them to her, one at a time. Eventually, she turned into someone's driveway and pulled up to the house.

"My house," she announced. "It's really just a rental, but I think of it as mine."

I couldn't see it very well in the dark. All I could see in the front porch light's bright triangle of light was an old, molded plastic trike and a window box filled with impatiens.

"It looks homey," I said.

Tori put the car in park and stretched her arms over her head. "It's not much—my place, my life—but at least it's mine, you know? The nearest neighbors are a mile away, so

I have lots of space and privacy. There's a dirt pile out back that Quinn digs in. He'll play out there all day with the hose and the bucket. He'll make a mountain or a river or a wall. It's better than any playground."

I nodded, thinking that that was the great thing about dirt. There were so many things you could do with it. "What color is the dirt?" I asked.

Tori snorted. "What kind of a question is that—what color is the dirt?"

"I was just wondering. If it's dark that means the soil is rich. Good for gardening."

"Well, it's black and really sticky. Quinn has to soak in the tub for an hour after he's been out there."

As if he had heard his name, Quinn started to wake up. Tori reached back and groped on the seat for his stuffed animal. When she found it, she expertly slipped it under his arm and Quinn settled back to sleep.

"You know," she said. "You could stay here."

"Here? With you?" I asked.

"Yes, with us," she said. "What did you think? That you'd get the house and Quinn and I would live in the car?"

"No. It's just . . . I didn't expect it. I'm—I don't know—touched."

She leaned away from me warily. "You're not going to hug me, are you?"

I finally got to the place where she was—that sarcastic place where the sarcasm didn't mean anything except that we were friends. "Not hardly. I haven't had a rabies shot lately."

Tori laughed and then sat quietly, just looking at the house and listening to the crickets.

I thought about the summer, stretching out in front of me, suddenly empty, and beyond that, the fall. I didn't know what was next for me or what my life would look like now that Michael wasn't in it. But what would have scared me a few months ago, all that empty space and uncertainty, didn't seem so scary now.

I thought about what it would be like to live with Tori and Quinn. Maybe Quinn and I could plant a row of peas, some beans, a few kinds of flowers. My African violet was nice, but I liked other flowers—daisies and tulips and rhododendrons.

It was easy to see myself in the garden, but when I pictured living here with Tori, it was like looking at a picture that had been printed backwards. Although I could recognize myself in the picture, something about the image wasn't quite right.

The other option was to go back home. My father would be smug about the break-up, but at least he wouldn't be able to pretend he was something he wasn't. I knew him a little better, now. It wasn't much, but it was a start.

I looked over at Tori, knowing she was putting herself out there for me. I hoped I could make her understand.

"It's really nice of you to offer," I said, "but I think I need to go home. My mom just started working part time, which may not seem like a big deal, I know, but in my family that's huge. I think she's going to need me for ballast, at least for a while."

Tori played with the gear shift. "Whatever," she said, shifting into reverse and backing out into the street. "It was just an idea."

I put my hand on her arm. "But is there still a cleaning position open with Virgins on the Verge?"

She shifted into first. I could tell she was trying not to grin. "Yeah, maybe, for the right person. You know somebody?"

"I might."

Tori stopped at a stop sign and looked around. "Which way do I go to get to your house?"

"It's a few blocks from the high school. Just drive toward town."

We passed Liv's darkened house on the way. I hadn't seen or heard from her since the night of the accident. Someone said that they'd seen her in South Bend, just over the state line, and that she was working her way south.

On the day I had gotten out of the hospital, my parents and I had found a package shoved into the door when we got home. It was Liv's bridesmaid's dress with a note scrawled in Liv's writing. *Maybe this will fit one of your other friends*, the note said.

It would have been kind of funny if it wasn't so sad. It wasn't like friends were interchangeable, especially the kind of friend you'd ask to be your maid of honor. Besides, I didn't even know anyone the same size and shape as Liv. Nobody was like Liv.

"Quinn would probably want to help you," said Tori, like we had been talking all along instead of riding in silence.

"I mean, if you did make a garden behind the house. You've already done the older man thing. Who knows? Hanging out with Quinn might be nice for a change."

"Yeah," I said. "He won't care about what I read or wear, right?"

"I can guarantee that he won't give a rat's ass about what you read or wear."

"Okay, then he's in." I knew it was a little late to start a garden, but there was a decent chance it would turn out all right, especially if we got going on it in the next week.

Eventually, maybe I'd ask Will out to see it, but not right away. I'd want things to grow a little first, so there'd be something substantial to see. I'd wait for the tendrils of the pea plants to intertwine so it was impossible to tell where one began and the other ended. I'd wait for the bean plants to get full and leafy and the corn to grow straight and strong and over my head. That would be the best time for Will to see it, if he wanted to see it at all, if I still wanted him to see it by then.

THE END

Discussion Questions for
How It's Done

1. What is the "it" in the title *How It's Done*?

2. How has Grace's relationship with her father changed since her childhood? Why?

3. How would you describe Michael? How would you describe Grace?

4. Why did Grace like Michael?

5. Why did Michael like Grace?

6. When Michael said, "There is something I should tell you, though. I've been wanting to tell you, but I was afraid you wouldn't believe me or that it would frighten you and you'd end it," what did you think he was going to tell Grace? Why did Grace assume it was something bad? Do you think Michael meant it when he said "I'm in love with you" to Grace? (Pages 83-84)

7. Why do you think Michael asked Grace to marry him?

8. How did Grace tell her father about her relationship with Michael? Why do you think she chose that way? Would another way have worked better? Why?

9. What does Rachelle, Michael's ex-girlfriend, mean when she says to Grace, ". . . it could be that you're asking the wrong question"? (Page 222)

10. How are Grace's father and Michael the same or different? What about Grace and her mother?

11. What functions do Liv and Tori play in Grace's story? Can you think of characters from other books or stories who play similar roles? What would Grace's life be like without these people?

12. How did things change once Grace found out about her father's affair?

13. How do you think the story would have ended if Grace were pregnant?

14. Do you think Grace regretted her decision not to help Liv cheat to get the scholarship? Why? Do you agree with Liv when she says to Grace, ". . . in your charmed life you can afford to be all moral and ethical and everything, but you know what? I don't have that luxury."? (Page 290)

15. What do you think happened to Liv?

16. What is the difference between saying yes to yourself and saying no to others?

17. Reread the prologue. What's happening in this scene? Why do you think Grace wants to "bring on that flash of longing"? (Page 3)

18. Do you think Grace could have "figured everything out differently"? (Page 4) What would have to change in the story for her to be more true to herself?

19. Grace says, "If you're lucky, maybe there's someone who can help you [be your own person] . . . The funny thing is, that person is never who you think it's going to be. It's never who you want it to be." (Page 4) Who do you think that person is in Grace's life?

20. If you had to designate one of the characters as the villain of this story, who would it be? Why?

Acknowledgments

Not many first readers have both the patience and stamina to read multiple drafts of a work in progress, but I was fortunate to have several. Ann Yodhes McKnight, Carla Vissers, Lois Maassen, Lynn Richards Stubbs, and Mary Hildore Peters, thank you for your careful readings and thoughtful critiques. Hope Vestergaard, thanks for your insights and generosity, which I've experienced in many forms.

A special thanks to my teenage readers, Alison, Anna, Avril, and Elyse, for boosting my confidence at the very end.

Harold Underdown, you were right; I hope it shows. Pat Bloem, thanks for playing devil's advocate. To Gordon and Celaine, two M. Divs who are also friends, thanks for not flinching. Michele Lonergan and Kristine Dozeman, thanks for your steadfast support. Doug Dozeman, it means a lot to me to know you've got my back. *Merci,* Wendie, for loaning me the wide, open spaces of Juniper Hill Farm.

To my editor, Andrew Karre, thank you for getting it, taking it, and making it better. Gavin Duffy, thanks for giving it an irresistible cover. Rhiannon Ross, thank you for saving me from myself—several times.

To members of *The* Book Club in Holland, Michigan, passionate readers like you give angst-ridden writers like me hope that our words will connect with someone eventually. Every one of our discussions, from *War and Peace* to "the book that shall not be named," has taught me something about writing and living.

I am grateful for Katherine Paterson's reassuring words, "A book can have faults and still make a difference in someone's life."

To my family, near and far, *ubuntu: I am who I am because of who we all are.*